RULA'S NOT STUPID ANYMORE

and other short horror stories

Illustrators:

Rory's Great Uncle: Illustrated by Elena Rogers, Ukraine.
Instagram: @elen_rogers_art

Arvin's Creature: Illustrated by Yornelys Zambrano, Venezuela.
Instagram: @missyozart

Rula's Not Stupid Anymore: Illustrated by Decky Yuriadi, Indonesia.
Instagram: @deckyyuriadi_00

The Yik-Yak Mine: Illustrated by Andriy Dankovych, Ukraine.
Instagram: @andriy_dankovych

Juliana's Child: Illustrated by Lautaro Allende, Argentina.
Instagram: @crawlingchaos_art

Edited By Vicky Skinner, @vickyskribenten

Published in 2023 by Grant Crowther. All rights reserved. No part of this publication may be reproduced, in any form, without the prior written permission of the publisher and copyright holder.

Copyright text © Grant Crowther. Library of Congress Cataloging-in-Publication Data Available. Rula's Not Stupid Anymore and other short horror stories ISBN: 979-8-218-30886-5

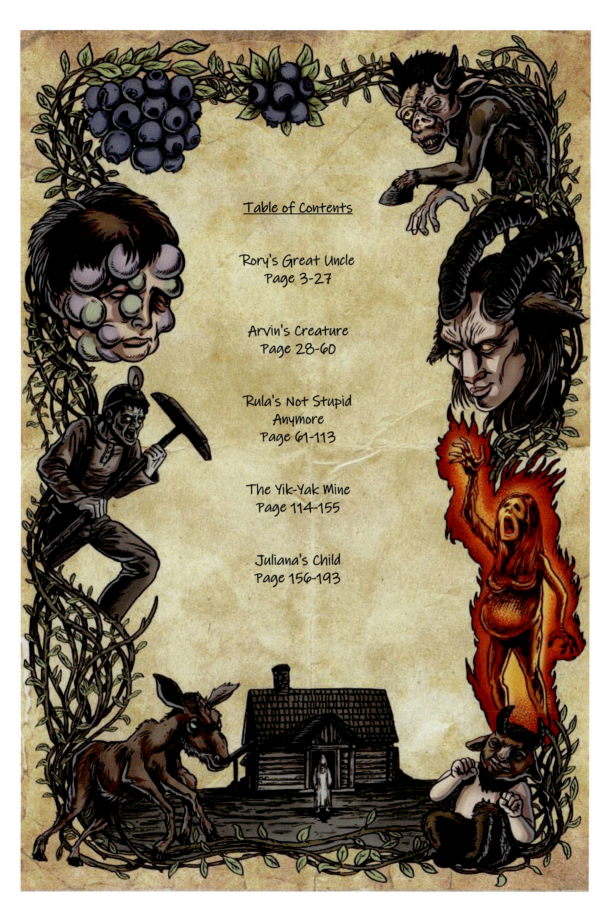

Table of Contents

Rory's Great Uncle
Page 3-27

Arvin's Creature
Page 28-60

Rula's Not Stupid Anymore
Page 61-113

The Yik-Yak Mine
Page 114-155

Juliana's Child
Page 156-193

RORY'S GREAT UNCLE

A lone carriage rattled along an age-old trail through the heart of a thick, untamed woodland. This forest, famed for its dense canopy and teeming wildlife, filled the air with an eerie symphony: fearsomely loud buzzing from enormous insects, strange and unknown bird calls, and the occasional distant howls of predatory mammals. At the reins of this horse-drawn carriage was Rory, a kind and resilient man, traversing a path that led towards an uncertain fate.

Rory was an intense man who bore an expression of chronically knitted brows and squinted eyes. His lean and wiry build came from years of hard labor, his smile was kind but terse, and he was a man of few words. Yet, beneath this rugged exterior lay a heart as tender as early spring's leaves. Known for his compassion, Rory often lent a helping hand and was always first to be called for when trouble brewed. He bore the badge of the "helper" with a quiet pride, his actions resonating louder than any boastful words could. Along with this, Rory had a genuine love for animals of all kinds, and it was common to see creatures flocking to him as if drawn by an invisible bond. Indeed, his kind nature was what had led him here to this eerie path.

Upon discovering a mysterious letter among his correspondences, Rory's attention was immediately captivated. The letter, penned by an unidentified scribe, detailed the frailty of his great uncle Harold and the pressing need to prepare his remote cabin for the harsh winter ahead. The penman claimed that, after his or her urging, the only name the old curmudgeon would give as a trusted caretaker was Rory himself. This revelation was especially startling, given that Rory had been informed of only two brief encounters with this elusive uncle during his infancy.

As he journeyed down the uneven dirt trail, Rory ruminated on the strangeness of his current predicament. The setting sun cast elongated, foreboding shadows that seemed to prance alongside him, heightening his sense of unease. He was en route to the dwelling of Uncle Harold, a figure whose elusive nature had been the crux of many whispered tales throughout Rory's life. This great uncle—his mother's own uncle—was an irascible hermit known for his odd behaviors and preference for solitude. Stories about him ranged from the darkly intriguing to the outright macabre. One particularly chilling rumor claimed Harold had committed murder years prior, seeking refuge in the woods to evade justice. Yet even more ominous whispers spoke of occult dealings, with one woman emphatically declaring that a curse from Harold had been the malevolent force behind her children's untimely deaths.

Rory, who was a man of good humor, diverted these ominous thoughts from his brain, by reciting aloud a somewhat humorous poem he remembered from an elementary school recital. As a child they had been forced to memorize it for Halloween:

"In the mist of moonlit night,
Where shadows loom and offer fright,
A gentleman sped in carriage fine,
To sound of hooves in steady line.

Abruptly, from the road's side,
A ghost appeared, eyes open wide.
The man gasped, reins in his grip,
But the ghost just sought companionship.

"May I join for a ride, kind sir?"
Asked the specter, voice a blur.
With a nod, the man made space,
And together, they set a casual pace.

Amidst the trees, side by side they rode,
One alive, one from an ethereal abode.
As the path twisted, ever so deep,
Man found company he would forever keep."

Rory chuckled softly, finding amusement in his own reminiscence. As he spoke, his voice, rich and resonant, echoed through the dense woods. Around him, the once-vibrant soundscape shifted. The cacophony of wildlife - the bird songs, buzzing of insects, and rustlings that had just recently animated the forest - seemed to pause and listen, casting the surroundings into an unexpected, hushed silence.

It seemed that the wilderness took on a different persona after Rory's little poetic recital. But perhaps that was also because dusk approached. Now the light cast odd shadows, and he could have sworn he felt eyes on him from the trees. The sounds of nature that had earlier offered company, now became a more foreboding sound, like chilling echoes of caution. Each rustling leaf, each hoot and howl a veiled harbinger of some impending doom. It felt as though the forest itself was pleading with him to turn around and return to the town he was from.

Bathed in the dwindling twilight, the young man pressed forward, his steel blue eyes flickered between apprehension and determination. Rory was not a man to be shaken from his decisions by a little fear, so he shrugged off the sensation, steeling his nerves. He was here for good reason, to turn back now would be dishonorable and cowardly, he scolded himself for even pondering the notion.

As Rory's carriage clambered along the ill-tamed path, the darkness grew thicker and more foreboding. Suddenly, a pitiful mewling sound pierced the silence. It was a raw and desperate cry that coaxed him to slow his horse. There, huddled near the side of the road, beside the underbrush, was a pathetic creature, wounded and left to die, lying helpless in the dirt. It was a baby moose, its minuscule form dwarfed by the surrounding gnarled trees.

Rory brought his carriage to a halting stop and gingerly descended from the driver's perch. He approached with a hint of trepidation, the sight before him demanding a more intimate inspection. This pathetic creature on the ground bore an unsettling deformity. Its front left leg, grotesquely mutated, sprouted an aberrant limb, jutting unnaturally. At the culmination of this limb was a fifth, fully formed foot. Although Rory was typically not one to indulge in superstitions, this eerie malformation hinted at something more sinister. With an audible swallow, he mustered his courage, drawn out of duty and sympathy towards the uncanny spectacle.

Upon deeper investigation the moose's pelt was matted with blood, bearing a tangle of cuts and gashes. He noticed the wounds weren't random. They were specific shapes etched deep into the animal's flesh, so specific they could only have been carried out by human hand - symbols, Rory realized with a shudder. What cruel human could carry out such a sadistic deed? Odd glyphs that bore a strange familiarity, a language he didn't understand but couldn't shake off the feeling that he'd seen before.

Despite the gruesome sight, Rory couldn't help but feel an overwhelming urge to help the creature. He was a beacon of compassion in a world that often harbored shadows, he could never just leave such a helpless calf to die. Hurriedly, he returned to his wagon and retrieved a kit he had brought full of medical materials. The contents had been intended for his uncle, if need be, but he had more than enough to spare. Kneeling by the baby moose, he gently cleaned its wounds with alcohol, then bandaged them, wrapping long strands of gauze around the body of the calf, who seemed to understand Rory's benevolent intentions. His large and calloused hands moved delicately, a gentleness that stood in stark contrast to his rugged exterior. The moose's wide eyes conveyed only trust, and obvious pain.

As he fastened the last of the bandages, a memory abruptly surged within Rory. The very letter he had received, penned by the unknown hand, bore peculiar scribblings gracing its margins. At the time, he had dismissed them as mere whimsical doodles. However, in this moment, their likeness to the symbols etched into the calf's hide became hauntingly apparent. The possibility of any connection between the letter and the afflicted creature seemed ludicrous, utterly implausible to his rational mind. He chided the fleeting thought, attributing it to his own timidity, mentally berating himself for his weakness.

Chastising himself for entertaining such a preposterous notion, Rory resolved then and there not only to dress the calf's wounds, but to take the creature under his care. Abandoned in this vulnerable state, it would inevitably fall prey to the forest's predators. Instead of surrendering it to such a grim destiny, with considerable exertion, he hoisted the calf and positioned it securely in his wagon's rear. True to his nature, Rory, the perennial protector, assumed responsibility for the beleaguered being, shouldering yet another charge in his life's litany of burdens.

The remainder of his journey was brief, and it wasn't long before Rory encountered the singular divergence in the woodland path. This side trail, recounted to him by his mother who had once traversed it many years prior, beckoned him. Guiding the carriage leftward, he embarked upon the less-trodden lane that surely led to his great uncle's abode.

Rory's thoughts wandered to the kind of existence one would lead in such seclusion. The sheer remoteness of the place suggested that even for a man of his own mettle, enduring a winter solitarily would be a monumental endeavor. Preparations for survival would be extensive: preserving food through canning, pickling, and meat curing; maintaining the integrity of the dwelling; perhaps tending to any livestock. The mere act of chopping and stockpiling the necessary firewood would be an arduous task. How, he mused, had his great uncle sustained himself in this isolation for so many years?

Before him stood a classic wooden cabin, neatly built with a small porch at the front and a peaked roof overhead, nestled perfectly at the trail's end. As Rory neared, the cabin's features became clearer. Orange light from lanterns streamed from the square windows, indicating that the old man was indeed home. He spotted hints of newer wood and recent repairs amongst the aged timber. It was clear that, despite his age, his uncle had put effort into maintaining the place.

The cabin, crafted from durable oak, had taken on a richer shade over the years. Time and weather had left their marks on its exterior. The roof, with its wooden shakes, appeared slightly bowed, as if weighed down by years of memories. Nearby, a sturdy barn stood. Simple in design, it offered a safe haven for animals seeking protection from the unforgiving wild. This barn, made of the same seasoned wood as the cabin, showed signs of careful upkeep. Stacks of hay were piled under a covered port. A large wooden tub of water sat at the rear, and he saw what looked like two goats standing, staring back at him.

Guiding the carriage to a halt, Rory directed both his horse and the injured calf towards the barn. As he entered, two goats bleated in curiosity, moving aside to allow passage. He led his horse to a vacant stall, making certain it was separate and settled. Nearby, a water pump caught his attention; filling a bucket, he ensured his horse was hydrated. After attending to his steed, he saw to the needs of the moose calf in similar fashion, grateful that two stalls were at his disposal. Aside from the goats, which had their own spacious dwelling and sheltered sleeping nook, there seemed to be no other residents. He gathered hay from nearby stacks, spreading it in each stall. As the animals settled in the cozy shelter, a comforting realization washed over Rory. Despite the oddities he'd faced, there remained a consolatory touch of the familiar in his surroundings.

Now, turning to the cabin, Rory steeled himself for what lay inside. He walked down the little pathway leading to the front door, making a conscious effort to remain calm, even jovial. As it was, he was here in good faith, and the anonymous writer of the letter had stated his uncle had specifically asked for him. So why did he feel such an edge of fright?

He knocked at the door and waited a few moments, with no reply. He tried once more. After waiting a laborious moment, he tried the door handle and found it was not locked, so he slowly pushed it open, its hinges whining in protest. Rory stepped into the amber glow of the room within. The cabin was small and neatly organized. The furnishings were functional and sturdy, worn by use: a wooden table and chair, a bookshelf stacked with an impressive assortment of leather bindings, an array of oil lamps hanging on all walls, and an old hearth filled with a perfectly stacked fire, looking as though it had just been set ablaze, warming the room. But there was no one to be seen.

"Hello?" he called out. "Uncle Harold? It's Rory, your nephew!" he tried to say cheerfully, but the anxiety in his voice was apparent. Still standing in front of the open doorway, he glanced around the room. He did not want to scare his uncle; his arrival was indeed unscheduled. The postman did not deliver mail to such a remote location, so he had had no way to contact the old man to tell him he was coming. He had hoped to arrive earlier in the day, but the delay with the baby moose had caused him extra time.

He closed the door behind him, took off his shoes and ventured further into the room. He saw a ladder that led up to a lofted area above the sitting room. He could just glimpse what looked to be many boxes and other storage items up there. He noticed a slightly opened door at the back of the house that must have led to the bedroom. Despite the humble arrangements, there was a certain homely appeal to the place, though with an eerie ambiance.

Drawing a deep breath, Rory fortified his resolve, pushing away the rising trepidation. Here he stood, entrenched in the enigmatic realm of his great uncle. Though the decor evoked a semblance of comfort, certain pieces starkly belied the eccentricity of the cabin's resident. The walls showcased a gallery of art, each crafted masterfully, yet their subjects teetered on the macabre. Among the still lifes and portraits, one painting particularly caught his eye: a banquet spread with apricots, apples, and corn. However, dominating the scene was a gruesomely rendered leg of lamb, its excessive sanguine spill meticulously depicted as it flowed off the table's edge. Another canvas showcased a woman, remarkable in technique but unsettling in portrayal. Her sparse, thin hair barely concealed a nearly bald scalp, and a pronounced underbite made her bottom teeth jut out unsettlingly. Her countenance bore the vacant, disconcerted look of a creature lost in its own world. He wondered what would draw a man to want to hang such work all about his home.

Rory's attention was next drawn to the unsettling array of literature adorning the bookshelves. A cursory perusal revealed titles that sent shivers down his spine: "Cambridge Studies of Biological Anatomical Anomalies: An Illustrated Compendium," "The Intricacies of Numerology and the Occult," and "An Archaeological Exposition of Balkan Death Rites."

Such arcane subjects gave rise to disconcerting thoughts. Were the whispered rumors concerning his uncle's dalliance with the darker arts rooted in reality?

Rory's feet creaked on the worn wooden floor as he crossed the cabin towards the bedroom door, where his great uncle must have been. The echo punctuated the eerie silence. As he neared the slightly open door, a peculiar sound reached his ears, a steady undercurrent to the quietness of the cabin. It was a low, persistent mumbling of words that Rory couldn't quite understand, spoken in a language that was alien and unsettling.

Venturing a peek into the room, he saw what had to be his great uncle. The man was lying flat on a worn bed, his unkempt hair a wild mess around his gaunt face. His eyes were glazed over and unfocused, giving off an empty stare that seemed to see into another reality altogether. His lips moved continuously, babbling an incessant stream of incomprehensible words.

Rory's gaze settled upon the man before him, evoking an involuntary shudder. The haunting image mirrored tales whispered amongst townsfolk of similar unfortunate fates: the chilling grip of catatonic psychosis. From his understanding, those consumed by this affliction became eerily detached from reality, trapped in the maze of their own mind. Such souls often exhibited rigid stances, unsettling motions, and a heart-wrenching disconnection from the world.

To Rory, it appeared as if his great uncle was submerged in a relentless nocturnal abyss, lost deep within his tortured thoughts, far from any comfort or understanding. It was as though he was imprisoned by his memories, re-living haunting episodes or trapped in nightmarish delusions, each more harrowing than the last. In this chilling revelation, Rory understood he was confronting a situation far more complex and menacing than he had imagined.

Yet, a more pressing concern tugged at his consciousness: if his uncle was in such a grievous state, who had been caring for the house? Who had ignited the lanterns and stoked the fire? A cold dread crept down Rory's spine as he grappled with these unsettling thoughts.

Positioning himself in a wooden chair thoughtfully situated by the bed, Rory's gaze was immediately captured by a disconcerting artwork hung above the bedstead. This particular piece portrayed an eerie landscape, rendered in meticulous oil strokes, depicting what seemed like an otherworldly terrain. The ground bore unnatural shades of deep purple and crimson, and the sky above was nearly black but illuminated by a far-off moon that gave off a sickly pale white hue. Dominating this desolate vista was a creature of bewildering design. Its features hinted at an aquatic origin, yet it stood defiantly on robust limbs. The being's yellow and black eyes seemed alive, piercing through the canvas and fixating on Rory with an unnerving intensity.

Hastily shifting his gaze from the grotesque masterpiece, Rory turned his attention back to his relative. "Uncle Howard?" he ventured gently, wary of jolting the man from his unnerving trance. Despite several gentle attempts to rouse his uncle, Rory was met with continued indecipherable babbling, directed mostly towards the ceiling. A sobering realization dawned on him: he would find no answers from his kin. Instead, the very walls of this chamber seemed to hold the answers. These timeworn barriers, having absorbed the peculiar events they bore witness to, whispered their cryptic tales to a wary Rory.

From the hushed shadows, a malevolent noise began to weave its way into the room, a ghostly sotto voce that caressed Rory's ears as if birthed from the very timbers encasing them. He pivoted sharply, endeavoring to pinpoint its source but was met only by motes of dust pirouetting in the singular moonbeam that pierced the grimed windowpane. He mentally chided himself, attributing the unsettling auditory illusion to his heightened state of anxiety and the oppressive atmosphere that seemed to cloak the cabin.

Yet, as if heeding this ethereal summons, his uncle's ceaseless, delirious mutterings began to morph. They took on a rhythmic cadence, echoing in a tongue unfamiliar to Rory but unmistakably deliberate, harmonizing with the enigmatic murmurs that filled the air. A bone-chilling epiphany dawned upon him: perhaps his great uncle wasn't merely ensnared by the clutches of his troubled psyche. Instead, he might have been the unwilling host to some spectral presence, a force from realms unknown, that sought to torment both mind and soul.

Rory jolted, as though physically attempting to dislodge the eerie murmurs that plagued his thoughts. They persisted, however, faint as the brush of a moth's wings yet undeniably present. Rising from his seat, terror's icy grip took hold. His uncle's eyes, previously lost in their own feverish world, suddenly and disconcertingly fixed on Rory, seeing him, it seemed, for the first time, yet his lips continued their strange recitation. Uncle Harold's fingers, reminiscent of gnarled talons, now clung fiercely to the frayed quilt draped over him, their pallor contrasting starkly with the fabric.

Taking a steadying breath, Rory addressed the older man, striving for calm in his tone. "Uncle Harold," he began, infusing his voice with as much authority as he could muster, "I must insist that you cease this unnerving behavior." He continued, "I am here to aid you, for it's clear you're unwell. Please, find some semblance of calm." Remarkably, his words found their mark. The frenetic chanting ceased, and Harold, seemingly mollified, returned his gaze to the cabin's ceiling. The spectral whispers that had haunted Rory also faded into silence. With a shuddering exhale, Rory embraced a momentary respite from the cabin's oppressive aura.

He quickly left the bedroom, needing to separate himself from the chilling experience he had just endured. He went out to the main room again and found a seat on the little couch that sat in front of the fireplace. Here, he took a moment to ponder his situation.

Rory couldn't help but draw a disturbing connection between everything. The stories told in town about his great uncle, the strange disfigured moose he had found, the disturbing artwork and books inside the house, his great uncle's unsettling condition, and then the haunting whispers in the cabin - were they all pieces of a terrifying puzzle? A dread-filled anticipation clung to Rory, a sickening certainty that he was on the precipice of discovering something that was profoundly and terrifyingly wrong.

As Rory tried to find some calm in the midst of the unnerving circumstances, he turned his attention to settling into the place for the night. There was definitely no hope in turning back. His poor horse couldn't do another long ride without rest, plus it was nighttime now. On top of that, he knew no matter how frightening the circumstances might be, he could never live with himself if he left the old man now. He was clearly incapacitated. Although the cabin was inexplicably clean and well-equipped, he could not leave him in the state he was in. The only other option would be to take him away from here. This was a thought that he would ponder, but there was no immediate danger to flee from, just his own tingling nerves.

"That's enough fretting about nonsense, you old lady!" Rory said to himself angrily. And so, he set about doing what he did best, getting things done. Rising from the couch, he returned to his wagon and began unloading all of his things, bringing them into the house. His dear mother had meticulously packed many items for his trip. She had been very worried before he left, and he wondered now if she had known more about the old man than she had let on.

There were crates filled with pickled vegetables, cured meats, bags of flour and sugar, and all sorts of other domestic items his mother had thought to pack with him. He also had a few suitcases full of clothes and some books to read. After getting everything back into the cabin, he set about looking for the best place for him to sleep.

The couch seemed inadequate in size, and the other chairs lacked the comfort needed for a night's rest. Contemplating a makeshift bed by the warmth of the hearth, an idea struck Rory. The lofted storage area above might have something to aid his comfort. Ascending the petite ladder, he discovered a space far more expansive than anticipated. To his surprise, it was replete with spare blankets, plush pillows, and even a modest mattress perched atop robust storage crates. It was curiously set up, mirroring a well-appointed bed, with its crisp sheets, snug woolen comforter, and cushions arranged to double as a sofa backrest. It bore an uncanny semblance of being pre-arranged for his visit. Could it be that his uncle sought refuge here during sweltering summer nights? Depositing his bags in this newfound alcove, Rory felt a touch more settled.

With his sleeping arrangements in place, his attention shifted to the care of the elderly figure. With newfound composure, Rory reentered the bedroom, the disturbing aura of his uncle now less pronounced. Bypassing the incessant murmurs, he set about seeking fresh attire for the man. The clothes his uncle donned were lamentably soiled, marred with drool and other mysterious stains; some bore a disturbing resemblance to blood. A thorough search of the neatly arranged drawers yielded a clean set. Carefully, and with some effort, he undressed the frail figure, finding, to his relief, no signs of injury. The bloodstains, it seemed, did not belong to his uncle. Rory shook his head, then reprimanded his own morbid thoughts. "Clearly it's not blood then," he whispered to himself. Thanks to Rory's youthful vigor, he managed to redress the rigid frame of the older man with minimal struggle.

Securing a fresh bed sheet, he replaced the old one—curiously marred with holes as if gnawed upon by an animal—and draped it over the recuperating calf in the barn. Back inside, Rory gently combed through the man's unkempt hair and attempted to hydrate him. However, his efforts were met with a sudden gush, the water regurgitated almost instantly. Hoping at least enough water had settled into the man's stomach to give a little sustenance, he resigned himself for the night.

Preparing for slumber, Rory chanced upon a modest wash area tucked away in the kitchen's recess. Rather than being a separate chamber, it seamlessly merged with the kitchen, a practical design considering the lone inhabitant. A sizeable washbasin, partnered with a robust water pump and accompanying pail, stood ready. The water it yielded was crystalline and inviting. Adjacent to the kitchen, a door led outside to an outhouse, underscoring the cabin's self-sufficiency. The intricacies of the home, like the strategically placed water pump, bore witness to thoughtful design and preparation.

Concluding his nightly ablutions, Rory felt drawn to the array of books lining the walls. Weathered shelves, their wood richly stained, cradled a trove of leather-bound tomes. Their well-thumbed spines whispered tales of decades, their titles spanning science, philosophy, and arcane knowledge, albeit almost all of which held a macabre tilt. Amidst this collection, Rory spotted one volume that stood out from the rest, a black leather book much larger than the others. The spine looked very well worn. The title, now almost illegible, read "Geomancy and Sigils of Abkhazia." Rory removed the heavy tome from the shelf and brought it with him to read through up in the loft.

In the dim, flickering glow of lantern light, Rory perched upon the quaint bed, drawn irresistibly to the foreboding book before him. With bated breath, he carefully opened its timeworn pages, only to be met with a ghastly array of illustrations and writings that sent chills down his spine. The book was a masterwork of dark arts, teeming with meticulously detailed drawings of arcane symbols, and step-by-step guidelines to rituals that bore unspeakably malevolent titles. Here were rituals for hexes, malefactions, and the invocation of infernal entities, each delineated with chilling precision. Foreboding and mysterious symbols, integral to the ceremonies, were sketched with unnerving care, accompanied by sinister chants — each meticulously annotated to denote the precise moment of recitation. Ghastly sketches of animals marked for sacrifice and eerily lifelike renditions of specific demons danced across the pages. As Rory's pulse quickened, a disturbing realization dawned upon him: the symbols etched into the tender hide of the young moose bore an uncanny resemblance to those that haunted the pages of this very book.

Under the lantern's muted glow, the foreboding contents of the book held Rory captive, their revelations even more chilling against the backdrop of his uncle's distant mutterings, emanating from the bedroom below. The enigmatic and twisted pronunciations of his uncle reverberated through the cabin's timeworn beams, but amongst the tangle of syllables he could hear, one clear phrase was repeated: "Ah-Tonk Gargonii Wachatt!" These unfamiliar words, otherworldly in their cadence, filled Rory with a shiver of dread.

Desiring to escape from the creeping unease, Rory hastily shut the book, yearning for the refuge of sleep. But as he reclined on the bed, a tangible sensation of fright took hold, rendering relaxation elusive. The ambient whispers, previously soft, now surged in intensity, becoming a maddening chorus in the night's stillness.

Within the room, the play of firelight created grotesque ballets of shadows that seemed animated with malevolent intent. But, as Rory's gaze flitted about, seeking something to comfort him, or at least ground him in reality, they fell upon a collection of crates stacked to the side. Nestled within were timeworn decorations and relics of bygone days, Christmas ornaments, flyers from a variety of entertainment shows he had saved, and a portrait of a solemn-looking couple, that very well may have been Rory's great grandparents. He had never seen pictures of them himself, his mother had always been a little secretive about her own upbringing. Seeing these forgotten remnants of his uncle's former life gave him a small shred of comfort. He found solace in knowing that, at least at some point in time, his uncle had been a normal member of society.

Then, his attention caught upon a finely crafted parchment, a calligraphy-sketched family tree that was set inside of a wood trim frame. The family tree was labeled with his mother's maiden name, Manix, and it traced his mother's lineage back many generations, through elegant lines and intricate loops. Rory's eyes landed on a familiar name - his own. And, curiously beside it, a delicately inked star had been scribed, seemingly penned in more recently, its presence a troubling enigma.

By this point, Rory was under no illusion; this cabin, these dense woods, were tainted with an evil that made his skin crawl. His great uncle seemed to be a part of the darkness that lurked in the very air of the place. Doubts started to gnaw at his resolve. Who had sent that letter asking specifically for his help? What was the true intention of those letters? And now, with the realization of his uncle's dark interests, why should he remain here?

The thought of spending winter isolated in this cabin unsettled Rory deeply. He imagined being surrounded by thick layers of snow, cutting him off from the outside world, with only the ceaseless mutterings of his unhinged uncle for company. It was a daunting prospect, amplifying the eeriness of his surroundings. After a few hours in this pondering state of torment, Rory's mind finally relented, allowing fatigue to take hold, and he succumbed to a troubled sleep.

***

Awoken from his uneasy dreams, Rory felt a cold wetness against his face. His pulse raced as his eyes snapped open to the disturbing sight of his uncle looming over him, saliva dripping from a gaping mouth, snarled and twisted to one side, eyes bulging with a madness Rory could only interpret as murderous. Glistening threateningly in the dim illumination was a sharp kitchen knife.

A surge of terror lent Rory unexpected agility. He jerked upright, narrowly avoiding a frenzied lunge from his uncle, whose knife whizzed through the space he'd just vacated. Slipping from the mattress to the ground, Rory instinctively grabbed at his uncle's ankles, causing the older man to lose balance. He spilled onto the floor slamming the back of his head against the boards, the knife skittering away.

A guttural sound of disgust and fear rose from Rory's throat as he took in the grim scene of what had just occurred. His uncle, now sprawled on the ground, squirmed in a pitiful and desperate manner. Like an overturned turtle, he flopped his arms about, utterly incapable of righting himself.

"What possessed you to come up here?" Rory's voice quivered with a mix of fear and incredulity as he addressed the man, though deep down, he knew his words would find no coherent reception. "Were you trying to kill me?" To this, his great uncle only responded with his continued nonsensical babbling and useless flailing about.

Drawing a deep breath, Rory collected himself for a few heartbeats before approaching the wretched man. He first secured the errant knife, tucking it securely out of reach. Then, with a mix of caution and concern, he hoisted the old man into a seated position. Their eyes locked, yet what stared back at Rory were orbs devoid of any semblance of recognition or humanity. His eyes appeared more like a fish's, blank and vacant.

"Are you even in there at all, Uncle Harold?" Rory whispered, but his words were lost, falling upon the dead ears and saucer-sized eyes of the aged man, who only stared aimlessly whilst he babbled.

The task of moving the unstable elder from the loft back to the bedroom below was arduous. Rory marveled at how his uncle, in his weakened state, had managed such a feat on his own. Safely back in the bedroom, Rory faced a heart-wrenching decision. For both their sakes, he had to restrict his uncle's movements. With a heavy sigh, he secured the old man to the bedposts, using a cord of rope he found in the kitchen, ensuring it was firm yet not painfully tight.

Exhausted and troubled, Rory retreated back to the loft. His thoughts spun chaotically. Could it be, he wondered, that the malevolent forces detailed in that accursed book were the puppeteers behind his uncle's disturbing antics? The mere idea froze Rory to his core. He was a simple man, unequipped to face such dark and ancient forces. Did he even have any hope to change things?

He pondered his options. Should he stay and try to wrestle his great uncle from the clutches of this malevolent force, or should he flee this haunted place out of the concern that maybe he, too, could fall victim to its curse? The answers eluded him as he once again tried to settle his brain and return to sleep. Knowing that his uncle had been secured to the bed did give him a little bit of relief, and eventually his exhausted brain succumbed to sleep.

***

Rory rose early the next morning. And as if in response to his predicament, nature seemed to conspire against him the very next day. A storm rolled in, bringing with it an ominous chill that hinted at the approach of snow. The thought of being snowbound here sent shivers down his spine. No matter what, riding home this day was not an option; it would be too risky to make such a long trip in that weather. So, Rory focused himself on household tasks.

He took care of the animals, attending once again to the grotesque wounds of the strange moose calf, cleaning the wounds and changing the bandages. Despite its horrific injuries, the calf seemed to be recuperating well, the dried blood forming protective scabs that showed no signs of infection but did bear the menacing shapes so similar to the symbols he had seen in that cursed book.

He decided to let his horse out of its solitary stall and allow him to roam in the larger pen with the goats. He watched them with care for a while, making sure they would get along. To his relief, all the animals seemed even-tempered. Rory had always loved animals and paid greater attention than most to their well-being. The pen was a bustling place now, housing his horse and two goats. He kept the moose calf separated in its stall just in case. There was no need to risk further injury to the little creature. He busied himself with filling their water troughs and feed buckets.

Despite the steady rain, he spent much of the day outdoors. Being a man of hard work, he couldn't help but give the stable a thorough cleaning and tend to the overgrown garden. The onset of winter made the tidying up all the more necessary. He was pleasantly surprised to find a variety of vegetables and fruits still thriving amid the neglected patch. The salvageable produce was promptly gathered and taken inside for storage. These activities served as a welcome distraction from the unnerving presence of his great uncle, who continued to babble incoherently, arms still tied to the bedposts.

Rory did make sure to attend to his uncle as well, giving him water and attempting to feed the man. The water went down this time, but the food did not. He also guided his uncle to the outhouse at one point, a task he had not even considered when he had first set out here as caretaker. He was always sure to secure the old man's wrists back to the bed posts whenever he left him alone. The unsettling event from the night before was still fresh in his memory.

As the day wore on, the rain intensified, keeping Rory indoors. He focused himself on indoor chores. It was while sweeping the cabin's floors that his attention was caught by something he had overlooked before - a hidden hatch in the floorboards just beneath a small carpet in the sitting area. He lifted the heavy door and took in a breath of shock. Instead of the expected rickety old ladder leading down to a small dirt cellar, there were actual stone stairs that went down to a sizable room. Intrigued, he thought that the cool, dark space could serve as an ideal storage area for all the freshly picked produce he had found in the garden.

After stacking the gathered fruits and vegetables into a few empty wooden crates, Rory cradled one of them in his left arm while carrying a pocket lighter in his right. Lighting his way, he began his descent down the darkened steps, only to find a series of lanterns mounted on the walls. He ignited each in turn, gradually dispelling the cellar's gloom. To his surprise, the underground expanse mirrored the cabin's ground floor in size. The foundation, crafted from masoned stone bricks and bolstered by heavy wood beams, hinted at a more formidable structure than the quaint cabin above.

In this shadowed realm, an unsettling tableau awaited him. Preserved animals, their lifeless glass eyes staring blankly, crowded the shelves, giving the cellar an ambiance akin to a macabre gallery. Drawn closer by curiosity, Rory's eyes settled on a red fox, its form meticulously posed mid-stride atop a wooden board. Its artificial gaze seemed haunting, yet what truly chilled him were the symbols etched onto its hide, eerily mirroring those on the injured moose calf. The grim revelation was clear: his uncle, it appeared, had repeatedly committed these heinous acts. Rory's heart plummeted; the depth of his compassion for animals made this discovery nearly unforgivable. Could he truly care for someone capable of such cruelty?

More unsettling discoveries lay ahead. Scattered on metallic trays were instruments of dubious intent. While their design hinted at surgical purposes, the sinister stain they bore hinted at far darker uses. Among them was a device seemingly meant to pry open wounds, another resembling pliers for tooth extraction, and a set of keen-edged knives. Disturbingly intertwined with these were objects of clear occult origin: wands, intricately designed bowls, and chalices adorned with stones and cryptic etchings. The unsettling fusion of arcane and surgical implements sent tremors through Rory's frame.

Next, the chalk inscriptions on the basement floor nearly had Rory retreating to the stairs. Their intricate and menacing patterns were filled with cryptic symbols he recognized from the cursed book. The realization that these markings were remnants of dark sorcery intensified the oppressive dread the cabin seemed to exude. He had unearthed more proof — the root of his uncle's apparent madness. The old man had either succumbed to insanity through his chilling beliefs, or, more unsettlingly, the dark forces he dabbled with had genuinely overtaken his soul. Such thoughts chilled Rory to the bone, and even as a generally non-religious man, he found himself entertaining the possibility of their truth. Clearly, the cellar was a sanctuary for this malevolent craft.

Distancing himself from such disturbing artifacts, Rory's gaze settled on the many canvases stacked against the walls. Evidently, the old man was indeed the artist of the paintings adorning the walls upstairs as well.

"Multi-talented," Rory remarked, surveying the surrounding artworks. Their subject matter held the same macabre tone as those above. A wooden easel stood in the center of the room, with a small chair positioned before it. On it was an unfinished portrait, a work in progress that was most likely halted by his uncle's deteriorating mind.

Approaching the painting, Rory felt his heart rate escalate as the subject became clearer. An icy grip of realization tightened around him: the exquisitely detailed portrait was of Rory. In his shock, the crate of vegetables he had been cradling under one arm fell to the ground, its contents spilling out. Panic coursed through him. He hadn't seen his uncle since infancy and in accordance with his mother's words, there had only been a few brief encounters. How could the old man possibly know his matured features with such precision? This revelation, combined with everything else he'd witnessed, solidified his belief in the supernatural events transpiring within these walls.

As if in response to the fallen crate of produce, suddenly, from the dark recesses of the basement, a deep, guttural growl rolled. The haunting echo resounded off the stone walls, infiltrating his bones. The raw animosity in the sound suggested a predatory intent. An overpowering sense of self-preservation drowned him, and Rory scrambled towards the steps, every fiber of his being desperate to escape the ominous basement. He could have sworn he heard something breathing behind him, but when he turned to shut the cellar door, there was nothing there. He slammed the hatch anyway, and placed the remaining crates on top of it, securing its closure.

Once safely above ground, Rory sought solace in a dusty bottle of whiskey he had noticed earlier tucked in the kitchen cupboards. He took a generous gulp, the liquor burning its path down his throat, an attempt to steady his trembling nerves. Now the storm outside was raging, rain pelting the roof with a vengeance, and the windows rattled under the relentless onslaught of the wind.

Rory was standing with his back to the main room of the cabin. As he stood there with the bottle of whiskey in hand, he could hear the sound of his uncle's incessant babbling above the raging storm, as if closer than from within the confines of the bedroom. The familiar haunting phrases echoing through the cabin. It was a disturbing symphony, the elements outside and the madness inside, playing off each other, amplifying the sense of chaos and dread that was quickly consuming Rory.

The soft screech of chalk against wood abruptly sliced through the cacophony. Heart pounding, Rory slowly turned around to face the main room behind him. His blood ran cold at the sight that unraveled before him. His uncle had somehow managed to free himself from his restraints and now sat hunched over the cabin floor. In his gnarled hand, he clutched a piece of chalk, using it to draw a complex circle filled with the same menacing symbols Rory had found in the cursed book and on the basement floor. His uncle had situated himself in the center of the intricate design, his gaze vacant and crazed, as he wailed the same haunting phrase into the cabin's air: "Ah-Tonk Gargonii Wachatt!" His voice echoed, each syllable dripping with an unfathomable darkness that made Rory's head ache.

Paralyzed with fear, Rory was jolted back to reality by a sudden knock on the cabin door. Everything was happening so fast; he could hardly keep himself from screaming. His heart was pounding like a wild drum, but a part of him had the irrational hope that someone had come to save him. He pictured his mother on the other side of the door. Perhaps she had sensed the danger he was in and had come out here to rescue him. He knew the thought was absurd, but he couldn't help but approach, a glimmer of hope emanating from within him. Even if it was just a passerby, he would be grateful for their arrival. Anyone to accompany him during this moment of terror would be embraced with zeal.

Opening the door, his eyes met an astonishing sight. The baby moose stood there, drenched from the rain, its bandages fallen away to reveal the strange, cryptic symbols that mirrored those now drawn in chalk on the floor behind him. The scars now seemed to glow green with a surreal illumination. The little creature's eyes, previously soft with innocence and pain, now blazed with a sinister crimson light.

Backing away from the cursed creature, a sudden force pulled Rory off his feet. His uncle had leapt at him from the circle and clasped his arms around him in a vice-like grip, pulling

him to the cabin floor with unexpected strength. A shriek tore from Rory's lips as he struggled against the old man's hold, but his efforts were futile. The unhinged senior seemed to be imbued with a supernatural might that kept Rory pinned to the ground. The baby moose advanced calmly, its haunting red eyes never leaving Rory. The creature leaned down, placing its face directly in front of his own, a mere breath away. As Rory screamed in pure terror, a plume of green smoke seeped from the moose's nostrils, snaking its way into Rory's open mouth. The world spun and faded to black, and he lost consciousness.

***

Rory woke with a jolt, finding himself sprawled face up in the middle of the chalk-drawn circle, the cold, lifeless body of his uncle lying beside him. The baby moose had vanished, and the cabin door was swinging open in the wind, letting in a chilling draft and splatters of rain. Rising to his feet, he felt a sudden, horrifying displacement of self, an alien feeling that his own body was no longer under his sole control.

A voice echoed within his mind, the timbre menacing and gleeful. "My apologies, lad," it said in a sickeningly sweet tone. "I required a new vessel, and your young, sturdy form serves my purpose perfectly. Your uncle was an ideal host for many years, but alas, his fragile mind can no longer sustain me. You, on the other hand, will prove far more enduring."

A cold realization pierced Rory, like a dagger through his heart. The demonic entity that had consumed his uncle's sanity had now claimed him. He felt the last vestiges of his own consciousness slipping away, subsumed by an encroaching darkness that threatened to erase his very identity. He moved to shut the cabin door, feeling the detached precision of his actions, as if he were a puppet controlled by invisible strings.

Whistling a tune, the entity within Rory began the macabre task of cleaning up, its cheerfulness a horrifying contrast to the grim scene. It contemplated reaching out to Rory's mother with a nicely written letter assuring his safety, soothing her worries with a web of comforting lies. After all, the woman had always been so anxious, and it would be a shame to add to her stress.

A lament hung heavy in the air, a final dirge to Rory's pure, noble spirit, now cruelly displaced. The haunted cabin had claimed another innocent soul, the darkness thriving on the vulnerability of a young man who had set out with nothing but good intentions. The new Rory picked up a journal from one of the many bookshelves and made a new entry:

In the dark woods, my cabin's set,
A stage for a sinister puppet's duet.
Tales are told, in whispers met,
Of a sorrow they'll never forget.

Old timbers groan, a grim delight,
Under the ghostly moon's pale light.
The cabin's new tenant's plight,
Sorry, but it's a demon's right.

Good folks, your fear's well-placed,
In the cabin, terror's embraced.
A fresh host, his life's effaced,
Apologies, it's just my taste.

ARVIN'S CREATURE

In the heart of a dense, haunting forest, where the trees towered like monstrous sentinels and the shadows whispered secrets of forgotten lore, stood a grim, solitary cabin. It was an outpost of humanity, defiant against the brooding wilderness, home to a man as fearsome as the forest itself.

His name was Arvin, a lumberjack by trade, a solitary figure scarred by life's cruel hand. He was a formidable sight to behold, his towering figure a silhouette of dread against the setting sun. The rhythmic fall of his axe, a relentless metronome, echoed ominously through the dark expanse of the woods, a grim melody of solitude and toil.

Arvin was a figure of terror, not just imposing in size and strength, but also imposing in his visage. His face, a grotesque canvas of weather-beaten lines and battle scars, was often pulled into a chilling scowl that would make even the bravest hearts quiver. His gnarled, calloused hands, every bit as hard as the timber he hewed, were a testament to a life of grueling toil and brutal encounters. No woman dared to share his life, no children graced his hearth, for his appearance and repute were as forbidding as the wilderness he called home.

His clandestine meetings with the town butcher offered a grim distraction from his harsh existence. The two weathered men, both with hardened souls, often shared a drink whenever Arvin trundled into town at night, delivering the bodies of whatever beast unfortunately found its way into Arvin's traps. Adept at the hunt, Arvin set elaborate snares and coil clamp traps in the darkest corners of the forest, luring and capturing the fiercest of beasts. The sinister thrill of the hunt and the prize of the coins it fetched added a dark spice to his otherwise monotonous life. The wealthier denizens of the town, drawn to the macabre allure of the wild game he traded, paid a pretty penny for the taste of the exotic and forbidden meats from the forest.

In the shadowed realm that Arvin called home, suffering was not merely observed, it was the cloth from which the tapestry of life was woven, an integral thread in the fabric of daily existence. Nature, in all her unyielding majesty, had revealed to him the eternal dance of death and rebirth, predator and prey, each step a testament to the cruelty that permeated this wooded world.

Amongst the towering timbers and under the watchful eyes of ancient oaks, Arvin had been a silent witness to the ballet of brutality that played out in the gloom. Once, he had stumbled upon the tragic tableau of two mighty stags, their magnificent antlers interlocked in a fatal embrace, their majestic heads bowed under the weight of their mutual imprisonment. After what were likely days of struggle, the two had finally collapsed to their deaths in exhaustion.

On another foray into the depths of the forest, his path had crossed that of a desperate mother bear, her hunger overcoming the maternal instincts that should have protected her young. From a far-off distance, across a rocky ravine, Arvin had watched as the emaciated mother bear turned on her cub, devouring it as its sibling looked on, frozen in horror.

Yet another memory etched itself into Arvin's mind, that of a lone wolf, its once proud visage marred by the scars of battle, left to die by its very own pack, its ravaged face a testament to the savagery of its kind. Now, the wolf lived a pitiful existence, limping through the forest, dragging its useless hind quarters, it had sustained itself by eating insects and other small creatures on the forest floor.

And then there was the haunting image of the wild cat, its savage instincts on full display as it feasted upon a hapless deer fawn, the baby's small head had been ensnared in the hollow of an ancient tree trunk. With an almost casual cruelty, the cat had ripped open the fawn's belly, pulling out its intestines, all the while indifferent to the heart-wrenching bleats of its victim. Such was the merciless world that Arvin had come to know, a place where nature's laws were written in blood.

So, when the tortured wail of another of the forest's inhabitants pierced the air that night, Arvin remained unmoved. His seasoned ears had grown accustomed to the multitude of cries that echoed through the shadowy woods, and the particularly distinct guttural groans of this unknown beast did little to perturb his steady nerves. Yet, the experienced trapper knew to tread lightly, for danger was always a possibility.

With the stealth of a cat, Arvin made his way towards the source of the tumult, guided by the symphony of snapping twigs and thrashings of what must have been an immense creature. There, nestled in the heart of the forest, lay one of Arvin's most formidable contraptions—a spring trap of gargantuan proportions, its iron jaws capable of holding captive the most fearsome of adversaries. As Arvin approached, he knew that whatever creature lay ensnared within its grip, its fate was sealed, for none had ever escaped the unyielding embrace of this deadly device.

Clutching his trusty ax in one mighty hand, and a keen-edged knife in the other, Arvin steadied himself for whatever grotesquery awaited him in the murk of the forest. His past escapades had seen him bring down the most bizarre and unimagined creatures, fetching him a handsome price from the fat and decadent elites who held their sumptuous feasts in high esteem, each course more extravagant than the last, in a relentless competition of opulence. And so, with the heart of a hunter and the light-footedness of a fox, Arvin plunged into the murky underbrush, every rustle of the leaves and groan of the branches serving to heighten his sense of anticipation.

Soon, the origin of the chilling wails was within his view, revealing a sight that would have had any greenhorn hunter turning tail and fleeing for their life. But not Arvin. His eyes widened, not in fear, but in incredulous awe, as they beheld the monstrous entity ensnared within the unyielding clutches of his colossal trap.

There, before him, writhed a nightmarish freak, a fantastical blend of human and goat, as if plucked from the most sinister depths of ancient mythology. The creature's lower extremities were a testament to its caprine lineage, powerful and muscular, ending in hooves that pawed at the earth in a futile attempt to escape its painful confinement. Towering above its grotesque visage, a pair of formidable, spiraled horns, their razor-sharp tips glinting malevolently in the ethereal light of the moon.

The contrast between the creature's lower bestial half and its upper human-like torso was startling, to say the least. Her torso was that of a human female, her bare flesh an incongruous element in her otherwise monstrous visage. The grotesque human likeness brought forth a macabre question—would the debauched elites even deign to feast upon the flesh of such a being? The very thought of consuming a creature with human features was horrifying.

Engulfed in its nightmarish ordeal, the creature writhed and thrashed in its metallic prison, its leg impaled by the cruel fangs of the trap that anchored it to the forest floor. Each agonized howl that escaped its lips seemed to weave an invisible shroud of dread that hung heavy over the shadowed woods.

Yet Arvin remained resolute, the specter of fear banished to the recesses of his mind, sealed behind the impenetrable walls of his battle-hardened spirit and a lifetime spent walking hand in hand with peril. He regarded the enigmatic beast before him, caught in the internal tug-of-war between his intrigue for the anomaly that was the creature, and the grim realities of his livelihood. When the creature lifted its hellish eyes to meet his, any inkling of sympathy that might have taken root in his heart was swiftly expunged. In its place arose the cold, calculating mindset of the hunter, as Arvin began to plot his next course of action.

She was too massive and still too healthy to approach. One swipe from those claws could mean death. But the trap had hit her artery; blood was coming from the wound at an alarming rate, creating a dark pool beneath her. Arvin watched the horrific scene with a detachment that only years of experience could inure one to. He had been the harbinger of death too many times, watched the light fade from the eyes of too many creatures, to be moved by the suffering before him. His heart had long turned into a chunk of ice, as cold and as unyielding as the winters of the woods he called home.

The creature, trapped and bleeding, locked eyes with him. The stare she returned was loaded with a primal hatred and terror, a promise of death should she break free. In the abyss of her dark eyes, Arvin saw a fierce, unbroken spirit, a mirror to his own hardened soul. The relentless iron jaws dug deeper into her flesh with each struggle, each futile attempt to free herself. She would bleed out; it was inevitable, he just had to wait.

There was a cruel simplicity to it all. The cold equation of life and death, the survival of the fittest, the inevitable cycle of predator and prey. The release of death would find her, in its own unforgiving time. If she looked weak enough, and it was safe, he would put her out of her misery, but only then. Under the spectral gaze of the moon, the woods bore silent witness to the grim tableau. And Arvin, as unyielding as the forest around him, stood guard over the dying creature, waiting for death to claim its next due.

In the throes of her final moments, the creature let out a guttural cry. It was a pained sound, a sorrowful mix of a growl and whimper that echoed mournfully in the silence of the night. Her eyes, still sharp despite her impending doom, darted frantically in front of her, to something that lay just out of reach.

Arvin followed her gaze, watching as she extended her arm in a final, desperate bid toward a hollow in a tree just beyond her reach. The pitiful sight was a stark revelation, a shockingly cruel twist in the drama before him. A maternal cry from mother to child had been in that dying wail—a plea interwoven with despair and love that echoed in the darkest corners of Arvin's hardened heart. Instinctively, he understood what it signified. He approached her body, and with one fluid, simple movement, he slit her throat. As he knelt down beside her, her body remained still; she had already succumbed to death.

Arvin's gaze was drawn to the mysterious shadows of the large tree hollow. Peering into the dim interior, he discovered a heart-wrenching tableau: nestled within the confines of the hollow rested a makeshift cradle fashioned from woven twigs. Within this rustic cradle, his fears of the tragedy he suspected were brought to life.

Gazing up at him, eyes wide with innocence and terror, were three diminutive figures— miniature facsimiles of the monstrous creature now ensnared in his trap. They were a bizarre yet pitiable blend of goat and human, their small faces etched with the terror of their mother's final, agonizing cries. Despite their unsettling appearance, there was something undeniably poignant about the tiny beings. Their odd features, a grotesque mixture of the fantastical and the human, were tempered by their tender age, giving them an otherworldly charm that tugged at Arvin's heartstrings. This awakened within him a flicker of sympathy and an unexpected surge of protectiveness.

The sight of these innocent, trembling creatures, whose lives were ripped apart even before they had begun, struck a chord within the gruff man. It reminded him, albeit in a twisted, haunting manner, of the cyclical nature of life and death he had come to accept in the woods. But for the first time, it was a cycle he found himself questioning.

As a flicker of pity began to kindle in Arvin's chest, it was swiftly quelled by the pragmatic survival instincts that had been his bedrock in these untamed woods. His gaze, once a tumultuous blend of revulsion and intrigue, now crystallized into a steely resolve as he weighed his options.

Life in the forest was a grueling test of endurance, and recent times had seen him falter under its weight. The previous year had been particularly cruel, robbing him of his health and, consequently, his ability to earn a living. With no other recourse, he had found himself on the doorstep of the town's clergy, hat in hand, seeking financial assistance. The clergy, for all their piety, had extended a loan to him with interest rates that bordered on usury. Gratitude for their timely assistance was now overshadowed by the looming specter of missed payments and the draconian penalties that awaited him should he default, penalties that included the unthinkable prospect of imprisonment.

His present situation, dire as it was, had left him with little room for the luxuries of morality or pity. And so, as he stood before the enormous creature and its diminutive offspring, he couldn't help but regard them as the godsend they were, a means to extricate himself from the financial mire he had found himself ensnared in.

The heft of the mother beast's lifeless form was not lost on Arvin, nor was the potential bounty it represented. He understood all too well the decadent predilections of the town's wealthiest denizens. Exotic meats were the currency of opulence, a tangible manifestation of status that they vied with each other to showcase. Here, in the grotesque form of this terrifying carcass, lay the epitome of the exotic, a terrifying treasure trove that held the promise of a tidy windfall, enough to see him through the lean months ahead.

With a world-weary exhale, Arvin bent down to retrieve the rustic cradle nestled in the tree hollow. His wagon, an essential requisite for transporting the hefty carcass of the mother beast, was parked at his cabin, a fair distance away. In the meantime, he decided to take the fauns with him, their ethereal innocence a stark contrast to the macabre tableau that had unfolded.

Hoisting the cradle, he commenced the trek through the dense woodland towards his home. Every so often, his gaze would be drawn downwards to the fauns that gazed up at him with eyes wide and brimming with an innocence that belied their monstrous lineage. The weight of their gaze was almost as tangible as the weight of the cradle in his arms, a silent plea that pierced the veil of his jaded heart.

Once at home, he arranged a makeshift bed in a secluded corner of his kitchen for the creatures. He lined an old wooden crate with hay and soft, worn-out clothes that had outlived their use. It was a poor excuse for a bed, but it was the best he could offer. As he laid the strange fauns in their new home, they made mysterious chirping noises that filled his usually silent cabin. At first, they were sounds of fear, but gradually the chirps became more curious, and the fauns showed interest in their new surroundings. He watched them, their innocent wonder stirring a strange sense of responsibility within him. Shaking off the unfamiliar feeling, he headed out to fetch his cart, leaving them behind.

When he returned to the lifeless body of the beast, he hoisted it up onto his old, rickety cart. The body, now limp and lifeless, lay grotesquely sprawled, its limbs hanging over the edges of the cart. Each bump on the path seemed to jolt the corpse, making it seem eerily alive, a morbid puppet dancing to the tune of death.

As Arvin made his way through the thick foliage, a strange disquiet settled upon him, unsettling in its novelty. With every step that carried him further from the sanctuary of his cabin, an invisible cord seemed to tug at his heartstrings, compelling him to return. The adrenaline-fueled excitement that had once been an integral part of the hunt now felt distant, its intensity diminished and replaced by an overwhelming compulsion to rush back to the three small beings who had, quite unexpectedly, become his charges. In his mind's eye, he pictured them huddled together, their eyes wide pools of innocence, fear, and confusion, strangers in a land that was as foreign to them as they were to it. The raw vulnerability etched in their expressions had kindled within him a protective instinct, an almost paternal desire to shield them from the harsh realities of their existence and offer them a haven of safety and comfort.

Ensconced within the inky veil of night, Arvin guided his cart, laden with its grim and grotesque payload, through a winding pathway toward the town's outskirts. He had captured strange creatures before—the forest was indeed home to many curious entities, and tales of the paranormal abounded in these lands. Three years ago, he had ensnared a frog so large he could hardly lift it; its eyes shone with a pink glow that, Arvin swore, had caused him to slip into a trancelike state. He had been forced to cover the fantastical reptile with a sack to shield himself from its gaze. On another occasion, he had encountered a giant badger, a beast of legends with claws longer than Arvin's own fingers; it was larger than a wild boar and only fell after taking five arrows. But by far, the greatest prize was the mutant wildcat he had snared more than five years prior. Its form was so strange that even now he struggled to recall its shape—a long, snakelike body with six legs, and fangs so enormous that the King himself was said to have purchased its head, now displayed in the royal gallery. The beast was the stuff of nightmares. Each creature he had taken to the butcher had earned him a sum of money that exceeded a regular year's worth of earnings. The reward for this latest creature was sure to be even more substantial.

The village that Arvin found himself nearing was ancient, its history etched into the fabric of its existence. Nestled upon a forested mountain peak and fortified by towering stone walls, it was a relic of the past, a testament to the bygone days of a vast empire that was now in its twilight. The landscape that approached its gates was marked by terraced farms that ascended the slopes, a mosaic of agriculture that contrasted starkly with the dense woodland that cocooned it.

In its heyday, the empire was a robust entity, its borders patrolled and protected by legions of well-funded monarchs. But as the years wore on, its robustness waned, leaving its furthest reaches, including this mountainous outpost, somewhat forgotten and neglected. The only reason it had not been completely forsaken was its location atop an enormous underground reservoir of salt, a valuable commodity that enriched a select few. The wealth derived from this natural resource funded the lifestyles of a handful of elites and clergy who took up residence in the ancient palaces and monasteries that were ensconced behind those formidable stone walls. Outside of this sanctum, the less affluent — the tradesmen and farmers — eked out a living, their abodes clinging to the exterior of the fortress walls like barnacles to a ship's hull.

It was a taxing climb for Arvin as he hauled his heavily laden wagon beneath the starlit night sky. Gradually, the silhouette of half-timbered houses emerged, their aged facades lit by the flickering light of lanterns that hung from rusted hooks. These structures, though worn by the passage of time, were redolent with stories from days of yore, standing as silent witnesses to the harmonious coexistence of civilization and the encircling wilderness.

Above this tableau, imposing in its authority, the town's governing body and its clergy occupied towering edifices that loomed over the walls, their penetrating gaze constantly surveying the hamlet below, ever vigilant for any deviation from their imposed righteous path.

Adjacent to the gate was the butcher's shop, a quaint two-story half-timber building that exuded an air of rustic charm. Its thick wooden beams framed walls of white stucco and brick, and hanging from its frontage was a sign that bore the painted image of a sumptuous ham hock, a visual enticement that even the illiterate could not fail to comprehend. This establishment was owned by Arvin's sole friend, Tibor, though to refer to the relationship between the two hardened men as a friendship might be a stretch.

Yet, for all its apparent adherence to ancient customs and its rustic appeal, the town harbored a dark secret. Its elite, comprised of aristocrats and clergy alike, were united in their pursuit of decadent pleasures, their taste buds titillated by exotic and forbidden meats. This gross indulgence stood in stark opposition to the holy vows they purportedly upheld, a hypocrisy that was all the more stark given the strange bounty that the surrounding forest seemed to provide. As darkness descended, the wealthiest among them satiated their gluttonous desires, partaking in an epicurean sin that the clergy conveniently chose to ignore, often joining in the debauchery themselves.

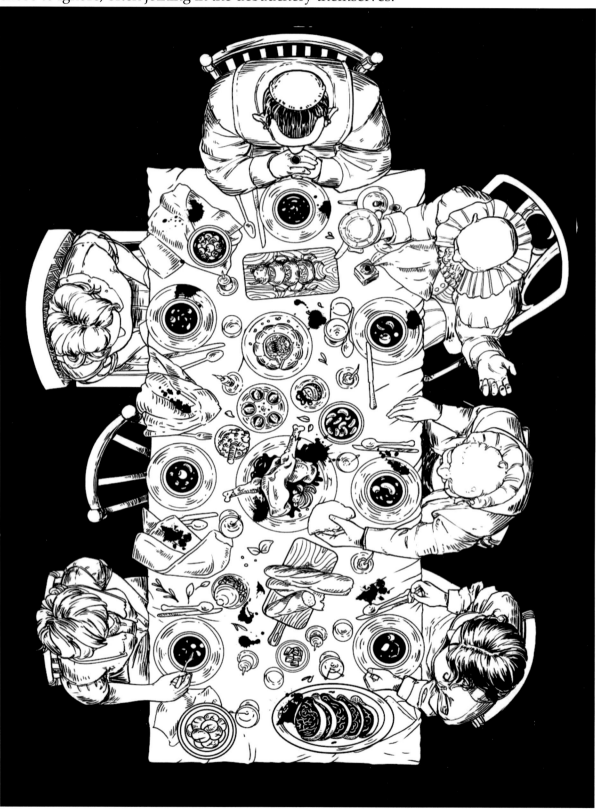

In this intricate dance of sin and secrecy, the butcher played an indispensable role. This strange creature was not the first, nor would be the last, to make its way to the butchering table. These forests were filled with undiscovered beasts, but this one was more ominous than most, and its unmistakably humanoid form would make it particularly sinful for consumption. Tibor, the epitome of cruelty wrapped in human skin, was such a carcass' trusted facilitator. His lanky form, draped in shadows, resided here near the town gate, making his sinister shop conveniently located for such a discrete delivery. As he saw Arvin's silhouette emerge from the darkness, Tibor' unsettlingly asymmetrical face broke into a carnivorous grin.

As Arvin's horse clattered to a halt in front of Tibor' establishment, the butcher emerged from the shadowy innards of his shop, a flickering lantern in his hand casting monstrous shadows on the surrounding stone walls. His long, skeletal fingers curled around the door handle, eyes glinting with a cold, avaricious anticipation that was all too familiar to Arvin.

"Evening, Arvin," Tibor drawled, his voice gravelly and as unsettling as the eeriness that hung in the air. "Looks like you have something mighty interesting for me tonight." He scurried to the side of the building where he opened the double doorway leading to his meat storage.

Arvin, the gruff stoicism that characterized his demeanor unbroken, nodded in silent affirmation and followed, pushing the overloaded cart over the threshold into the cold stone room. Here, massive hooks hung from the ceiling, for placing large animals on, to be drained of their blood before butchering. Arvin helped Tibor lift the body and hang it from one of the hooks. Its gigantic length hindered it from being totally suspended; its long hooved legs touched the floor.

"Have you ever seen such a creature?" Arvin asked quietly, looking in reverence at the great beast before them. Hanging upright like a ghoulish puppet, the creature's head flopped forwards, hiding the slash mark from Arvin's blade on its throat.

"I have never seen one, but indeed I have heard of such a creature. Have you never heard of the Ördög?" Tibor asked incredulously.

"No, I have heard many strange tales but nothing about a creature like this one." Arvin replied, intrigued. He leaned against the stone walls of the meat locker and listened to Tibor's tale....

"They say the first Ördög was born a woman. Exceedingly ugly, a mutant, she led an unfortunate life of loneliness and despair. She became so desperate for a child of her own that she delved into the dark arts. There, she found a way to bear a child without a man, but with the devil himself. After performing a ritual opening a doorway to hell, she became pregnant. When the child was born, it was so enormous that it killed her during labor. Those who bore witness to it said it was half goat and half man. Not knowing its demonic heritage, the priests declared it immoral to murder the creature, so instead it was abandoned, left in the forest to die.

"From that creature grew the Ördög, standing taller than the tallest man, and as strong as three combined. It has claws larger than a bear's, and walks on hooved legs. Its face is a mix of goat and man, horns spring from its head, and a long tail protrudes from its rear. That, my friend, is what we see before us now."

Arvin was astounded and did not know how to respond. He stared at the corpse hanging before him. Indeed, it had massive claws, and horns, and the tail could be seen dangling from behind it. He wondered if Tibor would make up such a tale just to scare him but thought better of it. Magnifying the rare and powerful nature of the beast would only increase its value, which meant paying Arvin a greater sum. This would not be in Tibor's best interest. He surmised that indeed he must be telling the truth. Arvin paused, and for a moment became fearful of the three fauns back in his cabin. But the memory of their cute little faces, and the innocence in those eyes, dispelled him of any such worries.

Returning to his natural cool demeanor, Arvin laughed. "You will have to pay me a pretty penny for her then." He smiled wryly, pleased with his witty response.

The negotiation that followed was a dance of two seasoned practitioners. The butcher, his eyes gleaming with anticipation, offered Arvin a handsome sum, his sinewy fingers stroking his purse thoughtlessly. Arvin, an old hand at this grim trade, held out for more, his counteroffer measured and unyielding.

Once the business proceedings had concluded, the two men vacated the confines of the icy meat locker, taking solace in the comparatively more hospitable environment of the butcher shop, as was their custom. Seated comfortably, Arvin took the opportunity to regale Tibor with the tale of his extraordinary encounter with the beast. He spared no detail, vividly depicting the heart-wrenching wails that had first alerted him to the creature's presence, and subsequently, his discovery of the behemoth sprawled out on the forest floor, cruelly ensnared by his bear trap. The crescendo of his narrative was the revelation of the three faun offspring secreted within the hollow of the tree. This crucial bit of information acted as a catalyst to Tibor's already fervent interest, stoking the fires of his avarice. His eyes alight with a greedy gleam, Tibor promptly doubled his original offer for the fauns, his voice betraying the intensity of his desire through its tremulous tone. Despite the allure of the proffered sum, Arvin's resolve remained unyielding, and he declined the offer.

"You're certain?" Tibor inquired, an edge of incredulity sharpening his voice. "Let's not forget the substantial debt you've incurred with those avaricious clergy. Even with this sum, you'd scarcely make a dent in your outstanding balance."

Arvin's response was terse and final. "This will suffice to keep them at bay." Accepting the futility of his entreaties, Tibor gave a resigned nod. Their camaraderie concluded, Arvin bade him farewell, stepping out into the crisp night air.

***

Upon his return, Arvin's wagon was void of its macabre cargo, and his pockets were weighed down by the heft of the coins he carried. A twinge of guilt flitted through his heart at the thought of the three little fauns nestled in their makeshift bed. The irony of having sold their mother to the butcher, only to return to them as their new guardian, did not escape him, and a sense of self-disgust tinged what should have been a celebratory evening.

As he opened the door to his cabin, a chorus of coos and chirps greeted him. There, in the dim light, three small Ördög fauns lay nestled amidst hay and old clothes. His heart was tugged at the sight of their odd, hybrid forms – a fantastical manifestation of the folklore narrated to him by the butcher. Their tiny goat eyes, luminescent in the flickering lantern light, watched him with a mixture of reverence and curiosity, capturing his every move with an intensity that was both endearing and unnerving.

In the subsequent days, Arvin found himself at the doorstep of the town abbot. He handed over the lion's share of his hard-earned money into the greedy, claw-like hands of the clergyman. As he did so, a cynical thought crossed his mind - had this very man feasted on the flesh of the Ördög mother? In his heart, he knew the answer.

Back at his cabin, Arvin adapted to his new role as caregiver. He discovered that the fauns had a penchant for goat milk and took to the feeding bottles he had used in the past for his own goats. They would spend the daylight hours nestled in their bed, lost in slumber, only to awaken as the sun dipped below the horizon. In the evening, he would cradle them one by one, feeding them as the others frolicked and bleated on the cabin floor, basking in the warmth of the fire.

This new regimen became Arvin's routine. His days were consumed by the backbreaking labor of felling towering trees, their colossal trunks chopped and stacked, ready for trade. His nimble fingers worked his traps, capturing a variety of animals, their pelts and flesh destined for the nearby town. Yet, as night fell, the peculiar sight of his cabin, filled with these mythical creatures, their otherworldly features illuminated by the firelight, imbued him with a newfound sense of purpose.

With gentle hands, Arvin brought the feeding bottle to the tiny, waiting mouths of the fauns. Their diminutive lips greedily latched onto the bottle, their small bodies quivering with the eagerness for the nourishment they so desperately required. In those moments, their eyes - wide and innocent - would lock onto his, creating an intimate tableau that, to an outsider, would have appeared comically tender. Here was this fearsome trapper, a towering figure amidst the shadows and whispers of the ominous forest, tenderly nursing three creatures of folklore - demonic beings, so they claimed - with a patience and calmness that bordered on paternal.

Before the arrival of these odd, little fauns, Arvin's life had been a monochrome of bleak practicality, a life measured in the simple metrics of survival. Now, his world was punctuated by the quiet companionship of these peculiar orphans he had unexpectedly found himself caring for. Beneath the rough exterior and harsh demeanor of the trapper, lay a surprisingly nurturing side, a facet of his personality that he himself hadn't been aware of. As days merged into weeks, Arvin discovered, much to his surprise, a growing attachment to the little beings. Their vulnerability and dependence awoke within him a profound and primal protective instinct, one that he hadn't known existed. He, who had never even owned a pet, was now the guardian of beings with an intelligence that gleamed in their eyes, beings that clung to life with a desperation that resonated with him, for it was a feeling that mirrored his own struggle for survival in this harsh, unforgiving world.

✳✳✳

In an ironic and cruel twist of fate, Arvin awoke one dawn to the horrifying realization that his cherished woodcutting tools and meticulously crafted traps had vanished. Some audacious thief had exploited the cover of darkness, leaving Arvin bereft of the very instruments that defined his existence. Initial shock swiftly transformed into a slow-burning fury, the intense blaze of indignation glaring from his eyes.

Arvin, with his forest-honed instincts, could weather many of the wild's hardships, but these tools and traps were not mere instruments. They were the lifelines that anchored him to his vocation. The cost to replace them would be exorbitant, especially under the heavy weight of his outstanding debt to the clergy. Now deprived of his primary means of income, the icy fingers of desperation began to grip him.

Cornered by his circumstances, a heartrending choice loomed before him. The memory of the butcher's insidious proposal - the ravenous gleam that danced in his eyes at the prospect of the fauns' tender flesh - reverberated darkly in Arvin's mind. The very thought was chilling, but it also presented an immediate respite from his predicament. Rationality and cold pragmatism edged out emotion.

With a heart as heavy as lead and a grim resolve, he selected one of the three Ördög fauns. The faun's eyes, alight with innocence and trust as Arvin lifted it, pierced his soul like the sharpest of daggers. Yet, he steeled himself against the guilt that threatened to overwhelm him. In the brutal dance of survival, as he'd observed in the very nature around him, sacrifices were inevitable. This was the grim logic with which he justified the agonizing choice he was compelled to make.

He traded the minuscule creature to the butcher, receiving in return a substantial sum of money, sufficient to replace his pilfered tools and traps. With his task accomplished, Arvin retraced his steps to his abode, only to be met with the disoriented and terrified wails of the remaining fauns that pierced the stillness of the nocturnal forest. Gathering them into his robust arms, their minuscule bodies quivered against his rough exterior, serving as a stark reminder of the price exacted by survival.

From that day forth, a specter of guilt dogged Arvin's footsteps. The vacant space in their little bed, where the faun once slumbered, served as an unrelenting reminder of his treacherous act against his trusting brood. Their destinies were irrevocably entwined with his in this unforgiving world, and he had chosen to be their guardian. How then, could he have dispatched one to the butcher's cruel blade? These were the ponderings that emanated from his sentimental side. Yet, his pragmatic self offered a different perspective, equating his act to that of a mother deer abandoning one of its own in the face of a looming predator, a harsh yet necessary sacrifice for the greater good of the remaining kin. This was the logic that underpinned his decision. And so, amidst the shadows of the menacing forest, Arvin and the two remaining fauns trudged on, their very existence emblematic of nature's harsh dance for survival.

Months passed and life was good. The fauns flourished, their burgeoning physiques a testament to their Ördög lineage. They had seamlessly woven themselves into the fabric of Arvin's existence, their presence a comforting anomaly amidst the adversities that characterized his days.

Yet, the wilderness had a penchant for dashing hopes and dreams to ruins in the blink of an eye. Arvin's humble abode, a rudimentary structure born out of necessity, boasted a singular valuable asset – a stove, essential for both sustenance and warmth during the biting winter months. This stove, a relic salvaged from the town in years past, was the linchpin of his survival during the frigid season.

Unfortunately, on one fateful evening, the ancient, dilapidated stove committed an act of treachery: a small burning ember escaped its confines through a hole in its belly, landing on the wooden floorboards. The smoldering coal ignited a conflagration that quickly enveloped the cabin in an inferno, all while Arvin and the fauns were deep in slumber. Awoken by the roaring flames, Arvin found all attempts to douse the fire futile. Faced with no alternative, he salvaged what few valuables he could lay his hands on and, cradling the fauns in a wooden crate, fled the incinerating cabin. By dawn, his home was reduced to ashes.

Winter's icy grip was fast approaching. He could rely on the forest's bounty for timber to reconstruct his cabin, but procuring roof tiles, a stove, and rudimentary furniture necessitated funds. His dire circumstances once again directed his gaze toward the fauns. The mere thought of parting with another was akin to a dagger to his heart, a gut-wrenching sacrifice he wished to avoid. Yet, the allure of a snug home and the prospect of hot meals in the face of winter's brutal onslaught proved too seductive to resist.

With his heart encased in a shell of stoicism, he made his decision. Another faun was handed over to the butcher. The unsuspecting creature, with trusting eyes wide, was placed upon the butcher's slab. The coins that filled Arvin's pockets in exchange ensured the procurement of a new stove, bed, and roof, thereby securing his survival through the impending winter. Yet, the haunting image of the faun's eyes, filled with a mixture of trust and betrayal as he lay it on the butcher's table, was etched in Arvin's memory, an indelible mark that would remain with him for the remainder of his days.

***

Upon his return to the makeshift tent that served as their interim refuge after the tragic fire, Arvin was greeted by the searching eyes of the lone faun he'd come to endearingly call Cody. Those eyes, vast wells of innocence, reflected bewilderment at the sudden absence of his brother. Arvin, reciprocating that gaze with unwavering determination, silently conveyed a promise birthed from their shared hardships. The sacrifices made, trading the lives of Cody's kin for the security of their future, weighed heavily upon him. But from that moment onward, Arvin committed to an unspoken oath: to place Cody's well-being above all else. Using the acquired funds, he began crafting a modest cabin, ensuring they'd face the winter's embrace shielded from its harshest touch.

As the two rebuilt their home and their lives, Cody flourished. Arvin couldn't help but be struck by the faun's uncanny aptitude, an almost human-like awareness glimmering in his eyes. Cody exhibited an understanding of gestures and commands that surpassed Arvin's wildest expectations for this uncanny amalgamation of animal and human.

Cody's gaze followed Arvin with an intriguing blend of curiosity and mischief as he wielded his ax to collect lumber or while meticulously laying traps amidst the trees encircling their abode. The fledgling faun's remarkable agility was evident in every step he took on his cloven feet. His upper limbs, shaped in the mold of human arms and hands, had burgeoned into powerful appendages, far surpassing the strength one would expect in a human boy. As the months rolled by, Cody's digits grew into formidable claws, necessitating frequent trimmings by Arvin. His nimbleness and velocity were a marvel, effortlessly keeping pace with Arvin as they navigated the dense tapestry of their woodland world.

In the tranquility of the evening, as shadows blended into the encroaching obscurity, Arvin would lounge by the comforting flames, with Cody nestled at his feet, often engaged with the simple wooden blocks that Arvin had crafted for him. Arvin's voice would weave the ancient tales once relayed to him by his own father. Bathed in the golden flicker of the firelight, Cody's eyes would shine with lucid understanding, his mental faculties mirroring those of a human child, marked only by the absence of speech. As each story reached its zenith, Cody would erupt in a cascade of delighted claps, his small hands meeting in gleeful acclamation. And as the narrative drew to its close, he would gently tug at Arvin's pant leg, a silent plea for another tale to fill the hushed nocturnal air. This mute communion, rich with unspoken gestures and implied emotions, stood as a testament to the intricate and indescribable bond that had blossomed between them.

Time, with its eternal dance of seasons, wrought a profound metamorphosis in Arvin. The once barren wastelands of his heart were now awash with the budding warmth of newfound sentiments. Cody, his steadfast confidant and surrogate offspring, was the catalyst that precipitated this transformation.

However, the ghosts of his past choices were inexorable, casting long shadows over his spirit. The acute sting of regret and the overwhelming surge of self-reproach that swamped him whenever he gazed upon Cody was nearly insurmountable. The realization that he had traded the lives of Cody's siblings—who would undoubtedly have been as extraordinary as Cody himself—in pursuit of his own welfare, was sufficient to bring a surge of pain deep within his guts.

In the face of these tumultuous emotions, Arvin found solace in the rhythm of their shared existence. The once burdensome tasks of survival now took on a new hue, their silent understanding illuminating their path forward. Together, they forged a life suffused with gentle happiness in their woodland sanctuary. Arvin found delight in the simple acts of making meals, maintaining their humble abode, and collaborating in their daily endeavors. The once burdensome tasks required for survival morphed into opportunities for shared growth and camaraderie. Their existence, harmoniously synchronized, became a beautiful dance of trust and reliance upon each other.

In the twilight hours, when the day's toil had come to an end, Arvin would sit by the fire's glow, his eyes fixed on Cody's earnest gaze. The flames cast dancing shadows on their faces, the hushed crackle of burning logs accompanying the unspoken conversations they shared. Arvin would hold Cody's hand, his touch a testament to his remorse, silently asking for forgiveness for a deed he could never admit to aloud.

As Cody matured into adolescence, the fabric of their once straightforward existence became threaded with complexity. The isolation that had once cradled them now became a burdensome shroud enveloping the maturing creature's growing self-awareness. A poignant realization of his unique place in the world and the solitary path it necessitated became increasingly troubling to him. Arvin, assuming the roles of both father and mentor, revealed to Cody the necessity of their concealment and the perilous consequences should they be discovered. In a harsh yet indispensable lesson, Arvin covertly led Cody into the stillness of the nighttime town, revealing the gruesome trophies of beastly heads adorning the walls of the town's elite. He did his utmost to explain the harsh realities of their existence, laying bare the grim fate that would befall Cody should he ever be exposed.

But, akin to any human adolescent, Cody harbored a longing for camaraderie and a kinship with those similar to him. In clandestine rebellion against his circumscribed existence, Cody would slip from the confines of their cabin under the cover of night's inky tapestry. Stealthily, he traversed the boundaries of their wooded sanctuary, and returned to the town perched atop the hill his father had shown him. Concealed amidst the shadows or perched upon rooftops, Cody would surreptitiously immerse himself in the townspeople's conversations. This stealthy eavesdropping was his sole connection to the outside world—a world he was barred from but longed to be part of. The murmured discourse of the townspeople wafted through the night air, each word a tantalizing glimpse into the realm he yearned to join.

One fateful night, he overheard the chatter of two farm wives. Hidden amidst the shadows of a storage loft, Cody crouched silently, his breath catching in his throat as he tried to remain undiscovered. Below him, the two women worked late into the night; bathed in the soft orange glow of lantern light. A mound of fresh peaches lay between them, and one-by- one, they skinned the fruits, dropping them into an enormous bubbling pot to reduce them into a compote. As they toiled, they chatted away:

"There was a woman, just like that," began one, her voice dripping with intrigue. "Haven't you heard the tale?"

"I have heard of the Ördög, of course, but not of anything recent, only myths from long ago." The other replied, eagerly awaiting a response.

The first woman leaned in conspiratorially. "Then listen well," she whispered. "In the heart of our very town, there lived a woman named Valerie. Her face was a landscape of oddities: a jutting, pointed chin, a nearly bald head, and eyes that were set so wide apart they seemed to watch the world from two different vantage points. Tall and gaunt, she resembled a lone tree in winter's grasp. Her visage might've drawn pitying glances and hushed chuckles, but her mind was a fortress, sharp and unyielding.

"Yet, behind the walls of that fortress lay a deep abyss of loneliness. And in her yearning, she turned to the legends whispered on nights like this — tales of the Ördög. In their haunting lore, she saw not just a reflection of her plight, but a potential answer. She didn't want the tragic fate of the woman from the myth, who met her demise when birthing the Ördög. No, she was too smart for that. Instead, she sought something more strategic. She wished to become an Ördög herself first, then to become pregnant by the beast, this way, she could live, and have a family of her own.

"She studied forbidden texts, and she learned how to summon the Ördög. In the months that followed her treacherous act of black magic, murmurs began to swirl about her. People noticed her hands were growing into the claws, and she covered her legs with long dresses so no one could see her feet. But people claimed they began to hear the clop of hooves as she walked. She grew taller, her silhouette more imposing with every moon. And then, as suddenly as her changes began, she vanished. Some claim she retreated to the heart of the forest where she could raise her freakish brood in peace."

The second woman scoffed, breaking the tense silence. "Such fables!"
The storyteller's eyes sparkled mischievously. "Ah, but there's one detail that might sway your disbelief," she murmured, dragging out a long pause to ignite suspense.

The skeptic listened intently. After waiting in silence for a few moments she leaned in, and asked, "What?"

The first woman's voice dropped even lower. "Soon after Valerie's disappearance, a fearsome woodsman brought the butcher a mysterious prize from his traps. It was the corpse of a female Ördög. Her carcass was secretly sold to the clergy, who roasted her to perfection, served in secret during one of the infamous royal gatherings. The Count, my husband's employer, was present. He confided in my husband about the feast, he still raves about the divine taste of Ördög meat."

"Absolutely revolting!" The second woman cried out, followed by a cackle of mischievous laughter from the both of them.

From his hiding spot, Cody's heart raced. Tears blurred his vision as he grappled with the ramifications of the tale, his mysterious heritage revealed to him now, like a knife in his guts. He tried to ignore the story as only speculation but continued his clandestine visits to town under the cloak of night to learn even more.

In light of the old hag's tale, Cody became obsessed with the notion of infiltrating one of these nefarious banquets. By eavesdropping in the town's concealed corners, he gleaned the details of the forthcoming exclusive gathering. That night, brimming with both dread and determination, he made his way into the palatial abode of the town's most opulent salt merchant. Finding solace in the shadowy confines of an enormous cabinet, he peered out at the grandiose banquet hall, which was abuzz with the town's most illustrious figures.

The resplendent room was a whirl of color and activity as the elites of society reveled in their secreted midnight banquet. Their conversations, refined yet superficial, swirled around the prodigious dining table that groaned under the weight of extravagant delicacies. The center of attention was a mythical bird of monumental proportions, its gilded and azure feathers meticulously arranged as ornamental garlands that adorned the table. The bird's colossal, plump body, now a glistening golden brown, sat proudly as the banquet's centerpiece.

"A most exquisite find, this Sabre Pheasant, wouldn't you agree?" declared an esteemed guest, the bones of the wing delicately held between her gloved fingers. "It's almost a pity that so few of them remain in the wild," chimed in a corpulent clergyman, his tone a nauseating mix of haughty indulgence and faux lament.

"It is quite satisfactory," agreed a portly nobleman, his obese frame enveloped in an extravagant, plum-hued velvet cloak. As he spoke, his jowls undulated in tandem with his whimpered utterances. "But, alas, it fails to hold a candle to the Ördög fauns that once adorned our banquet tables so many years ago." His melancholic sigh resonated through the air, promptly followed by vigorous nods from the surrounding elites. Their faces etched with an amalgam of wistful nostalgia and a calculated indifference, as they sought to affirm their lofty status by feigning nonchalance towards the lavish spread before them. Even the Count himself, seated at the head of the table, joined in the chorus of agreement. "Ah, now that was a true epicurean indulgence!" he declared with a flourish.

This confirmation of his suspicions, that his father was complicit in supplying such forbidden trade to the town's elites, sent rage through Cody's veins. His suspicions, once vague and nebulous, now crystallized into an irrefutable truth. The revelation of this past atrocity, a vile feast upon his own kin, likely supplied by his own father, was an affront to his very essence. Struggling to contain the wellspring of grief and fury threatening to escape, he bided his time until the revelry waned. Finally, under the cloak of night, he made his surreptitious departure, retreating to the sanctuary of his woodland home.

On the way back to the cabin, in the depths of the night, Cody absorbed these fragments of knowledge, connecting the dots of his peculiar heritage. The Ördög blood that flowed through his veins, the forbidden union of human and beast. The man he knew as his father, who taught him all he knew, and cared for him his whole life, was also the murderer of his mother and siblings. It was a revelation that stirred a mix of rage, sorrow, and an ever-growing resolve within him. From that moment on, his existence became intertwined with a haunting awareness, a profound understanding of his true nature.

By the time Cody had made it home, he was so filled with rage that he burst through the door of their humble abode, storming towards the tiny kitchen counter where he grabbed a large knife. Eyes filled with both tears and rage, he jumped upon the bed where his father lay. His now large and ox-like legs straddled his father's sleeping body.

Arvin, startled from his dreams by the sight of his son hovering above him, felt a primal fear seize his very being. A long knife glinted in the dim light, poised above his head, ready to strike. Terror coursed through his veins, his heart pounding like a distant drum. He had never imagined that the boy he had nurtured and loved would ever stand before him as he did now, as a harbinger of death.

But as their gazes intertwined, a tragic understanding pierced through Cody's haze of fury. He saw the profound weariness carved into the old man's visage, etched lines spelling out years of regret. Silent pleas for forgiveness hovered in the air, a burden that had hung between them, unspoken, yet palpable, for all these years. This tragic tapestry of guilt was now laid bare for Cody to see, a sorrowful truth his innocence had previously obscured.

In that suspended moment, Cody's arm faltered, the knife trembling in his grasp. The love that had been forged through years of shared existence surged through his veins, overriding the rage that had consumed him. He could not bring himself to strike down the man who had been his father in all but blood.

The room was steeped in a heavy silence, interrupted only by their uneven breaths, echoing the turmoil within. In the midst of this charged stillness, Cody emitted a heart-wrenching cry, a sound so raw and desperate that it needed no words to convey his plea. As the sound washed over him, tears pooled in the old man's eyes, a poignant reflection of his understanding. Years of unspoken communication allowed him to read his boy's thoughts without words. He knew the source of Cody's rage. His darkest secret had been revealed.

"I deserve death," Arvin said solemnly. "And now that you know the truth, you will abandon me. In the face of that, put me out of my misery," he pleaded. "I prefer death to that," the old man said, and tears flowed from both his eyes in a steady stream. Arvin braced himself for the punishment he believed was his due. In the flickering light, he nodded his head reassuringly. He was prepared to face the consequences of his actions.

But the blow never came. Instead, in the darkness of their shared pain and regret, the bond that had weathered the storms of their existence was too deep. Cody, overwhelmed by a mixture of emotions, lowered the knife, his trembling hand releasing its grip. It fell to the floor with a clatter.

Cody stood and jumped from the bed, running for the door of the cabin. He left Arvin, and disappeared into the depths of the night, into the forest beyond. At the same moment, Arvin raced to the door, but the old man was no match for Cody's youthful speed. Realizing that any pursuit would be useless, he stopped at the doorway, looking out into the trees beyond their little porch. He cried out in anguish, a ghostly echo of his boy's name, into the night air. Again and again, he cried out, pleading for Cody to return. But there was no answer, no sign that his beloved son would return. The wilderness swallowed him whole, leaving Arvin alone, calling out to the emptiness for hours until his voice left him, until he collapsed on the floorboards in front of his doorway.

In the following months, a relentless onslaught of torment befell Arvin, plunging him deeper into a realm of darkness and despair. Each attempt to gather wood or set a trap became an exercise in futility, as if an unseen malevolence conspired to thwart his every move. Sturdy logs, newly fallen, vanished without a trace, while the traps he so carefully placed would seemingly disappear minutes after they were set. It was as if the world itself had turned against him. He could barely earn a penny to survive.

For years, Arvin's heart had been encased in ice, a frigid chamber untouched by warmth. Yet, the brief span he'd spent raising his adopted son had kindled a fragile flame within. Now, with Cody gone, the cold seeped back in, intensified by the biting pain of loss. It's often said that the sting of losing something cherished is far worse than never having known it at all. For Arvin, the weight of Cody's absence was a burden too crushing to bear.

The forest, once his haven, now stood as a silent witness to his solitude. Despair became his constant shadow, wrapping him in its cold embrace. With his will to live dwindling, Arvin's life spiraled into degradation. The man who once hunted and chopped wood with pride now found himself groveling for mere scraps and stray coins at the town gate.

Once respected, or at least feared, Arvin became pitied, and a pariah. Whispered tales, steeped in pity and superstition, followed him like a cloud. Children mocked him from a distance, their parents casting wary eyes, seeing him as a manifestation of ill omens. The town's gates, once open, now shut him out, and the clergy, deeming him tainted, barred him from sacred gatherings.

His home, once a snug refuge amidst the wilderness, now bore the scars of neglect. Walls that had sheltered laughter and dreams now sagged with the weight of despair. The once crackling hearth, the heart of his home, stood cold and abandoned. Arvin, in the ruins of what once was, became a spectral figure, a living ghost, lost in the remnants of a life once full.

In the depths of this desolation, a flicker of hope was granted. A chance encounter with a mysterious figure ignited a glimmer of hope within Arvin's beleaguered soul. One day, while he was in the woods, an old wandering Táltos reached him, appearing out of the trees. A practitioner of ancient occult arts, this Táltos held the key to communing with the supernatural.

In times past, the appearance of such a foreboding figure would have instilled fear in Arvin's heart, but his current condition left him merely gazing in silent communion as the odd figure materialized from the forest shadows. Wild, unfocused eyes met Arvin's gaze, a mirror reflecting back his own fractured sanity. Here were two souls, both unraveled by their individual torment, each recognizing themselves in the other. The strange man, his body draped in a mosaic of unprocessed animal hides, bore an aroma of decomposition and filth. Amongst his morbid garb, enigmatic symbols and amulets pulsating with an inexplicable energy were woven. A small smile curled at the corners of Arvin's lips as the Táltos made his approach, the two disparate beings drawn together in the obsidian embrace of the woods, their disjointed psyches seeking solace in this unexpected union.

"How has one so fearsome as yourself become so pathetic?" The Táltos asked in a grizzled, whispery voice that almost sounded like the wind itself.

"I lost my son," Arvin replied, and the once menacing man, now so used to begging, raised his hand in the pathetic gesture of a vagrant. The two crazed-looking men stared at each other, eye-to-eye in that moment. Silence surrounded them as time lingered.

Then the Táltos spoke. "I can give you what you need," he replied in a sinister tone. "But it is an offer only fit for a man who has nothing to lose."

Any other man, given such a response, would have immediately declined, as the intention was clearly malevolent, but Arvin only stared back with hope in his eyes. "You can?" he asked.

"You will have to let go of any prior superstitious beliefs," the Táltos said eagerly. "Everything you previously have been told is forbidden is actually the solution." The Táltos followed this reply by revealing a large leather-bound book that he had concealed under his unusual clothes.

Arvin's eyes drifted to the book, fixated on it as though it were made of gold. "This book will help me find my boy?" Arvin replied in a pathetically desperate tone.

"A particular group of pages from this book, yes," the Táltos replied. "A ritual that can summon the forces that you seek." The insane shaman looked almost afraid to speak the next words. "An Ördög," he replied, much quieter than before. At this, Arvin reached out for the book, but as his hand came close, the Táltos snatched it away. "Not the whole book, fool!" he said cruelly. "You have no concept of what this took to create, but I will give you the portion you require… if you can afford to pay for it," he sneered.

Arvin was seemingly caught off guard. He paused for a long moment, lost in thought. He could only think of one thing he had of value. "My home," he responded. "It is small, and in disrepair, but it is all I have to offer."

"Take me there," the Táltos said and smiled broadly as Arvin nodded.

Arvin led the wild-looking shaman through the woods towards his home. The pair of men would have been quite the sight if seen by onlookers. Two crazed and disheveled men walking through the forest, with only the sounds of the forest around them, and the clanging of the Táltos' strange garb. When they reached Arvin's little cabin, the Táltos looked upon it eagerly.

They entered the home together. Arvin showed the man all of his belongings pleadingly, seeking the acceptance of the offer. His possessions were meager, and the place was in rough condition, having been neglected for some time now. Arvin had sold most of his furnishings and anything of value to people in town. All that was left was his bed, a chair, and the cupboards of his tiny kitchen, filled with only a few items. The Táltos inspected the cabin, wandering the floor, and looking into the drawers. Then, he nodded in approval.

"From one outcast to another," the Táltos cackled cynically, and he retrieved the great book from beneath his robe once more, flipping to the center of it. He then tore out three pages from its depths and handed them over to Arvin's eager hands. As the pages were transferred from one man to the other, a great howl from some unknown beast came from far off in the woods.

Arvin felt a powerful vibration as soon as he held them in his grasp. A paranormal vibration was clearly evident, and he knew the offer he had made was not a fraud. He quickly looked at the contents of those pages. His literacy was rudimentary, but there were many diagrams and simplified vocabulary, implying that the Táltos was of a similar literacy. The most important words to read were the incantation, and this he only needed to be able to sound out, for the language they were written in was clearly not his own.

"These pictures show additional items I will need," Arvin said worriedly, realizing he had already offered his home and all of its contents.

As if experiencing a sudden glimmer of regret, the Táltos spoke once more, "The consequences of such a ritual are not reversible. Know that once you open such a portal, there will be no turning back."

Arvin hardly listened to his cautionary words; he had only one focus now. Even when the Táltos offered him to stay for the night, Arvin declined. So, the Táltos rummaged through the cupboards and removed the items that Arvin would require. The Táltos gathered a dagger, a flint, a lantern, and a little pot.

"Take these," he said, handing them over. "Search now for a ring of oaks directly north from here. You will know it when you see it; they are like no others, and while you wander you will need to find nightshade berries," the Táltos instructed and then handed him one more thing from his own pockets. "Here are the bones of a crow, the main ingredient you will require. Consider it a final parting gift. The rest is up to you."

Arvin took the items gratefully and left immediately. Walking out the door of his little cabin he had lived in with Cody for so many years, he did not even look back. Now driven by a singular focus, Arvin headed northwards through the dense forest. He did not eat, and only drank water from streams. As he wandered, he found a nightshade bush and greedily collected its berries.

He walked, both day and night. Oftentimes doubling back, retracing his steps, ensuring he hadn't strayed off path, for five days in a row. Then, he finally stumbled upon the sight the Táltos had told him about. Just as the sun's last rays painted the horizon, a foreboding circle of oak trees emerged. Their towering presence cast long, ghostly shadows, and etched upon their ancient trunks were cryptic carvings, relics of forgotten ceremonies. At the heart of this circle, sat a pile of cold gray ashes, whispering tales of rituals long past.

With unwavering resolve, Arvin set his lantern alight. The flickering glow, hung from a sturdy stick in the clearing's center, pushed back the encroaching darkness. Laying out the timeworn pages, he meticulously went over the ritual's steps, ensuring he missed no crucial detail.

Taking a deep breath, he sketched a protective circle in the ground. Then, using this same stick, he carefully replicated the symbols represented in the book into the dirt around him. He then ignited a small fire and, using large stones as a base, placed his little pot above the flames. Into this pot, he added the nightshade berries and the brittle bones of the crow that the Táltos had provided him with.

As the contents hissed and released a thick, eerie smoke, Arvin steeled himself and then began to recite the incantation written on those pages:

"Zara Kalyn ordoth aznae,
Vithra ghanul tharza vinthae,
Narun zilthar, karza lithae,
Ordoth rizna, zarun fithae,
Marnul ordoth, zarun dithnae"

As he spoke these foreign words, sounding them out slowly to get them correct, he raised his left wrist above the small pot that was now sizzling. Using the dagger he had brought, he then slit his wrist, cutting deep into the veins. His blood gushed, and he directed the liquid into the pot.

At that same moment, the forest around him seemed to shimmer. The winds began to stir, whispering secrets carried from realms beyond mortal comprehension. The very ground beneath him trembled, as if awakened by the resonance of his words. As Arvin peered into the depths of the ancient forest around him, his eyes met a haunting spectacle. From the gnarled branches and twisted trunks, a multitude of eyes now loomed, staring back at him, bearing faces of otherworldly countenance.

Among the eerie gathering, he discerned a towering beast, its hirsute body standing tall on two legs, exuding an aura of primal power. Not far from that, a hybrid creature with terrifying features, its countenance a curious blend of reptilian and human form, with strange tattoos inked into the skin of its face. In the shadows, other forms that defied earthly norms emerged, with heads in place of torsos and multiple limbs, some intertwined in unsettling formations.

Alongside these, beings of indescribable alienness eluded definition, their shapes hinting at realms beyond human comprehension. These mysterious faces, each unique and unsettling, gazed upon Arvin with an intensity that spoke of ancient enigmas and hidden truths. They formed a congregation of the unknown, an eerie chorus of watchers that beckoned him towards a realm that lay beyond the veil of mortal understanding.

Amidst the congregation of spectral faces, Cody emerged. Enveloped in an aura of otherworldly majesty, he towered above the gathered spirits, his horns reaching skyward, symbols of his ethereal nature. Arvin's breath caught in his chest as he gazed upon his beloved son, now transformed into a being of fearsome power and authority.

Overwhelmed by the magnitude of the moment, Arvin knelt before Cody, a gesture of humility and reverence. His heart pounded with a mixture of awe and trepidation, for he knew that this was a pact that would forever alter his existence. Cody, the Ördög, extended his arms, an invitation for Arvin to embrace his destiny.

With unwavering determination and a surge of emotions coursing through his veins, Arvin clasped Cody's clawed hands, sealing their connection. The energies within the sacred circle intensified, their spirits merging in a symphony of light and darkness. A transformation began, transcending the boundaries of mortality and granting Arvin the power of the Ördög.

As the ritual reached its zenith, the forest became a stage upon which the realms intertwined. Time stood still, and the mortal and the mystical merged as one. The communion between father and son was sealed, an unbreakable bond that would span eternity. The trees seemed to release a sigh of sadness, while other voices laughed and cheered.

In the hallowed silence that followed, Arvin rose, his being now interwoven with the essence of the Ördög. The spirits of the forest whispered their approval, their forms fading into the tapestry of shadows. From that moment on, the two Ördögs would roam the depths of the forest, and many say they can be seen some nights sitting on rooftops in the town.

RULA'S NOT STUPID ANYMORE

As twilight's embrace began to darken the fringes of her yard, Rula was drawing her day to a close. Her evening clients had either collected their clean clothes or left their dirty laundry behind, leaving Rula to sort the piles into sets for tomorrow's washing. The clothesline bore witness to her toils with some freshly laundered garments still dancing softly in the evening breeze. Given the clear skies and no looming threat of rain, she chose to let them hang there for the night.

As she took a moment to admire her handiwork, Rula balanced a stack of folded men's uniforms against her hip. With her free hand, she tenderly wiped the beads of sweat that shimmered on her face with a subtle pride. Similar to the men's work shirts and women's house dresses she meticulously laundered time and again, Rula's life mirrored a rhythmic cycle of being rigorously worn, thoroughly scrubbed, and then hung out to dry, to be conspicuously displayed in her yard for all to see. Each cycle rendered the fabric of her life with a few additional holes and a few more frayed edges.

In this insular town, where every individual was under constant scrutiny, Rula was acutely aware of her station. To some she was the village idiot, to others the simple-minded laundry girl who washed their dirty clothes for cheap. But she held her head high, taking pride in her achievements. After all, as her friend Tanis liked to say, she was an 'entrepreneur'.

Relief swept over Rula as she anticipated her evening ritual. She appreciated her career as the town laundress, but it was the freedom after her work was complete that she truly savored. A typical dinner consisted of sandwiches, her favorite food, which then usually gave way to her beloved hobby of sketching in one of her numerous notepads. Her renditions of animal portraits on paper were amusingly inaccurate – a fox might more resemble a dog, a frog might resemble an elephant, proportions were a difficult concept for her to grasp. Yet, she was passionate about this quiet activity and had numerous sketchbooks filled with such drawings adorning her bookcase.

The tranquility she was hoping for, however, was disrupted. There, blocking her path, stood Jerry, the town's well-known menace, his ominous shadow falling toward her front door. His deceitful and cruel nature was infamous in their small town. Regrettably for Rula, this intimidator was her neighbor, living right across the split rail fence that divided her property from his. Jerry's presence, along with his disagreeable wife and two mischievous children, cast a relentless shadow on Rula's otherwise peaceful days.

Rula's eyes drifted from Jerry to her devoted goat, who stood staunchly by her, as if ready to shield her from any harm. She gently stroked its head, a gesture meant as much for her own comfort as the goat's. Together, they moved towards the house, trying to feign indifference to Jerry's presence. Since her father's passing, Rula had often let the goat inside—a move her father would have disapproved of—but one that brought her much comfort.

"Evening, Rula," Jerry said, his voice slathered in honeyed deceit as he blocked her path to the doorway. His grin was both wolfish and predatory, a look that had deceived many, but Rula knew to be wary of.

"Hello, Jerry. How can I help you?" she asked, her voice quavering with apprehension. The sun was setting, and Rula was not a fan of the dark. She tried to pass him, but he moved to block her.

"Actually, Rula," Jerry began, feigning earnestness as he held up a piece of paper, "I've run into a tiny predicament. My wife, bless her heart, can be so scatterbrained at times. She needs these ingredients to complete tonight's meal. Could you perhaps lend a hand?"

Rula squinted at the list before nodding. It was second nature for her to offer assistance. And Jerry, ever the opportunist, had mastered the art of exploiting her kind-hearted nature. As she maneuvered around, his intimidating posture barring her way, her loyal goat lunged forward, delivering a sharp nip to Jerry's thigh. Engrossed in unlocking her door, Rula remained oblivious to Jerry's swift, frustrated kick that sent the goat scuttling into the safety of the house. As Rula delved into her humble pantry, Jerry, silent and swift as a wisp, stole into her bedroom.

His target was a particular loose floorboard by the bed. With his predatory gaze fixed on the bedroom door, he knelt down and pried up the wooden panel. Below, the stacks of neatly wrapped notes and coins—Rula's savings—lay exposed. With practiced ease, he withdrew a few bills from one of the stacks and then replaced the floorboard, making it appear as untouched as he had found it. Jerry swiftly returned to the kitchen, so fast that Rula was still fully engaged in her search for the missing ingredients from his fabricated list.

Rula handed him a bag full of cooking supplies, completely oblivious to the theft that had just transpired. Jerry's smile, that sickening, self-satisfied smirk, was the only farewell he left behind. His footfall echoed into the eerie silence of the night, a steady drumming that marked the rhythm of his repeated betrayals.

***

The sun's first rays painted a new dawn, signaling the start of Rula's routine. Clients arrived in the morning light, each collecting or dropping off their clothes. As they left, Rula turned to the ever-growing piles, preparing for her evening clients. The never-ending cycle of washing, drying, and folding encapsulated her world.

In her yard, awash with buckets, soapboxes, and scrub brushes, Rula's hands moved with practiced precision. Reddened from the cold embrace of the rusty pump and chafed by harsh soaps, they danced a ballet of scrubbing and rinsing. Her glasses, often misted from steam, clung to her nose. Even with her impaired vision, her slightly crossed eyes remained unerringly on her task. An observer might chuckle at the fervor she displayed for such a mundane task.

Rula's every motion as she tended to the garments was a testament to an upbringing marked by severity, each fold and crease shaped under the shadow of her late father's formidable tutelage. From the tender years of adolescence, she had been schooled with an iron discipline that bordered on martial, compelled to master the art of laundry with the precision and solemnity of a surgeon. Men's starched collars and women's intricate pleats were her silent drills, every precise movement a reflection of her father's austere and unrelenting standards. Her diligent work ethic was not just a practice but a perpetual homage to the man whose stern expectations were as much a part of her as the very skills he had ingrained in her.

Rula's father stood as the sole authority figure in her life; he had raised her alone. To make things even more challenging, he had brought her into the world during the autumn of his life. At a time when most of his peers were transitioning into the role of doting grandparents, he found himself navigating the turbulent waters of parenthood, struggling to match the boundless energy and exuberance of a young child. After the untimely death of her mother, Rula was left with only the golden-hued stories about her. In her father's recounting, Rula's mother was elevated to an almost divine status—a luminous, ethereal figure whose time on Earth had been cruelly cut short, leaving a void that was impossible to fill.

To the townspeople, Rula's father was a figure shrouded in enigma. Towering at six feet seven inches, his formidable frame was topped with a broad, box-like head that seemed to cast shadows over his deep-set eyes. Those eyes, dark and penetrating, had the unsettling ability to pierce through one's soul, often leaving a chilling trail of intimidation in his wake. His voice, a deep and resonant baritone, added to the aura of an almost mythical giant that loomed over the village. Although he was known as Edward, in hushed tones laced with a mixture of respect and mockery, he was often referred to as 'Muttonhead'—a moniker Rula had accidentally caught drifting through whispered conversations.

School for Rula was less an institution of learning and more a gauntlet of unseen battles that she alone seemed destined to fight. Her departure from its unforgiving confines was precipitated by an uncanny occurrence in the fifth grade. In the throes of one of her mysterious fits—a catatonic paralysis that ensnared her in moments of high anxiety—a tormentor of hers was struck by an inexplicable disaster. As Rula stood frozen, a shelf gave way above her antagonist, sending books plummeting down like judgment from an unseen hand, striking the boy with such force that he was rendered immobile, his back so severely injured that he lay confined to bed for a month.

This strange and violent incident was the crescendo of Rula's educational strife, sending whispers of devilish blame onto Edward by the more superstitious minded residents of the town. More importantly, it underscored her difference in a way that the school could no longer accommodate or ignore. The local schoolhouse, with its limited means and understanding of Rula's complex needs, was ill-prepared to weave her into the fabric of their standard curriculum.

Following the accident, Rula's everyday supervision and instruction became the sole responsibility of her father, Edward. He undertook this duty with a quiet determination, making her a silent yet constant presence amid the aisles of the hardware store where he worked. Rula was both a specter and a staple there, often whiling away the hours in the storeroom amidst the cacophony of hardware and domestic wares. Over time, Edward diligently imparted to Rula the meticulous craft of laundry, instilling a skill that would tether her to a routine and offer a sustaining thread through the fabric of her future.

Their initial challenge had lain in overcoming the community's skepticism. Edward had faced the task of dispelling doubts not only about Rula's abilities but also towards his own intimidating persona. To counter these prejudices, they had begun by offering their services for free. As time had passed, through persistence and intensive training from her looming father, Rula had soon perfected the art of laundry, and the community's skepticism had shifted. The proof had been in the pudding as they say, and the laundry Rula had produced had always been done to perfection. Those who had mocked her abilities soon had become loyal customers, their jeers replaced by the clinking of coins in her pockets.

Today, Rula upheld this legacy. With the sun as her silent witness, she embarked on her daily ritual of laundering. The neighborhoods' perceptions, once blurred by her slow-witted intelligence, had evolved with every meticulously folded garment she returned. In a world quick to dismiss her, Rula had established herself firmly, a testament to her indomitable spirit.

Rula was submerged in her world of soap and water, the rhythmic scrubbing the only sound echoing in her yard. But this harmony was soon interrupted by the laughter and shouts of Jerry's mischievous children. It was a Saturday, and the children were not at school. They entered her yard with malevolent intent, having turned tormenting Rula into one of their favorite daytime games.

As one sneered and tipped over her washing basin, sending water and clothes sprawling across the dirt, the other made a beeline for her goat, tugging at its beard and poking at his hide. Rula's eyes widened, her internal alarm rising. She tried to communicate, to plead with them to stop, but her disability rendered her words a tangled web of distress.

Egged on by his sibling's antics, the elder of the two decided to rock the ironing board, laughing cruelly at Rula's mounting anxiety. But mischief quickly turned to horror as the hot iron wobbled precariously and then tipped, crashing onto the boy's face. A guttural scream tore from his throat, the raw anguish echoing through the yard.

Rula, overwhelmed, let out a terrified scream, her hands flailing as she struggled to process the accident. The world seemed to be crashing around her, each cry from the boy piercing her very soul.

Hearing the commotion, Jerry's wife Maggie, with her hawk-like eyes and a disposition nearly as cruel as her husband's, stormed into the yard. Taking in the horrific sight of her

son's burns and the toppled iron. She immediately directed her fury towards Rula, venom dripping from her voice as she shrieked, "You jangled-brained freak! Look what you've done!"

The scene unfolded with startling speed. Maggie's face, a mask of fury, was a clear threat as she surged forward, hand poised to strike Rula. But as fate would have it, the loyal goat, having borne witness to the entire chaotic scene and sensing its master's peril, surged towards Maggie with unexpected force. Jerry's wife, completely blindsided, stumbled and crashed face-first into the dirt.

As Maggie regained her balance, her burned-faced boy clung to her leg, his screams adding to the cacophony. His once boyish features now marred with raw, red, blistering scars.

The commotion didn't go unnoticed. Neighbors emerged from their homes, drawn by the chaos, and a few of Rula's arriving clients rushed forward, their faces etched with concern.

Rula, for her part, was losing her grip on reality. Every jeer, shout, and accusation seemed to play in a loop in her mind, pulling her deeper into a state of mental distress. Her eyes, once the windows to her kind soul, were now glazed over, locking her mind into an internal turmoil.

As Rula's clients arrived they were immediately drawn into the unfolding drama. In the middle of the chaos, Maggie, known for her questionable credibility, attempted to control the narrative by passionately sharing her side of the story to the arriving crowd. With every retelling, Maggie's tale grew and morphed, filling the air with a mix of sympathy and suspicion. Most townsfolk took her words with a grain of salt, resorting instead to whispered gossip that changed and expanded with each new listener. In the midst of the escalating whispers and sideways glances, a sensible person decided enough was enough, promptly fetching the police. It wasn't long before an officer arrived.

When the corpulent officer, his face contorted with annoyance, made his way through the throng, Maggie sprang into action. She capitalized on the situation, melodramatically displaying her son's recent injuries for maximum effect. "Officer, just look! See the harm she's inflicted upon my boy! This woman poses a grave threat to our community!" she exclaimed; her voice saturated with a sickly unconvincing despair.

However, Tanis, a steadfast pillar in Rula's life and a friend of her late father, stood firmly in her defense. As Rula's first client, Tanis had developed a strong bond with her. Placing herself protectively between Rula and the accusers, Tanis declared to the officer, "You're only hearing one side of the story. It was Maggie's children who instigated this incident. I witnessed the entire ordeal."

"Her yard is a mess! This is a hazard to everyone. It's ridiculous to allow a halfwit to run a business on her own. It should be illegal!" Maggie screamed.

The officer held up a hand, halting Maggie's derogatory slurs. His eyes roved critically over the yard. "This might be tidy for a girl like you," he said contemptuously, looking at Rula, "but there is enough evidence here to argue against your ability to handle dangerous equipment." Picking up a steel instrument used to swish clothes around in the wash tub, he waved it in Rula's face. "Service providers are required to conduct business with a certain level of safety!"

Rula tried to explain, but her voice wouldn't come. A few other clients murmured in agreement with Tanis, defending Rula's diligent care of her workspace. They argued there had never been any issues before.

He shot them a withering look. "What I see is a potential hazard." His gaze turned colder as it settled back on Rula. "And with you in charge? It's a ticking time bomb."

Tanis' indignation was evident. "Officer, this is uncalled for. She's a hardworking individual, and her yard is as tidy as any!"

His lip curled. "This simpleton might have fooled all of you with her innocent look, but not me. I knew her father well, Muttonhead was a vile and freakish menace in this town, and she's his blood." He stepped closer to Rula, his voice a low threat. "This may pass for now, due to the accounts here. But if I hear even a whisper of another incident, or if I find a single item out of place next time I come around, believe me, I will come down on this operation like a ton of bricks. You" –he jabbed a finger at Rula— "will regret it. Take this as your only warning."

The officer followed Maggie into her home with her son, telling the onlookers to disperse. Rula, still in her overwhelmed and uncommunicative state, was staring dumbly into the distance, wringing her dress in her hands. Tanis gently guided her inside, advising the lingering customers to collect their items and depart, reassuring them they could square their accounts the next day.

***

That evening, in the dim, flickering light of her home, Rula, now released from her psychosis, wrestled with the day's traumatic events. Though a sense of calm had begun to settle over her, a gnawing self-blame tightened its grip. Painfully aware of her limitations and the perceptions of others, she sometimes felt a kernel of truth in their assessments of her abilities. Perhaps she truly wasn't equipped to run a business or engage with the world in the way she aspired to. This very thought cast a long, dark shadow across her heart, raising an ominous question: if she couldn't succeed in washing clothes, how on earth would she fend for herself?

As if in response to her self-doubt, the ominous rumble of an approaching storm began, sending her nerves spiraling into fear once more. The deep rolls of thunder seemed to resonate in her very bones, and the gathering darkness of the storm cast an intimidating pallor over the evening. Her mental handicaps amplified these fears, making the thunderstorm seem like an insurmountable threat. In search of solace, she wrapped her arms around her goat, its warm presence a small comfort. Soon, the stray cats she looked after slinked close, their usual aloofness abandoned in favor of seeking warmth and protection against the encroaching tempest. Their anxious mews seemed to echo Rula's inner turmoil as they all huddled together, a small bastion of comfort against the storm's fury.

As the thunderstorm reached its crescendo, Rula felt her emotions spiral out of control, her mind teetering on the brink of the unresponsive state she dreaded. Frustration with her own frailty consumed her, and she would have given anything in the world to halt the encroaching paralysis of her faculties. Overwhelmed, she let out guttural sounds of frustration, before suddenly erupting in a burst of self-directed anger. "Stop crying!" she commanded herself, her voice echoing the familiar sternness of her father, as he would have demanded strength from her at such a moment.

Suddenly, an old memory surged forth so strong from within her that Rula violently rose to her feet. It was so abrupt that one of the cats she had been cradling on her lap fell to the floor. Without thinking, she shouted at the top of her lungs, "Throoog Tuuuk!!!" It was an exclamation she had overheard her father utter a few times when deeply angered. She had screamed these same words many years ago, only once…

She had been just a girl, around 10 years old, when she had been cornered and accosted by a group of schoolboys behind the hardware store. Rula had found herself screaming that mysterious phrase at the top of her lungs, right into the face of the boy in front of her. Alerted by the sound of his daughter's cries, her father had emerged from the back door to witness the confrontation unfolding. With fury in his eyes, he had chased off the boys. But then, surprisingly, he had turned his rage on Rula, admonishing her as well. His tone had been so severe she had momentarily feared a physical reprimand. That very night, the most aggressive of the boys—the one who had pushed her into the corner and instigated the harassment—had been severely injured by a horse kick to the head. The injury had left him so brain-damaged that he had subsequently been institutionalized.

The recollection of her father's face as he had informed her of the boy's fate the next day was still vivid in her mind. He had made her swear never to utter those words again, emphasizing their grave power. Now, the reality of having voiced them again weighed heavily on Rula. She quickly covered her mouth and reached down to comfort the dislodged cat, murmuring apologies.

As the storm outside reached its zenith, the sound of thunder reverberated through the foundations of Rula's home. Clutching the cat to her chest, she sought refuge beneath the frame of her bed. Each successive clash of thunder amplified her terror. In a climactic act of nature's fury, a fierce bolt of lightning struck the old oak tree in her yard.

The impact was monumental; one of the tree's gargantuan limbs gave way, crashing onto the roof of Rula's house. The resulting deafening crash echoed into the night, while a shower of debris descended, nearly burying one of the stray cats under a hailstorm of splintered shingles and broken beams. It was as if the storm harbored a personal vendetta against Rula for speaking those forbidden words again.

Even as the storm's fury abated and the harsh whistle of the wind wove a haunting tune through the gaping hole in her roof, Rula remained immobilized beneath her bed, paralyzed by terror. In the dusty enclave, surrounded by old trinkets and dust bunnies, she found solace and eventually drifted off to sleep, huddled amongst the stray cats that had sought her companionship in the turmoil. Contrastingly, the goat roamed the house freely, undeterred by the chaos, adding an element of absurdity to the spectacle.

***

As the sunlight poured in through the chasm above, Rula's heart sank. The damage to her home was catastrophic. The scene of devastation was pitiful, thankfully it was a Sunday and there were no clients to attend. Her beloved tree, once the jewel of her yard, was now but a charred monument of the previous night's terror.

There was a noticeable oddity to the embers, a strangeness to the dusty fine coals. They bore the same unnatural tones of the storm clouds from the night before; a glittering array of green and purple hues were scattered amongst the black and gray ashes. They looked surreal and possibly toxic, but Rula was her father's daughter. 'Waste not', she reminded herself, echoing his teachings.

As she cleared the debris with her dustpan and broom, she scattered the colored embers as fertilizer for her garden. Her blueberry bushes, which were her favorites, a small grove of them that flourished along the edge of her yard, received the bulk of the mystical coals. She wondered if they would bloom with a hint of those strange hues and stared in awe at the sparkly ashes before continuing with her chores.

The cleanup lasted most of the day, and Rula worked tirelessly. By afternoon a visitor broke her solitary routine - it was Jerry, her neighbor. Upon sight of him, Rula's stomach dropped. She knew this was not going to be pleasant.

Strangely, he didn't radiate the anger she expected. Instead, he approached at an almost eager pace, his eyes sparkling with peculiar anticipation. "Rula, yesterday was a challenging day for all of us." As Rula shifted her attention from the storm cleanup to his words, a pang of guilt pierced her stomach as she remembered the injured boy. "Maggie took our son to see the doctor," he continued, his attempt at sorrow not entirely convincing. "On a Sunday too, and as you know, medical care isn't free," he added, his voice dripping with a greed so blatant that even Rula, in her naïveté, could not miss.

Rula, shaken up and nervous, nodded her head. She didn't even ask him what he wanted. She turned and walked to her home, quickly heading to the emergency fund that lay beneath her floorboards. She fetched a decent wad, noticing the stack she grabbed seemed surprisingly light. But she was too distracted to focus on that now. Her heart raced as she hurried back to Jerry, who was waiting with open hands.

"It would be awful to have to get the authorities involved again, don't you think?" he said threateningly as he counted the bills in front of her. "I think a little more than this might be necessary." He stared back at her expectantly. Rula obliged and handed him more bills from her apron.

Jerry counted these, seemingly approving the sum. He placed the wad into his pocket. Then he looked around at Rula's damaged roof, "Hey, Rula, I know a guy who can get your roof fixed real quick, good friend of mine, real honest," he suggested, a wolfish grin on his face. Rula, tired and overwhelmed, agreed. She would need to repair the roof, and she knew it wasn't going to be free.

Jerry sprinted off in a hurry, and within only an hour following Jerry's extortionary visit, Rula found herself in the unsavory company of Mr. Simmons, a rotund carpenter with a tough and arrogant demeanor.

"Alright, Rula," Mr. Simmons grunted, examining the damage to her home. He stroked his stubby, grizzled chin. "I reckon it'll be about six hundred dollars to fix up this mess."

Rula's glasses slid down her nose as she looked up at the carpenter, her eyes wide with shock. "Six... six hundred dollars, Mr. Simmons?"

"That's right," he confirmed with an unapologetic shrug, nonchalantly lighting a cigarette. "Materials and labor ain't cheap these days."

A pit formed in Rula's stomach. That amount was more than she would usually use to subsidize herself for years. It was an incomprehensible amount to spend for someone with her means. But she needed her house; it was her sanctuary, her livelihood, and her father's dying gift to her. With a nod, she left Mr. Simmons in the entryway of her home and retreated to her bedroom for the second time that day, reaching into the floorboards to her secret stash of money.

As Rula carefully lifted one of the currency-strapped stacks of bills that represented her life's savings, she paused, a sense of unease washing over her. The stacks, once taut and robust under the firm embrace of the bank-issued currency straps, now felt unnervingly slack. Each strap had been designated to hold a precise amount, ensuring a quick tally of her funds, but now the stacks sagged, the straps loose around fewer bills than they were meant to secure. With a growing sense of alarm, she thumbed through her diminished reserves. The money that was meant to underpin her future was now drastically reduced, scarcely sufficient to cover the impending year's expenses. It was a silent testament to a thievery that had been quietly leeching away at her nest egg.

The room spun. Her savings, which should have lasted her a lifetime, were nearly depleted. Rula found herself grappling with an inconceivable reality. Her secret spot had been breached; her trust exploited. But as the cruel truth seeped into her consciousness, she found herself struggling not just with financial distress, but also the bitter taste of betrayal.

She returned to Mr. Simmons and told him she was short on funds for the repair. A sudden look of disinterest crossed the formerly cheerful man's face. And he bid her a quick farewell.

***

In the days following the catastrophe, Rula found herself steeped in sorrow, too heartbroken to fulfill her usual laundry duties. She gazed at the laundry baskets with a sigh, their overflowing contents a stark reminder of her responsibilities. However, her sadness had left her listless, with no strength for the tiresome chore.

Her clients, some with a genuine concern and others propelled by guilt, visited her humble abode. They cast empathetic glances at her, the lonely laundress that was often referred to cruelly as "that jangled headed girl." They handed her their payment, despite their clothes remaining unwashed, a testament to their pity for her plight.

But pity was a hollow consolation for Rula. These guilt-given pennies would only last a few days before her clients would turn away, that much she knew. She might have been mentally impaired, but she wasn't blind to the gravity of her situation. Without the buffer of her father's savings, she was teetering on the brink of an unfathomable crisis. Even if her roof were to be mended, her continued survival without those funds was a looming question mark.

Her heart ached with an indescribable pain; her eyes filled with unshed tears. In her darkest hour, she found herself reaching out to her father's memory, praying for his guidance.

"Dad," she murmured softly, clutching the sweater that had been his favorite, "I need your help. I don't know what to do." She paused because her father had never liked it when she used the word she was about to use. "I don't want to be stupid anymore!" she exclaimed angrily.

The defiance in those words rang through the house. She paused, regretting her rebellion. "I'm sorry. But I would know what to do if I was smart. Please help me be smart like you," she said, and she cried into the sweater.

It was oddly silent in the house. The goat in the yard outside stopped chewing on a rag it had found in the grass. Rula's whisper hung in the air, a simple plea, an appeal to the man who had loved her, raised her, and left her equipped to face a world that had always been unkind.

***

Under the silvery glow of the full moon, Rula's whispered words carried through the air. That night, the lunar light brightly bathed her backyard, and an ethereal glow, casting otherworldly shadows over her beloved blueberry patch, twinkled unnaturally in a manner that would have made any witness gasp in disbelief. The patches of soil, enriched by the strange, colored ash from the burnt tree, gleamed with an odd combination of green and purple, and at that moment, for only a few seconds, the ground below them flashed green and purple as well. And if anyone saw the boy's face next door, as he lay in bed that evening, they would have seen the same eerie glow come from the peeling skin that surrounded his red scars.

By the time dawn broke, something within Rula had changed. The torrent of despair seemed to have given way to a renewed sense of resolve. She decided she wouldn't let the circumstances break her spirit, wouldn't let herself crumble under the weight of the world's unkindness.

She rolled up her sleeves, tackling the debris left in the yard from the storm. Her goat, who had spent the whole night in her house, strutted outside in front of her as if to lead the way to a new day. Every scrap of wood, every loose leaf, was picked up and disposed of. She re-hung the laundry lines with an unshakeable determination, her forehead glistening with beads of sweat. Then, she filled the wooden tub with water and soap, the familiar scent bringing a sense of comfort. She saw the goat eating at her blueberry bushes and shooed him away. He skipped and jumped as if enjoying the negative attention.

Rula then turned to her clients, who started to arrive, dropping off their loads for her to wash with looks of apprehension in their eyes when they spotted her damaged roof. They asked if she was okay, and Rula replied with confidence and took every batch that arrived as if it were any other day. She worked tirelessly, her fingers rubbing the fabric of the clothes with a rhythm born of habit. By the end of the day, she had washed and dried all her clients' laundry, the clean, fresh clothes flapping gently in the late afternoon breeze.

Her goat had acted strangely all day. The beast seemed to have developed a sense of humor, knocking over buckets and then bleating in what almost sounded like laughter when Rula rushed to pick them up. He would watch her intently during the day, his eyes following her movements with a strange human-like comprehension.

When her customers dropped by, expecting to encounter a desolate Rula, they were greeted with the usual sight of immaculately washed and dried clothes. Their mouths opened in surprise, and the pity in their eyes was replaced with a hint of respect. Amid the chaos of her life, Rula had managed to find a sliver of normalcy in the one thing she knew how to do best - her laundry.

After managing to restore balance to her daily routine, Rula found herself with a moment to breathe and face the gaping hole that was her roof. She used some of the remaining funds in her savings to purchase a sizeable tarp from the hardware store her father had once worked in, hoping it could provide a temporary cover against the elements.

With the tarpaulin secured and all the necessary tools at hand, the only obstacle left was getting the bulky material to the rooftop. This was a task too cumbersome for her alone. So, she waited for Jerry to return home from his day.

As the sun began to dip, painting the sky in hues of orange and pink, she saw Jerry amble into his front yard. Gathering all her courage, she padded across the grass and approached his front door. It was a difficult thing for Rula to ask for help, especially from Jerry, but he did still owe her a considerable sum of money from all the loans she had given him over the years, and desperate times called for desperate measures.

She knocked on the rickety wooden door, and after a moment, it swung open to reveal Jerry, towering in the doorway. He looked down at her, his eyebrows knitted together in curiosity.

"Hello, Jerry. I... I need your help," she began, her voice quiet but steady.

"You've got some nerve seeking help from me," he drawled, leaning against the doorframe, the hint of a smirk playing on his lips. "My boy is unwell. The scars on his face seem to have gotten infected. The dullard was playing in the dirt by your yard and got it all over his burns. I beat him plenty for it, don't you worry, but we may be returning to the doc once more," Jerry said, hinting at future costs inevitably on Rula's dime.

Rula did not know what to say to such harsh words. The thought of Jerry beating his child for playing in dirt was beyond her understanding, so she decided to continue with her request; "I...I've got this tarp, see," she said, motioning towards the large blue sheet rolled up in her yard. "I need it over the hole in my roof, but it's too heavy for me alone."

Jerry glanced at the tarp and then back at Rula, his smirk morphing into a cruel smile. "And why ain't you hired that friend of mine I sent over? He'd have fixed your roof up nice and quick."

Rula looked down, her heart pounding. "I... I don't have the money, Jerry," she confessed. The words tasted bitter in her mouth, but she had to say them.

Jerry's smile disappeared, giving way to an icy, indifferent glare. There was no dawning comprehension of the cost of his larceny, nor a trace of contrition. With a nonchalant lift of his wide shoulders, he spoke with cruel indifference. "Well, that ain't my problem, Rula," he declared before forcefully shutting the door.

Left standing alone on Jerry's porch, Rula felt a stinging sensation in her eyes. But she swallowed down the lump in her throat and brushed off her apron, an instinctual gesture to regroup herself. The hurtful words from Jerry cut through Rula, but they also sparked a flame inside her. She knew Jerry owed her. He had been in her debt for years, constantly promising to pay her back but always finding some excuse to avoid doing so. And she had paid for his doctor bills; she had done everything right by him. Gathering her courage, she knocked again at Jerry's door.

Jerry yanked the door open, annoyance creasing his face. "What now, Rula?" he grumbled, not hiding his frustration.

"You owe me, Jerry. You owe me money," Rula said, her voice stronger this time. She was shaking, but she held her ground. "You could at least help me with this."

Jerry looked at her, seeming surprised. After a moment, he sighed and rubbed his forehead. "Alright, alright. But if I help you with this, we're square. All debts paid. You got that?"

Rula bit her lip. It wasn't fair. The amount Jerry owed was much more than the value of his help, but with the darkening clouds overhead promising a downpour, she had little choice. "Okay," she agreed reluctantly.

With that, Jerry lumbered over to Rula's yard and helped her haul the tarp onto the roof. His movements were rushed, his attention to the task minimal. He was doing just enough to appease Rula, but no more.

As they finished, Jerry dusted off his hands and looked down at Rula, a smug smile spreading across his face. "Y'know, Rula," he began, his tone unsettling, "I know some fellas who'd be more than happy to give you a few bucks for...a woman's company. If you catch my drift."

Rula looked at him, her brows furrowed in confusion. She didn't understand his crude implication but felt a knot of discomfort twist in her stomach. "No, Jerry. I don't want that," she said, shaking her head.

Jerry scoffed, rolling his eyes. "Suit yourself, Rula," he spat out, turning to leave. "Just remember, we're square now."

Rula nodded, watching him go. As Jerry walked out of the yard, the evening sky darkening the stone pathway that led to her gate, he tripped and fell over a stack of wood that had somehow been placed in the center of her pathway. He swore and kicked at the gate on his way out. Rula couldn't help but laugh.

Unfortunately, the laugh was loud, and Jerry turned to look at her, the hate in his eyes so extreme and vile that she stopped immediately, her smile falling slack. A chill ran down her spine, and then Jerry turned, heading to his home next door. At the same moment Rula's trusted goat trotted over to her, a mischievous look in his eyes as he joined her to go inside for the evening.

***

That evening, the weeping heavens unleashed torrents upon Rula's humble home. As the raindrops drummed on the hastily laid tarp, Rula offered shelter to the chilled and damp animals that flocked to her door. There was a small, covered shelter for the animals, but this storm was thunderous, and she couldn't leave them to be cold and wet. So, the motley crew of cats and the goat that lived in her yard filled the room with a warm, earthy din, a soothing contrast to the ominous drumming overhead.

The goat set to constructing an impressively intricate bed in the corner of the kitchen using nothing but straw and discarded cloth. Each corner was perfectly measured, and it even added a pillow of sorts by stuffing a burlap sack with straw. Rula noticed the bed but only chided the beast for having taken up so much room in her kitchen.

The tarp, a makeshift solution to a costly problem, held up well enough in the downpour, despite the beating it was taking. Drip-drip-drip. Here and there, a few stubborn leaks made their presence known, but some well-placed buckets contained the intrusion. And the goat drank from them as if curious to taste rainwater.

Inside this humble sanctuary, under the sympathetic rhythm of the rain, Rula found herself in quiet conversation with her late father's spirit again. A plaintive whisper slipped from her lips into the stormy night. "Father...I wish I wasn't so...muddled," she said, skipping the use of the forbidden word she knew her father would not approve of. "If only I had the brains of someone smart, I could handle all this. I know I could."

Her voice, full of longing and heartache, was barely a whisper above the storm. She was all too aware of the world's sharp teeth, its cruelty gnashing at her simple life. And she knew, if she could just harness more intelligence, more cunning, perhaps she could steer clear of its ravenous jaws.

Outside, her earnest prayer hung heavy in the rain-soaked air. The peculiar ashes, which she'd strewn over her beloved blueberry bushes, mingled with the rain, seeping deeper into the rich soil. And, at that same moment, the blisters on the boy's face next door shimmered and bubbled; a small cry came from his lips as he slept. Rula may have been none the wiser, but as she yearned for transformation inside her home, another transformation was taking place outside.

***

The following day dawned clear and bright, a beacon of hope piercing the dark shadow of the storm's aftermath. Rula began the day with the familiar rhythm of the laundry routine, so ingrained that she moved almost mechanically. More than once she had to shoo the goat from eating the blueberry bushes.

One by one, her clients arrived to drop their garments off for cleaning. Each was relieved to find her back at work, offering soothing words of encouragement, their gratitude manifesting in the routine exchange of dirty clothes and hard-earned coins. That day, the goat acted peculiar again, this time with even more elaborate revelations of ingenuity. It learned to pump the water pump, using its hoof with a finesse that surprised Rula. It even brought over the soap box a few times when she had run out, to which Rula stared, mouth agape in surprise. "How did you learn to do that?" she asked.

The last customer of the morning, Tanis, lingered longer than she typically would. A middle-aged woman known for her wisdom, Tanis held a reputation in town as a stern, mysterious, yet highly respected figure. Rula had heard others refer to her as "witch" in whispers – and Rula, troubled by anyone's derogatory remarks towards her cherished friend, had mentioned it to her, only for Tanis to respond with amused laughter. Rula deeply admired Tanis for her confidence and elegance. It had been Tanis's public praise of Rula's skills that had convinced some of Rula's first skeptical customers to give her a chance. Tanis was married to a successful lawyer and had been one of Rula's father's few friends. The pairing was indeed odd—a sophisticated lawyer's wife and a freakish hardware store clerk—but for some reason, Edward and Tanis had shared a special bond. Tanis's gaze fell upon the tarp that was haphazardly covering the damaged portion of Rula's roof.

"Rula," she began, her tone serious, "you must see to fixing that roof. The dampness can breed dangerous mold. It's not healthy for you."

Rula nodded, her face solemn. "I've spoken with a man about it, but I can't afford the repairs."

Tanis's brow furrowed. "What about the savings your father left for you?" She was one of the few people who knew about Rula's secret stash of money. She could trust Tanis.

Her question hung in the air for a moment before Rula replied. "It's almost spent," she said, lip quivering as she did. She knew this was an embarrassment, and Tanis would disapprove.

A soft tsk-tsk left Tanis's lips. "Your father was such a hard-working man. He didn't save all his life just for you to use up his money recklessly," she scolded gently, her eyes filled with concern, and a deep scrutiny, as though she knew there was something more to the story. She looked long and hard at Rula. She knew the girl did not spend frivolously. Tanis, wise beyond the average human, said no more. She knew something devious had occurred, but there was no need to upset the girl any further, troubling things had happened to poor Rula many times before.

Tears filled the stern woman's eyes, but she brushed them away before Rula could notice. "This world is too cruel for someone as pure as you," Tanis said, trying to ease her former critical words. She was never one to show affection, but she took Rula's hand and held it for just a moment.

As she turned to leave, Tanis paused, a thoughtful look on her face. "Rula," she said, "perhaps there's a way you could wash more laundry, faster. I don't mean work harder; I mean more efficiently. There's no shortage of clients in this town; if you could handle more work at once you would make more money."

Rula thanked Tanis for her advice. It was true enough. There were always more clients than she could accept. The idea sparked a glimmer of hope in her heart. As she stood there, the sun beaming, surrounded by piles of laundry, her mind began to whirl. She wished she understood the mechanics of such things. Could there be a way to wash more clothes at once?

***

Standing in the yard, with her hand on her chin, Rula suddenly felt a hard nudge into the backs of her knees, and she stumbled forward, face-first into the dirt. She found herself tumbling into a rather undignified heap. The goat trotted away gleefully; another successful mischievous prank complete. Behind her, she heard the snickering laughter of the youngest of Jerry's children, spying on her from the safety of his own yard. She felt her cheeks burning, not from the impact, but from the humiliation.

Rising to her feet, she found herself standing before the blueberry bushes, their foliage lush and vibrant from the recent rain, their roots drawing nourishment from the rich soil. The berries were especially remarkable. They gleamed, not reflecting the sunlight but radiating their own ethereal glow, a hypnotizing blend of greens and purples that seemed to pulse from within.

Rula, mesmerized by the spectacle, reached out to pluck one. Bringing it to her lips, she bit into the berry, the taste unlike anything she had ever experienced. It was a strange, potent mixture of bitterness and fire, so intense that her tongue went numb, and her lips tingled. She swallowed hard, her throat suddenly parched, and her cheeks flushed a deep crimson.

Panicked, she rushed into her home, making a beeline for the kitchen. There, on the counter, sat a large jug of water that she always kept filled. She gripped the handle, tilting it to pour a liberal amount into her waiting glass. As she gulped down the water, she could feel the warmth spreading from her stomach, up to her head. Her mind, which usually felt like a tangled ball of yarn, suddenly seemed clear and focused. The thoughts that were once jumbled now fell into a precise order, like puzzle pieces fitting together perfectly.

And there she stood, in front of her kitchen counter, the water glass glistening in her hand. Her heart pounded in her chest, as she felt an unfamiliar sensation grip her. Her world had suddenly shifted on its axis, and she felt the peculiar sensation of standing on the precipice of a vast, unknown chasm. Yet, amidst the chaos, there was an undeniable sense of hope.

As Rula stood reeling from the weird experience, she reflected on her goat's strange behavior over the past few days, as well as shewing it from the blueberry bushes numerous times. The goat had transformed from its previously predictable nature to demonstrating an astonishing level of intelligence and unpredictability. It had constructed an impressive bed in the kitchen, operated the water pump, and, rather conveniently, delivered laundry soap to Rula just when she needed it. In hindsight, these events were beginning to piece together a coherent narrative.

This cascade of realizations converged in Rula's heightened state of awareness, highlighting the undeniable impact the blueberry bushes were having on both her and the goat. This discovery, albeit overwhelming, filled Rula with an exhilarating sense of possibility.

***

Almost in a mania, Rula collected the ripest berries into baskets, even stooping to salvage those that had fallen to the ground. She was convinced that these magical fruits held the solution to her problem, greater than gold they could not be wasted. She plucked all the fully grown berries, leaving the smaller ones to mature, recognizing the importance of maximizing her yield from these miraculous bushes. A crucial question hovered in her mind - would the berries retain their effects if preserved? Blueberries, after all, were notorious for their short shelf life.

Leveraging her enhanced intellect, Rula swiftly formulated a plan. Her initial step was to prepare a test batch of blueberry jam to determine whether the berries would retain their extraordinary properties post-reduction. If successful, she would then proceed to preserve the entire harvest in jam form, aiming to capture their essence and prolong their beneficial effects.

With a newfound energy pulsing within her, Rula set to work. After reducing the berries in a pot with some sugar, she took a small taste of the half-cooked compote, gauging its effect. Just like the berry she had eaten before, it sent shimmering sparks of green and purple dancing across her vision, and her perception of the world seemed to expand immediately, but now with the added sugar, its bitterness was greatly reduced. The jam still set her tongue afire and made her lips numb, but the pain was enjoyable now that she related it to the source of her newfound intellect. She set to work furiously transforming the vast majority of the collected berries into a massive pot on the stove. After it cooled down a little, she transferred the jam into empty jars for storage.

Seeing her beloved goat watching her, she shared a spoonful of the final product with him. Despite the preciousness of the jam, Rula's generous heart wouldn't allow her to keep this gift all to herself. The goat was her companion, and she wanted it to share in her budding optimism. The goat's eyes seemed to gleam with comprehension, and Rula felt even more confident in her new direction.

When she had finished, Rula took a final, thoughtful taste of her creation. As the unique flavor unfolded on her tongue, it unlocked a floodgate of comprehension that filled her once-limited cognitive landscape. Concepts and insights that had once been like foreign hieroglyphs to her now stood decoded, clear and comprehensible.

Much of Rula's past learning had stemmed from a simplistic cycle of repetition and mimicry. The 'whys' and 'hows' of tasks and phenomena remained shrouded in mystery, her understanding only skin-deep, limited to the mechanics of the actions she replicated. But now, armed with her enhanced cognition, she possessed the ability to delve deeper, to peel back the layers and truly grasp the intricacies and underlying principles that governed the world around her.

Overwhelmed with gratitude, tears welled in Rula's eyes. She paused, her heart swelling with thankfulness as she looked skyward and whispered a heartfelt "Thank you" to her father. A radiant smile illuminated her face, and she made a solemn vow to not let this precious gift go to waste. With a clear purpose etched in her mind, she rolled up her sleeves and set to work, ready to explore the uncharted territories of knowledge that awaited her.

Rula moved swiftly, her focus shifting from the jam back to the mountains of laundry awaiting her outside. As she worked, her mind was awhirl with possibilities and inspirations, but she soon hit an obstacle. Her enhanced cognitive abilities, as phenomenal as they were, found themselves hampered by her lack of formal education. Her brain sought to connect the dots between the burgeoning concepts swirling in her mind, but she found herself needing a solid foundation in subjects like physics, chemistry, mathematics, and design – areas she had only heard referenced by her father in the past. As soon as she had attended to all her laundry duties, Rula made a beeline for her house, descending into the depths of her cellar.

The extensive collection of books her father had amassed remained undisturbed, a testament to his life as a self-taught scholar with a deep love for mathematics and physics. Rula eagerly scooped up the volumes, her mind craving the knowledge contained within their pages. Her afternoon was spent immersed in reading, the only interruptions coming when she paused to hand over freshly laundered clothes to her returning clients. Once these brief interludes were concluded, she promptly resumed her studies. Eating became an afterthought, with the occasional berry providing just enough sustenance to keep her mental gears turning.

Rula had always been capable of reading, her father having painstakingly taught her the alphabet and how to read simple fairy tales, be it at a snail's pace. But now, she devoured entire volumes with ease. What was once a tedious chore became a thrilling adventure, a journey into the realms of knowledge. Each word, each sentence, and each paragraph was a steppingstone to a deeper understanding, enriching her mind like sunrays nourishing a tree.

As she burned through candle after candle, reading long into the night, her goat companion stayed by her side. It was as if the creature understood her quest, its own intelligence amplified by the berries. With deliberate intent, the goat fetched a bucket, placed a chunk of cheese and an apple inside, and then carried it over to Rula, dropping it boldly under her nose - as if insisting she needed to nourish herself.

"Thank you," Rula murmured, stroking the goat's head and taking a bite. "We have a lot of work to do, don't we? And something tells me, my time is short." She bit her lip holding back a smile, feeling a strange sense of camaraderie with the animal. "This is a gift from heaven, and we're going to use it."

Rula allowed herself only a brief period of sleep, sufficient enough to recharge her body for the coming day. The cycle of learning and discovery had only just begun, and she was eager to embark on the journey once more.

***

Next door, the burn left by Rula's iron refused to mend; instead, it festered into something far more sinister. Over the past day, the boils, as if taken from a nightmare, had spread across the boy's cheeks, adopting those same peculiar shades of purple and green that sparkled in Rula's ashes. These unwelcome visitors swelled on his skin like grotesque berries, filled with a mucus that shimmered with the same eerie colors. Each blister, cloaked in one of the unnatural tints, seemed to mock the doctor's perplexity. Unbeknownst to the townspeople, the mysterious berries in Rula's yard shared a disquieting palette with these purulent swellings — a macabre echo that whispered of a dark and unknown connection between the fruit and the boy's now mottled complexion.

The physician had prescribed an antiseptic cream that Maggie applied to the wound consistently. But the boil's reaction only seemed to make things worse. The bubbles of skin blew up like little balloons on the poor boy's face, expanding until they popped open, oozing a colorful puss, only to then be replaced by new ones, never healing. It was as if the boy's skin was perpetually boiling.

To make things worse, Jerry's reaction was not one of empathy, but of pure disgust. He chided the boy and mocked the disfigured state of his face. A cruel man to strangers, Jerry was even more cruel to his own children. And he decided that until the putrid boils healed, the boy was to stay in bed.

***

The next morning Rula was awoken by the unfortunate return to her chronically muddled brain. The miraculous effect of the berries was, as she had expected, transient. But she was not disheartened, she had prepared for this. She went to the kitchen and grabbed a jar of the blueberry jam she had prepared the day before and spread a generous dollop of it onto a piece of bread.

And there it was! The familiar surge of clarity washed over her again, the fogginess receded, and her mind felt sharper than ever. A giddy laugh of pure joy erupted from her, and she jumped in triumphant delight.

Rula encountered her clients that morning with an eloquence and analytical ability that hadn't been present before. Her clients were taken aback, the changes in Rula's demeanor and vocabulary were glaring; after a few raised eyebrows and lingering looks, Rula became aware that she had better be cautious to conceal her transformation.

She did her best to look blank or nod dumbly when asked questions, she pretended to be perplexed with curiosity as one client explained to her, in excruciating detail, about the importance of using just the right amount of starch when ironing her husband's shirts. Rula might have just discovered a mind-altering source of intelligence, but the art of deception, she realized, would be crucial if she was going to keep her secret.

As the day progressed, Rula's elevated consciousness unveiled a cascade of revelations that weighed her heart down with sorrow. She couldn't help but perceive the myriad of disdainful comments directed her way and the palpable absence of respect she so often received. Her humble dwelling, too, revealed to her neglect and disrepair, poignant reminders of her previously muddled mind. The sight of a fractured chair, a barrel compromised by leaks, an unstable door hinge, and an askew picture frame all vied for her attention, crying out for immediate rectification.

This newfound clarity sent Rula on a journey of restoration. With skilled hands, she seamlessly restored the chair, secured the loosened metal strap around the barrel, and fortified the hinges of her front door. Even the askew picture frame was given its due respect, now hanging in perfect alignment upon the wall.

As Rula worked with unwavering dedication, past experiences continued to emerge from her deep within memories. Interactions with neighbors and classmates became clearer, casting the stark truth of their behavior into sharp relief. Many had taken advantage of and mocked her right in front of her face, each recollection serving as a painful reminder of her vulnerability and the exploitative nature of those around her. She fought to suppress these realizations; aware they would only deter her progress.

But the longer her newfound clarity lasted, more painful truths began to surface, one of which deeply troubled her. She vividly recalled a particular encounter with Jerry, who had lingered near her kitchen doorway, adopting a look of concern as he craftily inquired about any cough medicine she might have for his purportedly sick wife. His tone, dripping with feigned compassion, still echoed in her mind. As she had hastily turned to search her pantry, she distinctly remembered catching a glimpse of Jerry stealthily making his way toward the stairwell, only to later see him clutching bills in his hand as he exited her home. Her former naivety had prevented her from connecting the dots.

These fragments of her past now formed a cohesive picture, laying bare Jerry's betrayal. She saw a recurring theme: Jerry consistently concocted chores to divert her attention and then slipped from sight. She now understood that during those moments, he had stealthily entered her bedroom, pilfering the savings she had meticulously accumulated over the years from doing laundry—as well as the money her father had so lovingly made the effort to leave for her, only to be pilfered by Jerry's deceptive hands.

A tidal wave of anger consumed her, knowing her trust had been so brutally betrayed. She could almost see Jerry's malicious smirk, picturing him reaching into those hard earned savings, more than likely to be used for useless indulgences. The weight of her exploitation pressed down on her, the realization that she had been merely a pawn in his wicked game.

"He stole from me," she murmured, her voice quivering with a cocktail of fury and despair, a foreign emotion enveloped her… vengeance. "He preyed on my generosity, my stupidity," she thought to herself, and her heartbeat sped up, her cheeks flushed.

The weight of betrayal settled heavily upon her heart, but with it came a fierce determination to reclaim what was stolen. Rula vowed to confront Jerry, to demand restitution for his deceitful actions, and if that was not an option, she would seek retribution in another form. She would not allow him to continue preying on her vulnerability and using her hard-earned money for his own selfish whims.

A mischievous glint appeared in her eyes, and she savored this new sensation. She allowed herself a small smile as a daring plan took shape within her imagination. The next time Jerry visited, she would play along with his attempts to distract her, pretending to fall for his tricks. But this time, she would be one step ahead.

She ventured into the small storage pantry adjoining the kitchen, sifting through some of her father's old belongings she had never utilized yet hadn't discarded. A particular item sprang to mind: the menacing spring-loaded steel bear trap, an object Rula had implored her father to abandon. She had done so following the harrowing day they had ensnared a coyote, its agonizing howls and the gruesome sight of its nearly severed front paw etched indelibly in her memory. She had watched, tears streaming down her face, as her father had mercifully ended the creature's suffering with a swift blow. The trauma had left her inconsolable until her father acquiesced to her pleas, vowing never to deploy the cruel device again – a promise he had faithfully upheld. Now, however, with the seeds of hatred and vengeance taking root in her heart, Rula envisioned a new purpose for the sinister trap.

Having assembled her cunning trap, Rula harnessed her newly sharpened intellect for more pertinent matters at hand. She recognized that the books her father had cherished would not suffice to satiate her burgeoning thirst for knowledge. To genuinely augment her intellect and widen her horizons, she understood that she must seek beyond her current confines.

The allure of the city was undeniable, its prestigious university and the promise of its extensive library a siren song to her intellectually famished mind. Rula realized that amidst the towering shelves brimming with knowledge, she would uncover the answers she so ardently sought.

***

She set the cats and the goat up with enough food and water to leave for a full day, put a small sign up at her door that apologized, saying she would be open tomorrow, and headed out in the early morning the next day. She paid for a ride to the central market, and from there, she could walk to the university. She did not notice Jerry watching closely from his window as she left that day.

The journey to the city was a necessary expedition for Rula, a daunting task that brought a swirl of apprehension. The city's grand university was a world away from her small, insular town, its anonymity providing a perfect veil to her new abilities. Here, amongst the students and scholars, she would appear as just another eager learner, and her newfound intellect needed no disguise.

During her exploration of the university's sprawling halls, she encountered a professor. Aged yet agile, he was a distinguished gentleman with a weathered face that told a thousand stories. His eyes, peering from behind a pair of wire-rimmed glasses, had the serene quality of a tranquil lake, reflecting years of knowledge and wisdom. His attire was somewhat disheveled, giving him a lived-in look of a man more interested in the labyrinthine corridors of the mind than in mundane external appearances.

Rula found herself drawn to this professor, her instincts guiding her to approach him. His office was a scholar's sanctuary, crammed with teetering towers of books and papers. Amid the organized chaos, the professor seemed as much a part of the office's decor as the time-worn bookshelves and the antique desk that bore the weight of numerous volumes.

In this scholarly sanctum, Rula presented her unusual request. She was no student of this university, nor a scholar with a known pedigree, yet she asked for access to academic textbooks, a privilege typically reserved for students only.

The professor, taken aback initially, looked at her with a hint of intrigue. He might have dismissed her outright, yet something about her fervor, her untamed thirst for knowledge, compelled him to consider her plea. It was a spark he had seen in many students, yet rarely in someone who wasn't a part of the academic world. It was the unassuming passion in her eyes, the raw curiosity, which persuaded him to trust her, and he agreed to lend her a selection of books that could quench the intellectual thirst she described. Rula headed for home, her backpack and arms filled with a hefty stack of textbooks.

***

On Rula's return, Jerry blocked her path once again, a sneer curling his lips. His eyes narrowed as he looked her up and down, his gaze fixating on the bulging backpack and armful of books she carried.

"Well, well, Rula," he taunted, his voice dripping with condescension. "What do we have here? Looks like a pile of books. How did a retard like you suddenly take to reading?"

"It's for a friend of mine," Rula lied unconvincingly.

"Don't waste your time," Jerry replied. "You are a pitiful liar. I know you are up to something. But currently, I have a more important reason for my visit."

"More money I would assume," Rula said, with a sarcastic sneer that Jerry was not used to. He was taken aback but then replied.

"Yeah, more money, you petulant bitch. And when I show you what it's for, you won't give me sass any longer. Be prepared for what you are about to see," Jerry said angrily, and with that, he yanked the backpack from Rula's shoulders and threw it towards the door of her home. Her armful of books spilled to the ground beside her, and she was dragged violently towards Jerry's home.

Rula did not fight back. She allowed herself to be brought over to Jerry's home. She had never been inside before. The house was tattered and worn on the exterior, and the interior reflected that same lack of care. The scene inside the home was frightful, and Rula did her best to keep her eyes away from Maggie, who sat in a tattered old lounging chair, a look of sorrow on her face. She said nothing as Rula was dragged through the front door.

She was led to a bedroom at the back of the tiny house. Inside were two beds for Jerry's children. And laying in one of the beds she saw the boy… the boy whose face had been burned. She felt her heart sink as the horror of his injury was revealed to her.

The boy's face was grotesquely altered, enormous boils obscuring his lips, cheeks, and forehead. The sight made Rula's stomach turn. The swollen, bulbous shapes of the boils bore an uncanny resemblance to something all too familiar—she bit down hard on her lip, forcing her mind away from visions of the blueberries that flourished in her garden.

It was an unnerving sight, tears threatened as she made eye contact with the boy, his anguish mirrored the raw pain of the coyote from her childhood, the one caught in her father's cruel trap. Its eyes had haunted her, and now, the same pained expression was reflected in this boy's eyes. "This is your fault!" Jerry's accusation rang out, yet his voice lacked genuine conviction, oddly dispassionate given the boy's dire condition.

"He needs a doctor!" Rula pleaded, her voice tinged with tears. "It looks like an infection."

Jerry's response was mocking and cruel. "Oh, how touching!" he sneered. "Maggie, the town idiot is giving us medical advice."

Rula's reply was firm despite her rising disgust. "I'm not giving medical advice," she insisted. "I'm saying he needs medical attention."

"We agree there," Jerry conceded with a cold stare. "And medical help isn't free, right?" His insinuation was clear.

Overwhelmed with guilt, Rula quickly promised Jerry whatever she could spare and fled toward the solace of her own home.

Jerry didn't follow; he merely watched from the threshold, a smug gleam in his eye. His manipulations had worked.

Once inside her house, Rula was overcome with sobs, frantically collecting the remnants of her savings. Though she knew the boy's condition wasn't entirely her doing, the guilt was suffocating. She reserved only a fraction for herself before delivering the rest to Jerry, a capitulation to a fate she felt powerless to stop.

Upon Rula's return Jerry awaited her, standing in the doorway of his home. He snatched the money from her trembling hands. But just as Rula gathered the breath to speak, Jerry silenced her with a chilling gesture—his finger pressed against his lips. They stood in the shadowed threshold, beyond Maggie's prying ears. A sinister grin curled the corners of his mouth as he leaned closer, his breath a whisper of malevolence. "I know your secret," he hissed, his eyes gleaming with deceit and the weight of unspoken threats.

Rula's heart skipped a beat, her feigned ignorance a fragile shield. "I don't know what you're talking about," she lied, her voice a mere wisp of sound. She pleaded with a fragile hope,

"Please, make sure he sees a doctor." But her words seemed to dissolve before reaching Jerry, who regarded her with a cold, calculating gaze. With every intention of intimidation achieved, Jerry watched her retreat, his smile never faltering. And as Rula put distance between them, he slammed the door shut, the sound echoing like a gavel, sealing her fate in the quiet of the neighborhood.

***

The next day, as the first rays of dawn crept across the sky, Rula was roused by the unsettling bleat of her goat. She shuffled to the kitchen in a haze, her mind murky without the aid of the jam's clarity. She reached the pantry, intent on retrieving the already opened jar of jam and a loaf of bread. However, her eyes widened in alarm when she saw gaps in the orderly row of jars on the shelf—three jars were conspicuously missing. Her breath hitched in a gasp of realization, and she spun around to scan the room, her gaze landing on the goat staring in through the front door, which was inexplicably ajar. With a sense of urgency, Rula quickly dipped one finger into the open jar of jam to revive her muddled brain, savoring a sizable taste, and then headed towards the door.

As her mouth began to tingle, her mind felt the immediate charge of clarity the wondrous jam provided. With her heightened intelligence surging, Rula took in the severity of the situation that had occurred. She observed the small steel keyhole on her front door. The sense of security offered by the modest lock had always seemed sufficient in her tranquil town. Yet, it seemed she had been naively mistaken. Her sanctuary had been compromised; the door's latch, once securely shut, now sat unlocked.

With a growing sense of dread, Rula stepped into her garden, following the goat's persistent bleating to the perimeter of her yard. A foreboding feeling settled over her as she walked, her intuition telling her what she would find—or rather, what she wouldn't. The blueberry bushes had been a beacon of hope, a precious gift from her father's spirit that she had come to revere as sacred, the foundation of her newfound intelligence. But as she neared the familiar spot where the bushes should have been, her heart plummeted.

Her blueberry bushes were gone, savagely uprooted under the cloak of night. The thief had not only trespassed but stolen the very essence of her miraculous transformation. It was more than a mere theft; it was the loss of her salvation. The bushes, once lush and bountiful, now existed only in her pained memory, all that was left behind was a gaping hole in her yard.

Rula collapsed to her knees where the bushes had once flourished, her fingers clawing through the cold, empty soil. Tears blurred her vision as she grieved the abrupt end of the gift she had been so blessed to receive. But within the hollow despair, she clung to a sliver of hope. Something deep within her had warned her that this moment was going to be brief. It was as though she had already prepared herself for this loss. Instead of wallowing in grief, her mind immediately set into action, seeking the most urgent course of action. Although her bushes were gone, she still possessed the precious jars of jam she had preserved, minus a few that the thief had pilfered. She quickly realized the most important thing to do now was to devise a more secure hiding place for them, this thief may very well be back.

Returning to the house, Rula's actions were deliberate and calculated. She crafted a hidden compartment beneath the false bottom of a large chest, one that held her linens, crafting a concealment far less discernible to intruders. Here, she carefully hid the remaining jars of jam.

The security of her treasure restored a semblance of peace to Rula. She had always felt the urgency to make the most of her fleeting window of lucidity, a foreboding that had driven her to preemptive action. Yet, as she stood back and surveyed the chest that now guarded her secret, she couldn't shake off the nagging worry. The culprit of the night's devastation was out there, and the few remaining berries on the pilfered bushes wouldn't last, and she highly doubted they would survive to be replanted. If Rula's suspicions were correct, the culprit was close by — very likely right next door.

***

In the days that followed, a gentle stillness settled over Rula's world. This respite, though shadowed by the knowledge of her dwindling time, became a crucible for her creativity. Each day unfolded into a flurry of resourceful activity, as she harnessed her extraordinary intelligence to its fullest potential. Serendipitously, Jerry seemed to have disappeared from the scene, offering an unexpected relief. His absence was noted one quiet evening when Maggie appeared on Rula's doorstep to inquire if Rula had by any chance seen or heard from him, Maggie's face etched with worry. Despite Maggie's often abrasive demeanor, Rula couldn't help but feel compassion for her; entangled as she was in a life marred by Jerry's cruelty, a life that extended its misfortunes to her innocent children.

Maggie's distress, as palpable as the humid evening air, spoke volumes of a mother's fear for her ailing son — whose health, Rula deduced, had not benefited from the money she had given them. The thought of how Jerry might have squandered the funds elsewhere caused a tremor of anger to ripple through her. Offering a look of empathy, Rula assured Maggie she would keep a watchful eye out for any sign of him. With a nod burdened by her troubles, Maggie retreated to the life she could not escape, and Rula watched her go, the moment leaving a poignant silence in its wake.

All that week, in between the grueling task of laundering clothes and attending to her patrons, Rula embarked on a journey of discovery, immersing herself in university books. From the vast knowledge within those pages, she extracted concepts of mechanics and engineering, constructing a solid foundation for her mechanized laundry aspirations. Once she had digested enough knowledge, her real work began.

Capturing her ideas required precision and an analytical approach. Rula started by conceptualizing the overall structure and layout of the machines. She visualized where each component would fit, how they would operate synergistically, and the spatial demands for optimal laundry processing. These formative thoughts provided the foundation for her meticulous documentation.

To ensure accuracy, Rula painstakingly documented every component of the machines in detailed drawings. Using her newfound insights into engineering and architecture, she sketched each part, focusing on its size, shape, and function. Each sketch was supplemented with exhaustive descriptions and then followed by even more intricate illustrations of the complete machines.

Rula further dissected these general concepts into individual components. For every piece, she crafted multiple perspectives: front, side, and top views, encapsulating every nuance and dimension. Measurements were crucial. Armed with rulers, calipers, and measuring tapes, she documented precise dimensions, knowing that even a minor discrepancy could jeopardize her machines' functionality. Her sketches, accompanied by annotations, detailed the function and intent behind each component, ensuring craftsmen could fully grasp her vision.

The process of drafting and detailing was both exhaustive and time-intensive, but her previous hobby of sketching had enhanced her ability considerably. Days blurred into nights as Rula dedicated herself, often forgoing rest and sustenance to perfect her designs. Two voluminous books were the culmination of her endeavors, filled with intricate drawings and notes. These books bore witness to her tenacity, ingenuity, and unwavering commitment, proudly displayed in her living room as if they were masterpieces. Even amidst this fervent planning, Rula maintained her manual laundry services, ensuring a steady inflow of funds. She also remained vigilant, safeguarding her home from any potential intrusions, especially from the troublesome Jerry, who continued to remain elusive.

With her comprehensive blueprints in hand, Rula's next step was clear. She had to bring her vision to fruition. Using her diminished funds judiciously, she sourced the necessary materials and enlisted the expertise of adept metalworkers and carpenters. The task of constructing her immense machines was monumental. Rula's limited hands-on experience posed challenges, but her unwavering determination and the clarity of her blueprints guided the craftsmen. They referred to her meticulous documentation at each step, ensuring her dream machines took shape exactly as she had envisioned.

***

Amidst an electric atmosphere of palpable anticipation and skepticism, Rula's machines had slowly taken form in her expansive yard. Upon their completion, Rula prepared for a grand unveiling of her magnificent washing and drying machines. Whispers and sideways glances had been exchanged by the townsfolk for days, their curiosity piqued by the colossal structures that had taken shape under Rula's direction. She had overheard numerous skeptical murmurs from her clients: how could this simple-minded girl birth such complex inventions?

Finally, the day of unveiling was here; a sizable crowd, including Rula's dedicated patrons, had congregated, eager to see her machines spring to life. Among them of course was Tanis, who, in a show of faith, had brought along her entire household's laundry. "This should fill them up!" she laughed, as she came forward with her bulging bags of dirty garments and bed sheets.

With a confident stride and an air of suspense, Rula addressed the crowd. "Greetings, everyone! Today, you will witness a revolution in laundry," she announced, her voice echoing with a mix of pride while also trying to maintain her demure persona. "Through these inventions, I promise more efficient washing and, consequently, savings for all of you!" As she dramatically whisked away the bed sheets she had used to conceal the machines, to enhance the drama as she uncovered her masterpieces for the big day, a collective gasp filled the air. Before the townspeople stood marvels of engineering.

The washing machine was a monumental spectacle, combining robust wood and gleaming metal. Its barrel-like shape was intricately adorned with pipes, levers, and wheels. Within its belly, a maze of wooden paddles churned, designed to create a torrential flow that would cleanse the clothes. Rula explained the dual-cycle process, highlighting her unique soap concoction derived from local flora and chemicals. As she elaborated on the draining and rinsing systems, many stared, mouths agape in disbelief.

Heat, she pointed out, was the silent hero of the process. A substantial tank emitted steam, feeding into the barrel, and accelerating the washing. The combination of swirling warm water and enveloping steam promised to eliminate even the most stubborn stains.

Next came the drying machine, a monolithic spinning wheel that loomed over the heads of most grown men. Its wooden lattice-like design was a testament to both form and function. Connected to the washer's steam tank, it spun to extract water before blasting the clothes with warm air. Its foundation was a complex labyrinth of gears, belts, and cogs, powered by the steam's might.

What truly captured the imagination of the townspeople was the symphony of nature and machines that Rula had orchestrated. Her contraptions used the earth's resources - water and heat - and channeled them through the marvels of mechanics to perform a task as mundane yet essential as laundry.

As the machines churned and spun, people gathered around, their eyes fixed on the colossal spinning wheel and the large barrel. The air was filled with a cacophony of mechanical sounds as gears meshed, water splashed, and steam hissed. It was a symphony of invention, a testament to Rula's ingenuity and the power of her newfound knowledge.

That morning, as the first load ran its course, onlookers marveled at the mechanics in action. The clunking and whizzing sounds alone were impressive. The doubt that had shrouded Rula's reputation began to dissipate as people saw those machines run. Their skeptical glances were replaced by awe and admiration. There was even some applause and cheers when Rula emptied the washing machine and transferred the clothes to the dryer. She couldn't help but blush.

Then, just before noon, the moment everyone had been waiting for arrived. The load from the drying barrel was ready to be revealed. Rula carefully opened the barrel, and as the warm air escaped, a fragrant breeze swept through the onlooking crowd. Their anticipation grew, and all eyes were on Rula as she began to retrieve the dried clothes, one by one, showing the miraculously clean and fluffy garments to the crowd. Everyone clapped and cheered with approval. It was everything Rula could have dreamed it to be.

As each piece was meticulously folded, its freshly dried scent filled the air. Rula's hands moved with practiced grace, her touch gentle yet purposeful. The townspeople watched in awe as she handed out the perfectly folded garments to Tanis, a symbol of the transformation that had taken place.

Tanis, with her keen eye for detail, inspected her freshly dried clothes with scrutiny. A smile crept onto her face, and she nodded in approval. Her trust in Rula had been rewarded, and her faith in the young woman's abilities was cemented.

One by one, her clients handed over large bags of laundry, all of them eager to try her new inventions, their expressions ranging from surprise to delight. The newfound efficiency and quality of Rula's laundry service became apparent to all. The once skeptical townspeople had become believers, and word spread like wildfire throughout the community.

The demand for Rula's laundry service soared. People flocked to her humble abode; their arms laden with dirty clothes in hopes of experiencing the magic of her machines. The laundry queue grew longer by the day, but Rula handled it with ease.

***

It was only a little over a week after the great reveal when Rula heard the troublesome sounds coming from her yard. She had just tidied up the kitchen after a meal, and now sat relaxing in a chair in the little family room, her goat by her side, when she heard the commotion. Distinctly jarring crunching and clunking sounds were emanating from the direction of her laundry machines. She ran to the window in her kitchen to see what was happening when she saw Maggie in her yard. She was storming around Rula's machines, yelling obscenities.

Feeling anxious, Rula yelled outside her window at Maggie. "Maggie, what are you doing out there? Stay away from those machines!" she called. But the woman continued her strange and violent actions. It was when Rula observed a large canister of oil in Maggie's hand that she became very alarmed.

Rula sprinted towards her door, her goat bleating in distress and chasing after her. Swiftly, she commanded her pet to stay inside, closing the door behind her. In the brief moments she had taken to safeguard her cherished friend, Maggie had already commenced dousing the machines with oil, her demeanor wildly manic.

Rula approached with caution, intent on thwarting Maggie's malicious actions, despite the potential peril she faced by getting within reach of this woman who was clearly in a deranged state. "Maggie!" she bellowed, maintaining an arm's-length distance yet ensuring her voice would cut through the air, gaining Maggie's attention.

Upon hearing Rula's voice, Maggie swiveled her head, her eyes ablaze with fury, void of reason or sanity. The malicious sneer that twisted her lips spoke volumes; she was there with the sole intent of obliterating those machines, and should Rula dare to interfere, violence would erupt. Unperturbed by Rula's presence, Maggie resumed her sinister task, the oil glugging onto the machines as she made her way around them.

"You freak!" Maggie yelled out, spittle flying from her mouth as she did. "Do you know where my husband is?" she asked. "What did you do to him? He never came back the night after he came to visit you. I think you killed him, you evil spiteful demon's spawn!" she yelled. She stopped once again and turned towards Rula. This time, she faced her dead-on, and her stance implied she was pondering an attack.

Rula backed away, fearful that Maggie was about to charge at her. But what Maggie did next was even worse. She withdrew a package of matches from her apron and lit one of them. As she did, Rula ran towards Maggie to stop her. "No!" Rula cried as the match was thrown onto her drying machine. The thing lit up with a cool blue flame that spread all over its surface and then onto the adjacent washing machine.

Rula lunged towards the machine in hopes of smothering the flames, but Maggie pounced. She was on Rula in an instant, and she began punching her in the face and stomach repeatedly, screaming insanely as she did. Rula took the blows hard, dazed. She only covered her head in defense. But when Maggie paused for a moment, to look down at Rula, who was crumpled up beneath her, a crazed smile crossed her lips. She was about to speak when Rula used that pause to buck Maggie off of her.

With all of her might, she heaved her body upwards, and in doing so lifted Maggie from the ground. The woman tumbled to the side as Rula rolled onto her stomach, exhausted and in pain. At this same moment Maggie rolled into the flames of the now burning machines.

The woman's apron caught flame first, and the matchbook in her pocket lit up with a popping sound. The oil from the ground around the machine must have rubbed off onto Maggie's dress because it lit up like a gas lamp. With a look of horror on her face, Maggie jumped to her feet. A ghastly scream came from her lips as she darted towards her home.

Maggie ran all the way to her home, her entire body ablaze, she hurtled herself against her front door, desperation palpable in her movements. Engulfed by the merciless flames, she could not see to find the doorknob, so instead she hurled her body repeatedly at the closed door. Eventually, overcome by the burns to her body, she crumpled to the ground in a heap in front of the door. A final surrender to the inferno that consumed her, she writhed in her death throes, the air was pierced by the most harrowing, guttural screams that Rula had ever borne witness to; a sound that would forever be etched into the recesses of her mind.

Having caught sight of the gruesome event, Rula pulled herself to her feet and ran to retrieve a blanket from her laundry pile. She promptly saturated it with water from her pump, then rushed to Maggie, draping the soaked blanket over her still blazing body. Alas, Maggie's life had already been mercifully snuffed out.

Rula's focus was so singularly tunneled into her actions that she remained oblivious to the opening of Maggie's front door, which revealed her two children standing in the threshold. The older boy's face, still grotesquely marred by bulbous boils, stared out in shock at the horror that lay before him. Rula's eyes met his, and she instinctively screamed for them to retreat inside. Much to her relief, they heeded her command.

Hearing the screams, neighbors began running over, and the fire department was quickly fetched. As the scene unfolded, Tanis arrived and guided Rula away from the burnt corpse of Maggie, while others hastened to extract the children from the house. The police officer who eventually arrived on the scene, was the same one who had visited on that terrible day of the ironing board accident. He subsequently took stock of the calamitous scene with a sharp, analytical gaze. By now, Rula's innovative machines lay in ruin, their former glory blackened by scorch marks. Fortunately, the oil had fully combusted, averting the peril of an uncontrolled fire.

"How did this happen?" the officer asked Rula as he charged forward to where she sat atop an empty barrel in her yard, he looked at Rula with anger and vengeance.

Rula gulped and tried her best to keep the fright out of her voice. "She came over and started ranting and raving. She threw oil on the machines and lit them on fire," Rula explained. "I tried to stop her, and she attacked me. She was on top of me, punching me."

And indeed, the bruises and black eyes from the assault were welling up on Rula even as they spoke. But the officer showed little interest.

"And how did Maggie end up on fire?" he asked sternly.

"I pushed her off of me, and she fell into the flames," Rula said, and as she spoke, she began to cry, the horror of what had happened hitting her once again. "The oil, it must have gotten on her dress…"

"Why would Maggie light the machines on fire?" the officer asked, but even as the words left his mouth, he realized the answer.

Tanis stepped forward, defending Rula while fighting back her own tears, "You saw what happened to her boy. Maggie was angry, furious at Rula. She wanted to destroy her success as revenge."

"That's a convenient story, Tanis," the officer replied, his gaze hard as he turned to Rula. "But she can't defend herself now, can she? And as for you, I've told you before that people like you shouldn't be running businesses. It's not right. Your machines were a curiosity, sure, but this? This is what happens when we let someone of your... capacity, try to play in the real world. I'm telling you now, shut this business down. I won't have any arguments or excuses."

The weight of the officer's words hit Rula like a physical blow. Her machines, her precious creations that had brought her so much pride and hope, now lay in ruins. The laundry service, her path to independence and normalcy, was being forced to close. On top of all this, she now had to doubt herself. Perhaps the officer was right; maybe she wasn't capable of handling the responsibility of running a business, especially after such a horrific event. With a heavy heart, she nodded in acquiescence.

The officer's eyes narrowed as he leaned in, his voice a threatening whisper, "And just so we're clear, if I catch wind of you continuing this little venture of yours, I won't just shut you down. I'll make sure this whole incident is investigated as murder. Do you understand me?"

A sickeningly heavy feeling weighed down Rula's guts. With a numb nod, she looked to the ground in front of her, unable to meet the officer's eyes. Her dreams shattered; her world had collapsed around her.

***

The following weeks were a blur of sadness and hopeless resignation. If it had not been for the jam she had on reserve, her poor brain never would have managed to navigate through those coming days. She dismantled what was left of the machines and closed down her laundry service. Some of her former clients now looked at her with scorn, others with pity.

Rula herself had mixed emotions. When she heard the two boys had been sent to an orphanage for care, her heart broke. Jerry was gone, he had taken the money and run off, leaving his family to fend for themselves.

Then, one dark evening, as Rula was organizing her yard, the moon only allowing a sliver of illumination, she saw a man approach her yard. Rula stopped what she was doing and walked towards her gate. "Is that you, Jerry?" she called out tentatively, recognizing his frame.

"You betcha!" Jerry called back sinisterly. "You ain't stupid anymore, are ya?" he said joyously, but with such a hateful ring, it sounded murderous. Rula took a step backwards, and she heard the goat bleat from far behind in the garden. She did not want the innocent animal to come any closer. In Jerry's right hand was an extremely long machete.

"What do you want?" Rula asked, but she knew the answer already. She had anticipated the possibility of his return, but not the knife and the threat of violence.

Jerry nodded as though he knew that she already knew. "The jam, all of it," he said and raised the blade up, making sure she could see it.

"You would kill me for jam?" Rula retorted, her hatred for him welling up at his bold request.

"I'd kill my own wife for that jam, you muddled wench, and don't act like you don't know why. If it can make an idiot like you smart, imagine what it does for me," Jerry sneered and took a few steps forward.

"How do you know about the jam? I never gave you any." Rula replied, attempting to gain an admission of guilt to his thievery.

"I watched you gather those berries, the look on your face was something I'll never forget," Jerry replied. "I ate some of them myself later that day, stole three jars of it and the bushes too… But you knew that already I'm sure. You're no dummy, at least, not at the moment," he said mockingly.

Rula shook her head slowly. Jerry said nothing, only paused for a moment, before entering her yard.

At that moment, she heard the goat's hooves trotting towards her from behind, and Rula turned quickly, crying out to stop the loyal creature. But the goat, in a move of protective instinct, disregarded Rula's pleas and charged past her, leaping at Jerry with all its might. Time seemed to slow down as Rula watched in horror. The goat's brave act of honor was met with a swift and brutal strike from Jerry's blade.

Rula's cries filled the air as the machete pierced the goat's stomach, causing blood to gush out. The once lively and spirited creature let out a winded, pained bleat, its body collapsing onto the ground. Rula's legs carried her swiftly to her fallen companion, her hands shaking with grief and disbelief.

Kneeling beside the goat, Rula's tears mingled with the blood staining the creature's fur. She softly stroked its head, whispering words of comfort and love as the goat's breaths grew shallower. It was a devastating sight, the life force of a dear friend slipping away before her eyes.

In that moment, grief consumed Rula's heart, leaving her shattered and vulnerable. She couldn't comprehend the cruelty that had taken place. The weight of loss settled heavily upon her, suffocating her spirit.

As Rula mourned the loss of the goat, a voice broke through her sorrow. It was Jerry, his sneer audible in his words. "Shut your mouth, or I'll do the same thing to you!" He spat back at her.

Rula cut her cries short, stopped breathing completely for a few moments, trying to gather herself. Her tear-filled eyes widened in shock and confusion. Jerry had been observing her all along. He had stolen her berries and her jam. He had likely eaten it all and was looking for more. Her mind raced, trying to make sense of his motives, but the pain of her grief for her beloved pet overshadowed her ability to think clearly.

"It's all gone," Rula said cautiously, trembling, her voice tinged with both sadness and a welling anger. "I could only imagine what you did with your share of it," she said with a great sardonic sneer.

A grin spread across Jerry's face, amused at her new cynical sense of humor, the only kind a brute like him could appreciate. "I learned to count cards, my dear. I've been winning all month in gambling dens across the coast. But I need more of the jam. I was richer than any man in town a few days ago, but I got a bad run. A few more jars of that jam, and I bet I can triple what I had."

Rula's mind raced, trying to comprehend the situation. Jerry had deserted his family, stolen her money and her berries, only to use the power to win at cards? The simplicity of his actions made her laugh out loud. How pathetic and shallow was this man? A true miracle at his fingertips, and that was what he had done?

"I won't give you the jam, Jerry," Rula said firmly, her voice laced with determination. "You've already taken enough from me. You stole my money, you stole my jam, you killed my friend. I won't let you exploit their magic for such degrading desires. You are repugnant!" she yelled.

Jerry's expression hardened, his eyes narrowing with a mix of anger and frustration. "You don't understand, Rula. You're smart now, but you're stupid at heart," he growled. "With that jam, I can continue to win, to amass wealth beyond imagination. You're the fool, not me, sitting around in this dump doing laundry. What great deed have you done?"

Rula stood her ground, a fire burning in her eyes. "No, Jerry. I won't be pushed around by you anymore. The magic of those blueberries is not meant for greed and cheating at cards. It's a gift from Heaven, from my father, that should be used for something greater, something meaningful."

Jerry's face twisted with rage, and he lunged towards Rula, his intentions clear. But Rula was not one to go down easily. She swiftly stepped back, evading his grasp, and held her ground with unwavering determination.

"You won't get the jam, Jerry," Rula declared, her voice firm and resolute. "I will protect what's left of that magic, and I will use it for good."

With that, Jerry punched Rula dead in the face. The world spun, and blood splashed from her now busted nose. The pain was like lightning, far more powerful than the hits she had taken from Maggie. It shook her already shaken soul. She stared blankly back at Jerry, who grabbed her by the hair and dragged her into the house. "The jam," he said again flatly. "No more messing around." And she knew he was not going to stop. Dragged by the hair, knife pointed at her back, Rula led him to her secret hiding place. Jerry grunted, seemingly impressed by her false-bottomed storage chest.

Rula, trembling with fear, followed Jerry's command and began placing the precious jars of blueberry jam into a sack he provided. Each jar clanked against the others, a symphony of shattered dreams. Tears streamed down Rula's face as she realized yet another fortune her father had given her was about to be stolen.

But then Jerry said, "The rest of the money too!" In a threatening tone, yanking her towards the stairs leading to her bedroom. A spark of hope ignited within Rula. She saw an opportunity to turn the tables, to take back control and dole out a bit of revenge to this man who had taken so much from her. With a quivering voice, she pretended to comply with his demand, her mind racing to conduct a cruel revenge.

As Jerry's attention switched from the jam to the money, Rula guided Jerry towards the floorboards of her bedroom, urging him to the place that she knew he was already aware of. She pretended to meekly reach for the floorboards, quibbling and gibbering like a woman in terror. She intentionally took a painfully long time, fumbling with her fingers at the loose board. The plan worked. Jerry's impatient and greedy nature took him over. He pushed her out of the way and reached for the floorboard he knew all too well.

As Jerry's hand descended into the depths of the hidden compartment, searching for her remaining stacks of bills, Rula held her breath, her eyes fixed on the hole in the floor. And in an instant, her plan bore fruit. The trap's sharp jaws clamped down on Jerry's wrist, trapping him in a vice-like grip. A cry of pain echoed through the room as Jerry's face contorted with agony.

Stronger than she had anticipated, the device not only clamped down on Jerry's wrist, it nearly removed his entire hand from the bone. Just like the poor coyote from Rula's youth, Jerry screamed and howled, and as he assessed his dire situation, Rula ran out the front door screaming for help. Gauging the danger he was in, Jerry pulled his wrist out of the hole with one horrendous tug, leaving his severed hand behind in the hole. With his one good hand, he grabbed the sack of jam and fled, leaving a trail of blood across Rula's floors as he went.

Rula ran screaming all the way to the police station in town and reported what had occurred. Unfortunately, by the time an officer came to the scene, Jerry was long gone.

***

In the aftermath of the police investigation, Rula found herself standing in her yard in a state of apathy. The continual battery of misfortune had reached its saturation point, her grief could reach no further heights. With her goat now included in the carnage of her life, she had lost all hope. She returned to the goat's little body, lifeless and limp on the dirt of her yard, she sat and cradled his head in her arms.

Under the cold, uncaring moonlight, while Rula pet her loyal companion on the ground of her lawn. Life would dole out one final blow to poor Rula, for it was in this very moment of profound tragedy, that the last vestiges of her sharpened intellect, bestowed upon her by those magical blueberries, began to fade. Her mind, once clear as a cloudless sky, was quickly succumbing to the encroaching fog that had been held at bay by the transformative power of the jam. The brilliant tapestry of thoughts and ideas that had briefly illuminated her world began to unravel, leaving her to grapple with the cruel reality of her limitations.

Surrounded by the darkness of the night and the weight of her sorrows, Rula's soul ached with the unfairness of her circumstances. The fleeting moments of exceptional capability, the depths of human cruelty she had witnessed, and then the immense loss of her beloved pet, all seemed to merge into a quilt of despair. The world transformed before her eyes into a bleak and unforgiving abyss, where even the smallest spark of hope could be snuffed out by the darkest of intentions. And yet, as her intellect receded, giving way to the simple-mindedness that had defined her life, a strange sense of relief washed over her. The nerve-wracking introspection and the torment of understanding the depths of her plight diminished, leaving her with a bittersweet solace in her unadorned perception of the world.

As time passed, Rula's wounds began to heal, though the scars of her past remained. She carried the memory of her goat and the bittersweet taste of the stolen blueberry jam with her, a reminder of both loss and possibility. While her intelligence may have faded, her spirit endured, unyielding in its pursuit of a brighter future.

Rula diligently carried out her daily chores, returning to the rigid teachings of her father on how to conduct herself. But now, without a laundry service to run, the days seemed much longer than they used to. It was during one such long day that her father's old friend Tanis paid her a visit. Tanis, who had witnessed Rula's transformation and subsequent downfall, had remained loyal to her.

As Tanis stepped into Rula's humble abode that afternoon to pay a friendly visit, hoping to encourage Rula to move forward with her life, her eyes widened with astonishment. Spread out before her on Rula's little sketching table were the meticulously crafted manuscripts from the two machines Rula had invented, filled with intricate diagrams, detailed measurements, and comprehensive descriptions of materials. Tanis' heart skipped a beat as she realized the true significance of what lay before her.

"Rula!" Tanis exclaimed, unable to contain her excitement. "These manuscripts, these instructions, they are wondrous! You have created something truly remarkable!"

Rula, still carrying the weight of her past losses, regarded Tanis with a mix of confusion and curiosity. She had poured her heart and soul into those manuscripts during her time of heightened intelligence, but they felt like remnants of a distant dream. When she looked at them now, she barely understood any of their contents. She had never pondered their potential value.

Tanis, overcome with enthusiasm, continued. "Rula, you have the opportunity to share your brilliance with the world. These manuscripts can be patented, safeguarding your inventions and securing your rightful place as an innovator!"

Rula's eyes widened with a glimmer of hope as the gravity of Tanis's words sunk in. Could her creations truly have value beyond her own small town? Could her designs and ideas find recognition and provide a better future for herself and others?

Eager to seize this chance, Rula followed Tanis as she led her to her husband, a lawyer with expertise in intellectual property. With his guidance and support, Rula embarked on the process of patenting her manuscripts. Her intricate drawings and detailed instructions were carefully examined, and after months of dedicated effort, her inventions were granted the protection they deserved.

As the marvels of Rula's washing and drying innovations reverberated through surrounding cities, they inevitably landed on the ears of a leading manufacturing conglomerate. Sensing the game-changing potential and monumental market value of Rula's machines, representatives from the company wasted no time in seeking her out for a discussion.

Complex negotiations unfolded, guided by the steady hand of Rula's legal counsel, who happened to be Tanis' astute husband. After intense deliberations, they cemented an historic agreement wherein the manufacturing behemoth acquired exclusive rights to Rula's groundbreaking machines. But Rula didn't simply hand over her brainchild for a pittance. She was duly rewarded with a substantial initial sum and was also guaranteed a monthly allowance for the entirety of her life. This phenomenal turn of events was nothing short of a miracle for Rula, who had once grappled with destitution and seemingly insurmountable adversities.

Leveraging their vast resources and unparalleled expertise, the manufacturing company honed, enhanced, and embarked on the mass production of Rula's machines. It didn't take long for these marvels to sweep the market, radically transforming the realm of laundry. These devices laid the cornerstone for a new era of advanced washing and drying mechanisms, forever altering the domestic world. As for Rula, she gracefully retired her hands from the toil of laundry. In an ironic twist, she entrusted her own garments to a burgeoning service that exclusively employed her inventions.

In the wake of Jerry's precipitous exit from their community, whispers began to waft back to the townsfolk. Tales of a one-handed rogue masterminding audacious cons in casinos and shadowy gambling nooks across the coast were rife. Jerry's warped genius was indisputable as he artfully evaded the clutches of many a foe, always seeming to be one step ahead of his enemies.

But a life drenched in treachery and subterfuge is rarely sustainable. Fate finally caught up with Jerry in a dimly lit alley of a sprawling metropolis far away from Rula's little town. There, his lifeless form was found, bearing the grisly marks of a brutal altercation. The true events leading up to his grim end remained a mystery, but it was evident that his path of deception had spawned formidable adversaries who had exacted their revenge.

THE YIK-YAK MINE

The mid-morning sun cast an ethereal glow over the jagged peaks of the western mountains. The air was thin but crisp and ringing with the strange songs of the mountain birds. Forests dense with towering pines stood like ghostly sentinels, their shadows stretching out and dancing in the wind. It was a world that was as eerie as it was beautiful.

Three men, each burdened not just by their heavy backpacks but by the weight of golden aspirations, meandered the serpentine path that promised to lead them to fortunes untold. From the smog-choked cities of the east coast, where industry roared and dreams often withered, they had ventured forth, riding the iron beast of a train to the vast, untamed expanse of the western mountains.

Their journey, the day before, had brought them to a sparse, almost ghostly town, where the train tracks ended, and stood in defiance of the wilderness around it. The price of a night's stay had been exorbitant, a clear exploitation of their unfamiliarity with this frontier. The locals, with eyes like vultures, had sized them up quickly, identifying them as out-of-place seekers of wealth.

Come dawn, under a sky that had been painted with the hues of early morning, they had negotiated a ride up the mountain. The Waggoner, a man whose wrinkles had told tales of sun and wind, had demanded a fee that was nothing short of daylight robbery. The trio, resilient and determined, had chosen to have him take them only halfway, confident in their resolve to trek the rest of the way on foot. Their absence of mining equipment would, after all, make their ascent less cumbersome.

When the men had shared their plans to procure their mining gear from the town nestled high in the mountain's embrace, the Waggoner's laughter had held no warmth. With a sardonic smile, he had offered a wish of luck, the undertones of which had spoken of challenges and mysteries yet to come.

Now they pressed forward, Mitch at the forefront, embodying the essence of their determination. His lean physique, sculpted by years of grueling labor, paired with a penetrating gaze, lent him an air of intensity that was almost predatory. Yet, this fierce demeanor was skillfully balanced by a magnetic charisma, one that captivated those around him, compelling them to embrace the realm of the impossible.

Then there was Jack, their most experienced member. A sturdy, barrel-chested man, time had claimed the hair atop his head, leaving a frame of silver around his bare crown. His ruddy nose and round belly, indicative of countless hearty meals, bore witness to his long-standing duel not only with the passage of time, but also with the seductive allure of whiskey.

Last but not least was Jacob. Barely out of his youth, his wide-eyed optimism and innocent enthusiasm made him the dreamer of the group. It had been Mitch's persuasive charm that had lured this young man into the gold rush adventure, pulling him away from the comforting embrace of his sweetheart back in the city they'd left behind.

Amidst the rustling of leaves and the distant cries of unknown creatures, Mitch paused. The soft glow of his cigarette flared brightly as he inhaled, casting an orange glow on his face, revealing a meditative look. He held the smoky air in his lungs for a second before exhaling a large plume of smoke, letting it mingle with the crisp cool air of the mountains.

"Look around, fellas," Mitch said in a tone filled with reverence, as he gestured to the sprawling landscape. "This isn't just nature. This is our salvation, our freedom. These wild, untouched lands are our ticket out of that wretched life back at the wheel factory."

Jack, panting from the exertion, beads of sweat forming on his brow, replied with a smirk, "You see freedom, I see fortune. Don't get me wrong, Mitch. This view? Worth every step. But it's the glint of gold that brought me here."

Mitch turned to Jack, eyes glinting with mischief. "Always about the tangible with you, eh, Jack?" Then, looking to their younger counterpart, he asked, "And what of you, Jacob? Any regrets about embarking on this madness with us old-timers?"

Jacob's eyes, alight with dreams yet to be realized, sparkled with conviction. "Not one, Mitch. I swear, it's like I can sense the gold beckoning me. Picture it: a year from now, owning a swath of land somewhere on the plains, where the earth blesses you with its own kind of gold. Susie and I, married and starting a family. That's the dream."

Mitch's smirk widened into a genuine smile, his hand landing heavily but affectionately on Jacob's back. "That's what I wanted to hear! Onward, then—to glory and untold treasures."

Their conversation ebbed as they continued their arduous climb, the mountains whispering old secrets in their ears. The towering pines seemed to sway with an ancient rhythm, rustling eerily in the wind. Every now and then, the mournful hoot of an owl or the scurrying of unseen creatures would punctuate the silence, lending an aura of mystery to their journey.

As the gold rush town emerged over the horizon, a wave of anticipation washed over them. The treacherous path, the eerie forest, and the exhausting journey - all seemed to fade into the background. Their dreams were within reach now, and the real adventure was just about to begin.

The sight of the town almost seemed like a mirage against the sprawling wilderness. Any settlement this far up in the mountains seemed surreal to the three men who hailed from a huge coastal city. A single, dusty road ran through the heart of it, undulating with the contours of the land. It was flanked on both sides by a collection of makeshift buildings, each one standing as a monument to the entrepreneurial spirit that the booming gold rush had sparked.

Every structure appeared hastily constructed from rough-hewn timber, yet there was an undeniable charm to the elaborate facades facing the street. The builders, savvy in the art of marketing, had adorned their door and window frames with intricately patterned trims. Colorful awnings and luxurious drapery hung from exteriors, their garish hues striking a brilliant contrast with the earthy tones of the dirt road and the plain wooden frames of the buildings. Bold lettering and illustrations adorned the facades, ensuring their wares were clearly visible to the scores of prospectors, many of whom were illiterate.

The barber's shop, its pole spinning in red and white, beckoned the unkempt prospectors for a trim and a shave. Beside it, the bank stood solemn and resolute, its door a gateway to the dreams and riches that men hoped to extract from the unforgiving earth.

The post office, humming with activity, was a lifeline for the many men who left everything behind. Its presence served as a poignant reminder of the world they had left, promising news from home and civilization.

A few steps away, the hotel, with its slightly more polished facade, promised warmth and rest for weary bodies. The glow from its windows spoke of the luxuries of a soft bed and a hot meal - rarities after the hard journey.

But perhaps the most strategic establishment was the hardware store, its shelves laden with shovels, pickaxes, and pans - the tools of the prospectors' trade. As the old adage went, why dig for gold when you could get rich selling the shovels? The store stood as a testament to this wisdom, thriving on the hopes and dreams of those who came seeking their fortune.

And finally, there was the saloon, the undeniable pulse of the town. Even from a distance, the laughter, the clinking of glasses, and the discordant notes from an old piano filled the air, promising camaraderie and respite from the relentless pursuit of gold.

The town teemed with a heady mix of hope, tension, and anticipation. Each man eyed the other with a wariness born from the shared dream of striking gold. Amidst its riotous colors and noise, this town represented the heartbeat of the gold rush, a place where dreams were bought and sold, and fortunes were made or lost with the swing of a pickaxe.

When the men finally reached the town, the sun was beginning to dip beneath the serrated peaks of the mountain range. The gold-flecked rays cast long shadows on the bustling street, stretching out the hubbub of the day into twilight.

To their disappointment, the bank had already shuttered its doors for the day. It was the bank they needed. The hunt for gold wasn't as simple as picking up a shovel and digging. The stories of brutal confrontations over lucrative patches of land were all too common, whispered around campfires and echoed in the dank corners of watering holes. Greed had a way of twisting men's minds, and the promise of gold was the most potent elixir of all.

To prevent such deadly disputes, land leases were implemented. A prospector had to secure a plot of land from the bank, designating a specific territory where they had the exclusive right to dig. It was a system as vital as the veins of gold they sought. Choosing the right plot was as critical as choosing the right tools for the job. A wrong decision could spell the difference between striking it rich or returning home empty-handed.

But with the bank closed until morning, the men were left with little to do but find a place to rest. They rented a room at the hotel, a welcome luxury after the grueling journey. But after only a few minutes rest in the room, the lively notes wafting from the saloon lured the men, who all too often enjoyed a good brew. The promise of a stiff drink and a respite from their impending work was a siren's call they couldn't resist.

Mitch, always the most level-headed of the three, cautioned his friends. "Not too much, boys," he advised, eyes twinkling under the dim light of the saloon. "We've got a long road ahead of us, and every cent counts." So, they settled into their seats, the warmth of the saloon and the camaraderie of their shared adventure wrapping around them like a comforting blanket. Their journey was just beginning, and the coming morning held the promise of gold.

The saloon was a hive of activity, filled with hardened prospectors whose eyes had seen fortunes rise and fall in the blink of an eye. The locals, cunning and hardened by their pursuits, were a stark contrast to the trio, who wore their inexperience like a badge, standing out among the crowd of seasoned miners.

As Mitch, Jack, and Jacob scanned the bustling establishment, they drew more than a few curious glances. The city slickers stood out like sore thumbs amidst the throng of grizzled men whose faces told stories of laborious days and lonely nights. These men, weathered and seasoned by the unforgiving elements, eyed the trio with a peculiar blend of amusement and predatory interest.

The evening began innocently enough. Laughter flowed as freely as the alcohol, and the other patrons welcomed the newcomers, listening intently as the trio boasted about their determination and future exploits. Encouraging words and tales of legendary hauls were exchanged, painting vivid images of instant riches and dreams within arm's reach.

However, as the night wore on, the atmosphere began to change. The men of the town, sly as foxes, began to show their true colors. A few strategically convinced Mitch to join a game of poker, baiting him with the promise of an easy win. Jack found himself ensnared in a drinking game that quickly turned costly, where each loss translated into a round of drinks. And Jacob, the youngest and most naive, found himself under the spell of a seasoned harlot, lured away from the revelry under the guise of a romantic encounter.

Morning found the three men nursing splitting headaches, their pockets nearly empty and their spirits heavily dampened. They had gambled away a significant portion of their savings, seduced by the heady promise of easy wealth and the deceptive camaraderie of the saloon. The harsh morning light brought with it a bitter realization - the road to gold was fraught with more dangers than they had initially thought, and some of these perils were not buried within the earth, but walked on two legs, hiding in plain sight.

The morning air was crisp and biting as the three men met on the town's main street, the somber expressions on their faces a stark contrast to the joviality of the previous night. All around them, the town was waking up. Dust swirled around their feet as they converged, their heads throbbing, spirits dampened, and pockets much lighter.

"What the hell happened last night?" Jack groaned, rubbing his temples to alleviate the pounding in his head.

Mitch grimaced, admitting with a sigh, "We were fools, Jack. Got taken in by the charm of the place and let our guards down. We were swindled out of our savings."

Jacob, still trying to shake off the effects of the alcohol, remained silent, letting the older men argue.

"How much do we have left?" Jack inquired, his brow furrowing with concern.

Mitch reluctantly dug into his pocket and pulled out a small bag of coins. "Not much. Barely enough to buy the tools we need, let alone secure the land lease."

A disagreement began to brew. Jack, believing in the importance of securing their plot, argued, "We need to lease the land first, Mitch. There's no point in having tools if we've got no place to dig!"

Mitch, however, had a different view. "No, we get the tools first. What good is a plot of land if we don't have the means to mine it?"

As the two older men continued to argue, Jacob watched them, his mind a whirl of regret and uncertainty. But he chose to remain neutral, allowing Mitch's assertiveness to eventually overshadow Jack's argument.

Resigned, the trio trudged towards the hardware store, their hope now hanging on the promise of gleaming shovels and sturdy pickaxes. As the men entered, a cold shiver passed down Mitch's spine. He saw the rows of tools, all tagged with exorbitant prices, and his heart sank. The dimly lit room smelled of earth, metal, and the undeniable scent of greed. The establishment was monopolistic, the only one of its kind for miles around. Their wallets didn't stand a chance.

The store clerk, a wiry man with a crooked smile and sly eyes, approached the trio. "Gentlemen," he inquired, "looking for something specific?"

"We need digging equipment," Mitch said, his voice steady despite the sinking feeling in his stomach.

With a glint in his eyes, the store clerk guided them through the store. "You'll need a sturdy shovel, a lantern for those dark mines, and a good old pickaxe, of course," he enumerated, pointing to each item in turn.

Mitch frowned at the outrageous prices. "Five coins for a shovel? Two for a lantern? And four for a pickaxe? That's highway robbery!"

The store clerk only shrugged, his smile never faltering. "Supply and demand, sir. The tools are here; the gold is out there. It's your choice."

The three men exchanged worried glances. Their options were limited. Reluctantly, they dug into their pockets, their faces hard as they forked over the precious coins.

As they left the store, each clutching their newly acquired tools, the hardware store clerk leaned back in his chair, a satisfied smirk on his face. "Ah, the price of dreams," he chuckled to himself as he counted the coins. The day was off to a good start.

The morning sun still shone brightly down the single street of the gold rush town, casting a warm golden hue over the colorful buildings lining its path. While each structure had its own distinct charm and craftsmanship, the bank stood out—a tad more majestic, a hint more regal, as if it wore an invisible crown.

As they approached, its grand façade seemed to beckon them, showcasing an extra touch of elegance and polish that set it apart. Pushing open the heavy oak doors, they were greeted by an interior that seemed out of place in such a remote land. Gleaming mahogany desks sat under the sunlit glow from tall, arched windows, while the gold accents on the walls and fixtures shimmered subtly. The plush red carpet, softer underfoot than any they had trodden upon, was a nod to the prosperity this gold boom had ushered in.

From a dim corner of the lavish chamber, a rich laughter rippled, drawing their gaze. The figure that emerged was the bank manager. Short and stout, his very presence seemed to consume more space than his stature suggested. His mustache, enormous and meticulously groomed, held an air of mischief, while his eyes - warm on the surface - concealed a calculating glint. "Gentlemen." The manager spoke in the velvety tone of a seasoned salesman. "You've entered the very lifeblood of our burgeoning enclave. Most newcomers inevitably find themselves here. Thus, I wear the dual hats of greeter and gatekeeper." With a grace that belied his rotund figure, he motioned them into his inner chamber. While this room echoed the bank's opulence, it gave off a palpable sense of privacy and secrecy. Mitch nodded in appreciation; this room would have hosted every gold prospector who had come before them. As they settled into the inviting chairs, a mix of comfort and subtle tension hung in the air. The manager leaned in and inquired, "How might I be of service today?"

Mitch took a deep breath and said, "We're looking to lease some land for prospecting."

The manager's eyes twinkled. "Ah, prospectors! Always excited to help new gold miners find their fortune." He gestured grandly for the men to come forward; "Leave your tools by the door; don't worry your things are safe in here." His jovial demeanor turned solemn when asking the next question. "So, what is your budget?"

Mitch, always the diplomat, chimed in first. "Well, let's see, what do you have?"

The manager opened a drawer and pulled out a large surveyor's map and spread it on the desk. "Blue dots represent currently leased lands; green dots are available," he explained, his finger tracing over the map. "Each available land is noted with a price tag per month, depending on location and potential yield."

Huddled closely around the vast map spread out before them, the trio meticulously studied each section under the warm, golden light of the ornate chandelier hanging above. Its luminescence deepened the furrows of worry that etched the faces of the three spirited adventurers. Every parcel of land, boldly marked with its daunting price tag, felt agonizingly out of reach given their rapidly depleting funds. The manager, bearing the tired eyes of someone who had watched countless dreams crumble in the face of stark reality, was clearly inching towards impatience.

Then, Mitch's gaze narrowed onto an anomaly—a corner patch seemingly marred by time or neglect. A faint impression suggested a blue or green emblem might once have graced it, but now, hastily scribbled, were the words "Yik-Yak Mine," with a price that seemed absurdly humble: just 10 coins per month.

His finger landing squarely on the anomaly, Mitch looked up, questioning, "What's the story behind this one?"

For a moment, the bank manager's mask of affable authority wavered, replaced by genuine unease. He took a deep breath, as if bracing himself against an old, chilling wind. "Ah, the Yik-Yak Mine," he began, reluctance evident in every word. "That particular claim, gentlemen, is not up for lease," he stated, his tone final, shutting down any inkling of negotiation.

"Why 'not for lease'? It's displayed clear as day on this map," Mitch asserted, a challenging glint in his eyes.

Beside him, Jack added, "If it's on the map, it's fair game," while Jacob, though less confrontational, nodded in agreement, his eyes showing a hint of desperation.

The bank manager leaned back, intertwining his fingers and taking a moment to collect his thoughts before responding. "Gentlemen," he began cautiously, "there are places on this earth that hold stories, stories that are better left buried. And the Yik-Yak Mine is one of those."

Mitch raised an eyebrow, skepticism evident. "Stories? Is that all? We're not paying for tales; we're paying for land."

The manager's voice lowered, a sense of gravity settling in. "You misunderstand. These aren't just stories. Horrible events have happened up there."

Jack, ever the realist, cut in, "Sounds to me like a ruse to keep the best plots for the town's elites. We aren't greenhorns, sir. We've heard enough tall tales to last a lifetime."

Jacob, chiming in for the first time, added, "Look, all we want is a chance. A piece of land to call our own. And to deliver on our promises to our loved ones back home."

The bank manager seemed to waver, caught between a genuine concern and the determination of the three men. Then, with a heavy sigh, his resistance crumbled. "Alright, alright! But on your heads be it. Know that it's haunted, cursed with demons of unknown origin."

Mitch, unable to resist the urge to be brash, laughed outright, dismissing the bank manager's warning with audacity that only further aggravated him.

Visibly agitated, the manager continued tersely, "The lease spans a compulsory three months. That's 30 coins, plus an additional 10 coins for insurance and surcharge. So, you owe 40 coins in total."

Pooling their resources, the trio scraped together the required 40 coins, leaving a meager 7 coins remaining. They finalized the agreement with each man's signature, though Jacob struggled to pen his own name, and in return, received the lease agreement and a detailed map leading to their new territory. Rising from their seats, they exited the room with a mix of jubilation and defiance. As they left, Mitch couldn't resist one last derisive snort, dismissing the bank manager's foreboding story.

The stout mustached man watched them depart, a knot of regret forming in his stomach. His momentary lapse in judgment had potentially doomed the men to a fate he dared not utter aloud. He trotted behind them into the bank's main room and yelled out one more offer. "You can still take the money back. You really shouldn't go!" But the men were deaf to his plea and did not respond to his words. Instead, they headed out onto the street.

After pooling their money, the trio meticulously allocated their funds for provisions. They secured large burlap sacks of coffee beans, flour, and sugar, a few pounds of lard, a basket brimming with eggs, several hefty cans of beans, and a bottle of syrup. For the cold, lonely nights, three large bottles of whiskey were deemed essential. A stroke of fortune allowed them to strike a deal with an old-timer, acquiring a sturdy wagon to haul their supplies for the meager price of one of their whiskey bottles. With deeply etched lines marking years of hard living, the grizzled man claimed he had no further use for it. This transaction felt like a triumph to Mitch, Jacob, and Jack, not only facilitating their immediate needs but bolstering their morale for the journey ahead.

As they trekked away, the elderly man's voice trailed after them, his words tinged with foreboding. "Watch out for the ghosts up there!" he cackled with a disturbing glee. Dismissing it as the ramblings of a decaying mind, the men continued on, albeit with a slight unease.

***

The lease agreement, now their most treasured possession, was accompanied by a detailed map. This map, rich with topographical markings, showed footpaths and the hand-drawn silhouette of a cabin. Such a luxury was more than they had dared to hope for. No longer would they need to endure nights on the uneven forest floor, shielded only by their threadbare tents. Now, they'd have a sturdy roof overhead and solid wooden walls to shield them from the cold nights ahead. Their journey was beginning to seem less a gamble and more a well-thought-out adventure.

As the afternoon sun cast shimmering reflections off the map, they plotted their course to the Yik-Yak Mine. Dismissing the haunting echoes of the wilderness, the men's journey was filled with laughter and banter. They took turns pulling the wagon, spirits high and full of anticipation.

The forest was a dense tapestry of towering conifers, swaying bushes, and babbling brooks. The air was alive with a chorus of birds, their melodies weaving seamlessly with the rustling of leaves—a true symphony of nature. But had they listened more intently, they might have detected the odd cadence in the birds' calls, and the faint whispers beneath the rustling leaves. It was as though the forest, disturbed by their intrusion, watched with a malevolent gaze as the miners delved deeper into its heart.

As they navigated through the dense woods, Mitch's voice echoed with an almost manic glee. "The greatest men in history are those who dared, those who took the road less traveled," he proclaimed, slashing a branch out of their path with a makeshift machete. "Who are these country rubes to believe in ghosts and devils? Such primitive superstitions will be our winning hand. Just imagine the gold left untouched because of those ludicrous fears." He paused to look back at Jack and Jacob, a wide grin stretching across his face. "They'll sing songs about us, boys. The three brave souls who saw past the ignorance and superstition, who dared to venture into the accursed Yik-Yak Mine and came out millionaires!"

Jack chuckled, his eyes dancing with dreams of wealth and success. "Once we strike gold, I'm buying a saloon of my own, but not anywhere near this desolate place. Nah, I'm heading back to the coast. I'll buy the old Duck and Barrel. The finest whiskey will flow freely, and the patrons will raise their glasses to our names."

Jacob's expression turned wistful as he imagined a life beyond the grueling labor and squalor they were used to. "And I, I'll finally marry Susie. I'll buy a grand ranch for us, with green pastures as far as the eye can see. With hired farm hands, so she never has to lift a finger, and we can enjoy the rest of our days in leisure."

Mitch seemed to mull over their dreams and then shared his own grand plan. "When we're done here, I'll buy a grand ship and sail the seven seas. I'll dine with the elites in all the world's best restaurants. Oh, the tales I'll tell them! Of three brave men who dared to confront the unknown and emerged victorious."

"And the best whores!" Jack chided with a sideways grin, and the other men laughed.

As dusk settled, the once vibrant hues of the forest shifted to darker, more haunting shades. The inky shadows that danced between the trees grew increasingly foreboding. Noises once dismissed grew louder and more ominous, making Jacob flinch with every eerie echo. Even the familiar hoots of distant owls or the sound of twigs snapping beneath their feet took on an unsettling quality. A tangible, chilling aura was arising in the shadows around them.

"What's that!?" Jacob yelled suddenly, with a jarring pitch that made the other two men jump.

"What are you talking about?" Mitch asked, his voice tinged with annoyance.

"There," Jacob said, pointing to a spot beside the path. In the waning light, a stark white shape was unmistakably affixed to a tree trunk – the eerie visage of a human skull.

As the others looked, they saw not just the skull but also arm and leg bones arranged in a macabre design, fastened securely to the tree, whether by nails or some other adhesive.

"Just one of the former tenants' idea of a sick joke," Mitch grumbled, resolutely pulling the wagon forward, his intent clear: to move away from the morbid sight as quickly as possible.

Jack nodded, pausing just a moment longer before stating, "Mitch is right. This is just someone's twisted sense of humor." He quickly rejoined Mitch, continuing down the path, while Jacob lingered, his gaze fixed on the unmistakably human skull.

"You guys aren't worried?" Jacob's voice quivered slightly.

"It's sick," Mitch called back, his voice tense, "But remember, the banker warned us about the legends surrounding this place. People have died up here. I never denied that, and that... display... could've been crafted from one such unfortunate soul."

"But how did he die?" Jacob asked, his voice trembling just a tad.

"Miners die." Jack said, matter of factly. "These old mines aren't safe, and accidents happen. We knew this when we signed up for it." Jack reasoned.

Jacob nodded, taking a moment before catching up with the others. Their earlier lightheartedness had evaporated, replaced by a sober intensity. Mitch, bearing the brunt of their load, steadfastly pulled the wagon ahead.

As hours dragged on and their path inclined, the weight of fatigue bore down on them. Yet, in a way, their weariness dulled the edge of the forest's growing eeriness. As the last light of day began to wane, shadows danced and expanded around them.

"Is that it?" Jacob's voice pierced the stillness, tinged with hope. He gestured toward a silhouette breaking the tree line.

Peering ahead, Mitch nodded, a hint of a smile playing on his lips. "It is." The dark outline gradually sharpened, revealing a solid cabin framed by towering trees. The small details - the porch, a window, the moss-covered shingles, and a sturdy chimney - all signaled that a decently constructed little domicile did indeed await them. This haven amidst the ominous woods brought palpable relief. Even Mitch, usually so stoic, looked visibly heartened. "We made it, boys."

But the forest's malevolent grip wasn't going to release them just yet. Nearby, a disquieting rustling came from the bushes, punctuated by the stark crack of a sizable branch just off to the side of their path. A chilling, guttural growl swiftly followed. And this time, it wasn't just Jacob who jumped; an unmistakable wave of fear washed over them all.

"Run!" Jack's urgent cry sliced through the mounting fear. Darting a quick glance behind, he was certain he saw the hulking silhouette of a massive bear barreling down on them. The pounding cadence of its approach sent shivers of panic through each man, propelling them into a frantic sprint toward the cabin, their gear jostling violently with every step.

Mitch, ever determined, clung to the wagon, dragging it despite its jostling contents. A few eggs tumbled out, smearing the path behind them. As the cabin's entrance neared, he finally released the wagon, which careened to the side, and joined the desperate race to the door.

Reaching the refuge, Jack's trembling hands struggled with the doorknob, precious seconds passing before they stumbled inside. Slamming the door shut, they secured it, their rapid breaths the only sound. The bear's menacing growl eventually retreated, but its haunting echo lingered in their ears.

"Where are our supplies?" Jack's voice bordered on panic as he rushed to the cabin's little front window. He half-expected to witness the bear ravaging their provisions, but to his astonishment, nothing was there.

Mitch joined him, taking a closer look. Their wagon lay toppled just short of the porch, its contents scattered. While some tools and food sacks lay strewn about, the wagon was largely undisturbed, and more importantly, no bear in sight.

After a few tense moments of vigilant scanning, relief replaced their alarm. Convinced of the beast's absence, they ventured out to retrieve their belongings and secured them inside the cabin.

The cabin itself was a bastion against the looming wilderness outside. Its sturdy walls seemed to shield them from the forest's oppressive mood. Stepping inside felt like entering another world.

To their delight, a spacious living area awaited them, with a grand stone fireplace taking center stage. Its dormant hearth hinted at countless cozy evenings spent by its flames. While the furniture bore the weight of years, its charm was undeniable. Four sturdy little armchairs, a sofa with worn out plaid fabric, a robust table, and a quaint rug underfoot transformed the space into a homely retreat. For a moment, the forest's malevolence faded, replaced by the comforting embrace of their newfound haven.

Beyond the living area, they discovered a compact kitchen, surprisingly well equipped with pots, pans, utensils, and even a sink. Outside, a water pump and an outhouse stood at a convenient distance.

At the back of the cabin were the sleeping quarters. Three sets of bunk beds, each with its own worn yet clean set of sheets, were lined up against the walls. Each could have comfortably accommodated two miners, speaking to the cabin's past life.

The men's spirits lifted further as they took in their surroundings. This was more than just a shelter; it was a base, a home they could return to after their arduous mining efforts. It was the beginning of their golden dream. Mitch lit a fire in the fireplace, its warm glow reflecting in the men's faces, as they settled into their new abode.

While the forest still whispered its creepy tales outside their door, inside the cabin, the men enjoyed a few glasses of whiskey and indulged in cheerful banter. The chilling episode in the forest was slowly forgotten, replaced by the excitement of their gold-seeking dreams and the comforting familiarity of their new dwelling. Despite the dust and cobwebs, which were quickly dealt with, the cabin offered more comfort than they had hoped for.

"We really hit the jackpot with this place, didn't we?" Jack remarked, his eyes twinkling in the firelight.

"Makes you wonder why no one claimed it before us, doesn't it?" Mitch replied, a half-smile playing on his lips.

The men enjoyed a few more rounds of chatter and calming whiskey before they began the pre-bedtime chores of shaking off bed sheets, brushing teeth, and peeing off the deck... The men might have calmed down from earlier, but they were all still a little too weary to venture to that outhouse in the dark. Outside, the forest remained daunting, filled with animal sounds, unidentifiable noises occurring sporadically, which the men tried their best to ignore.

Jack ventured to a previously unexplored corner of the cabin. Hidden in the shadows, a weathered desk sat, cloaked in layers of dust and cobwebs. As he carelessly brushed his teeth, Jack's curiosity got the better of him. He began to sift through the desk's contents. His fingers stumbled upon a brittle piece of paper, yellowed and curled with age. Cautiously, he unfurled it, revealing a poem penned in a fading, hurried script. The weight of the words pulled the others closer as Jack began to recite with a mouthful of toothpaste:

"Where shadows of the past reside,
In cabin's heart, they chose to hide,
Spectral whispers do confide,
Of gold's curse and deadly pride."

"What's that you're saying?" Jacob asked nervously, not liking the sound of the words.

"Just a weird poem I found in this desk," Jack replied warily. He returned to the kitchen, swished out his mouth with water, and put down his toothbrush. Then he went back to the little desk for further inspection.

Beneath the paper, a worn leather-bound journal sat. As Jack picked it up and flipped through its yellowed pages, skimming the entries, he surmised it was a logbook from past miners. "There are numerous dates and names here," Jack mentioned, continuing his scan of the journal.

"Aw, come on!" Mitch chimed in swiftly, attempting to dispel the unease. "A journal from past miners? They probably filled it with horror tales just to scare us. That's probably where all the hogwash about this place comes from—a ruse to keep people away from the good finds they discovered here." Mitch seemed thoroughly convinced by his own words, but Jack and Jacob looked skeptical.

Jack took the journal, sat in front of the fire, and became engrossed in its pages, while the other two men awaited his review with anticipation. "Um…" Jack began cautiously, "You guys, this stuff ain't good."

Jacob, now entirely unsettled, leapt onto the couch next to Jack and tried to read over his shoulder, but it was futile—Jacob was illiterate. "What's it saying?" Jacob inquired, his voice betraying his fear.

Clearing his throat, Jack began to recite a passage aloud. "'Today we settled into the cabin. The place seems great. We've all eaten and will get a good rest. Tomorrow, we will head down the shaft and start working. I'd be more excited about everything if things didn't feel so strange. I swear I keep hearing whispers, and it feels like there's someone else here with us. Even just now, Chuck said someone kicked him. He raged at us, demanding to know who did it, but he was in the kitchen when it happened, and we were all seated. This place might be haunted.'" Jack paused, exchanging a concerned glance with Jacob.

"Oh, please!" Mitch interjected, feigning nonchalance. "This is obviously a joke."

"How do you know?" Jacob retorted angrily. "Keep reading, Jack. What happens next?"

Jack continued, turning to a subsequent entry. "'Today, we ventured into the mines. The mountain is indeed rich in gold. We barely began our work when Chuck, unnerved by something, swung his pickaxe haphazardly. Before we knew it, Donny was injured. We restrained Chuck and hurriedly brought Donny out. Now, we're back in the cabin. Night approaches, so our return to the mine must wait. Chuck seems in denial, and Donny… Donny's in bad shape. He's unconscious and losing blood.'"

"Oh my God!" Jacob exclaimed, horrified. "What's next?"

Jack leafed through the journal and paused. "What is it?" Jacob pressed.

"Nothing," Jack answered. "The next entry is from a different group, many months later."

Seizing the opportunity, Mitch grabbed the journal. "Boys!" he cried jubilantly. "You overlooked the vital part: the mountain is rich in gold!" He returned the book to the desk. "They must've left with their fortunes!" he speculated; excitement evident. Yet the other men remained doubtful. "No more ghost stories tonight," Mitch declared.

After some reflection, Jack seemed to concur. Nodding to Jacob, who often sought guidance from the more experienced Jack, they all decided to retire. They were excited yet apprehensive about the following day's excavation.

Despite the foreboding feeling, they clung to their dreams: the glint of gold, the promise of a brighter future and a better life. The fear of failure was even more terrifying than the ghostly voices carried on the wind. With these thoughts swirling in their minds, one by one, the men succumbed to a restless sleep.

***

A new day dawned, the harsh light of morning piercing through the grime-encrusted windows of the cabin. The men groggily prepared their morning sustenance, the air laden with the aroma of freshly brewed coffee and frying pancakes. Their tools, newly purchased from the crafty hardware store clerk, lay scattered around them - a symbol of the backbreaking labor that awaited. They didn't talk much, their joviality from the previous night replaced by a silent determination. They understood that this was it; they had ventured this far for this very moment.

Gathering their tools, they ventured out, lanterns swinging from their hands, casting long dancing shadows onto the dense undergrowth. Their map guided them to the remnants of a pathway. Despite its decay, the path's direction was clear, leading them directly towards the looming, rocky mountainside.

The twisted pathway gave way to a clearing where the mountain's raw, exposed rock stood tall. In its core was the gaping entrance of a mine shaft, shrouded in darkness. Above it, a weather-worn wooden sign hung precariously, its letters faded yet still decipherable. They read the words aloud as a group, their voices echoing in the cold, morning air: "Yik-Yak Mine." Suddenly, the wind picked up, slicing through the quiet like a knife. A howl emerged from the depths of the tunnel, echoing outwards, chilling their spines and causing the hairs at the back of their necks to stand on end.

Jacob jumped, a sharp yelp escaping his lips. His eyes widened with fear as he turned to his companions. "Did you hear that?" he asked, his voice trembling. "It sounded like...like...a laugh!"

Mitch sneered, crossing his arms over his chest. "Don't tell me you're scared, Jacob," he mocked. His voice was strong, commanding, a stark contrast to Jacob's frightened whisper. "We came here for gold, not to run away at the first sign of danger."

"But Mitch, that wasn't normal! It sounded like..." Jacob's voice trailed off, as he struggled to find the words to describe what he heard.

Mitch cut him off. "Like what, Jacob? A ghost?" He let out a derisive laugh. "This is a mine, not a haunted house. We all just read the sign out loud. That was just an echo of our own voices. Now, unless you want to go back to living off your girlfriend's money, I suggest we carry on."

Their argument echoed off the rocky mountainside and was swallowed by the gaping entrance to the Yik-Yak Mine. Mitch's stern words and relentless pressure overcame their resistance. Mitch pointed out two large mining carts discarded near the entranceway. "These could come in handy, but let's check things out first." And with lingering trepidation, they finally agreed to venture into the mine.

***

As the men ignited their lanterns, the yellow glow barely penetrated the deep obsidian of the mine. The shaft was just over six feet tall, barely tall enough to accommodate the tallest of the men. With a width no greater than five feet, the mine felt claustrophobically tight yet also alarmingly deep. What struck the men as they delved deeper into the Yik-Yak Mine was its seemingly unnatural straightness. It was almost as if it was bored straight into the mountain, rather than having been dug out following a vein of gold. Its linear layout was far removed from the more traditional, branching structure of most mines they'd heard of. Usually, miners would follow a vein of gold deep into the earth, carving a network of tunnels and shafts.

Indeed, the linear nature of the Yik-Yak Mine tunnel felt strangely out of place. Anyone with a basic knowledge of geology would know that mineral deposits, especially gold veins, were seldom, if ever, found in such a consistent, straight line. A gold vein formed when hot, mineral-rich fluids flowed into cracks in the earth's crust. These veins could meander in any direction - left, right, up, down - following the path of least resistance. But not this one apparently.

The mine was supported by a series of wooden 'sets', each one made up of two posts and a horizontal beam or 'cap'. This traditional method of timbering was widely used for its simplicity, though the sight of timeworn, weathered wood bearing such an immense load was disconcerting. Each echoing footstep reminded them of the colossal weight of the rock above their heads.

As they delved deeper into the mine's passage, a stifling atmosphere settled around them. The air grew colder, and an unnatural silence seemed to mute even the minor echoes of their footsteps. Every instinct screamed at them that something wasn't right. Their gut feelings, those primal instincts that had long protected ancestors from unseen predators, clawed at their resolve, urging them to turn back. But greed, curiosity, and perhaps a touch of hubris drove them onward.

Each miner could feel it — the tangible weight of unease pressing on their chests, growing heavier with every step. The spine-chilling tales from the journal were no longer just stories; they felt like prophetic warnings. Whispers of dread wormed their way into their ears, a constant chilling reminder of the ignored cautionary tales from the journal.

Suddenly, the endless forward march was halted by a sheer wall of cold, gray stone. It was a jarring end to the relentless tunnel, and all three men momentarily lost their bearings. One would have expected the prior excavators to taper off their tunnels, their pathways becoming narrower as resources dwindled or they gave up on the vein, but this...this was different. The termination was abrupt, with the rock face bearing the scars of hasty pickaxe blows.

Illuminating the area with their lanterns, the dancing amber light revealed patterns that seemed strangely deliberate. Upon closer inspection, those random gashes began to form shapes — primitive symbols, some geometric, others more arcane, etched into the rock. The uncanny carvings sent shivers down their spines.

But as they neared the rock wall, scrutinizing it with an intense gaze borne of desperation and hope, a glint caught Jacob's eye. He blinked, crouched down, and shone his lantern onto the seemingly innocuous patch of rock right at the center of that wall. It gleamed, the warm light bouncing off a yellow metal embedded in the stone.

"Look at that!" Jacob exclaimed, disbelief lacing his words. The others turned; their curiosity piqued.

"Is it real?" Jack asked, his voice hushed as he squinted at the golden streak that Jacob's lantern illuminated. Mitch, ever the cynic, leaned in skeptically, scrutinizing the gold vein with a hardened gaze.

And then he saw it too, the undeniable glimmer of gold. His skepticism melted away, replaced by a greed-fueled excitement. The men erupted into shouts of joy; their previous apprehensions forgotten in the face of this golden promise. They eagerly brandished their picks, Mitch leading the charge. The ring of metal on rock filled the tunnel as they began chipping away at the stone, each strike a step closer to their dreams.

The echo of their tools reverberated through the depths of the mine, the only sound breaking the otherwise eerie silence that enveloped them. The shards of rock that fell away revealed more of the precious metal, fueling their enthusiasm further. Soon, they had chipped out a chunk of the vein, its lustrous surface catching the lantern light and making their hearts leap with joy.

Their initial disbelief morphed into giddy laughter and backslapping as they admired their find. "We've hit the mother lode!" Mitch crowed, holding up a chunk of gold as big as a baseball.

"We're going to be richer than a railroad tycoon!" Jacob chimed in, a triumphant grin on his face.

Jack, usually more reserved, couldn't hide his excitement either. "We've done it, boys!" he cheered.

It seemed as if their dreams of wealth and success were coming true. The hardships of their journey, their dwindling funds, the foreboding mine – all of it seemed worthwhile at the sight of the gleaming gold. They celebrated their victory, not noticing the echoing laughter that joined in their jubilant shouts.

Amid the overwhelming rush of discovery and the magnetic pull of gold, the trio plunged into their toil with an intensity previously foreign to them. Every swing, every strike into the rock, was a symphony of burning muscles and taut sinew. With hands reddened and raw and backs drenched in sweat, they bore the brunt of their endeavor. And yet, every wince and hiss of pain was promptly forgotten with each glimpse of the treasure they were revealing. Veins of gold, some as robust as their own wrists, embedded within the rock, stood as luminous tokens of their unwavering dedication.

As they toiled, the excavated chunks of rocks were neatly stacked into pyramidal piles, creating a gold laced testament to their day's labor. Time seemed to warp and twist in the cavern's embrace; hours melded into mere moments. Their sole measurement of its passage was the dwindling light from their lanterns, which began to waver and dim, projecting elongated, capering shadows against the rough cavern walls. Realizing the need to wrap things up before their fuel ran out, they made their way back towards the entrance of the mine to retrieve the ancient mining carts they had spotted there. As they returned to the outside world, an unsettling chill gripped Jacob. Amongst the play of light and dark from the flames, he spotted the eerie resemblance of elongated faces in those shadows.

Emerging from the cave's maw, the men were momentarily blinded by the waning light of the setting sun. A blanket of shadows crept ominously across the landscape, threatening to obscure their path back to the cabin. Time was of the essence. With a combination of elbow grease and a liberal application of lubricant to the old rusty axles, the abandoned carts groaned, creaking back to life. Conversation was kept to a minimum with a singular focus on each of the men's faces. Single word instructions and answers were all that passed between the men as they hurried. The carts clattered and protested along the decrepit track. They were thankful for the tunnel's linear formation. When they finally arrived back to their haul of rocks the men were hit with the realization that the volume of their find was staggering. A daunting task lay ahead – attempting to fit those mountainous piles into the limited confines of the rickety carts. Undeterred, they set to work, cramming in as much as the carts could bear.

The men pressed forward, muscles tense as they pushed the heavy carts back along the path they had just traversed. Jacob, sweaty and tired, primarily supported Jack as they pushed the heavy cart together. Every so often, noting Mitch's fatigue, Jacob would switch over, trying to balance the workload. Their sheer determination was evident, driven by their overpowering greed and excitement. The carts' wheels shrieked loudly, echoing within the confines of the tunnel. As they emerged from the cave's darkness, the encroaching night greeted them, its dimness combined with the noises of nocturnal birds and other creatures, giving the men an eerie welcome.

When the day's work was finally done, the men howled and cheered in excitement and celebration. "Good work boys!" Mitch cried out in good cheer.

Their joyous celebration had only just begun when it was brought to a sudden halt. Jack, who wanted a better look at some of those thick, yellow veins of gold, sifted around in one of the carts, trying to find a good sample to examine. But as he perused the rocks, his stomach dropped. The first chunk he held up had no gold in it at all. Holding it under the dim light of the moon, he squinted, trying to find some hint of metal but failed. He dropped it to the ground and grabbed another. The result was the same. "What the hell!" Jack yelled.

The other two men, who had been observing Jack's actions, quickly ran to the cart to do the same. Grabbing chunks of rock, one by one the men examined the cartload with hysterical excitement, along with cries of "this is just rock!" and "it's all worthless!" They threw each chunk of rock to the ground as they inspected them. Not a single one had any gold to be found. The metallic treasure they'd worked so hard to chip from the mountain's core seemed to have vanished upon exiting the shaft. The previously brilliant veins that ran through the excavated rocks now appeared to be worthless gray stones in the dwindling twilight.

"It's a trick. It must be the light!" Mitch said with a glimmer of hope returning to his voice.

"Let's bring some back to the cabin!" Jacob shouted, and all three men were in agreement. No one could believe that there was actually no gold in these rocks. They had all seen it; they had touched it.

So, the men filled their pockets with as many chunks of rock as they could carry, and they headed back down the now almost invisible pathway back to the cabin. Full of enraged disbelief, they were all but sprinting their way home. More than a few times, the men tripped and fell, bruising their sides and scratching their arms and legs on branches.

Once back in the cabin, Mitch ran around, lighting every possible lantern in the place, and Jacob set the fire ablaze. They wanted full illumination to make sure this wasn't just a trick from the shadows. Jack and Jacob threw their stone chunks onto the little table and took a seat. Once Mitch had lit every lantern he could, he joined them, slamming his own rocks down amongst the others.

Sitting there together, the men were silent. The anticipation in the air was as thick as pea soup. Anxiously, each man grabbed a chunk and examined it. It was silent for a few moments. No one could believe this was happening.

"It has to be some kind of hysteria," Jack said, his voice so hopeless it would have been humorous had the circumstances not been so grave.

"You mean, like maybe there is gold, but we have convinced ourselves that there isn't?" Jacob asked, the youthful optimism shining through in his voice as he discarded the chunk he had been observing back onto the table.

"Yeah, like we are creating our own worst nightmare. Maybe we just worked too hard. We probably need water and sleep," Jack reasoned. Finding his own argument convincing, he nodded his head to himself.

But Jacob, usually the most positive of the bunch, was not buying it. "No…That's not it," he said, solemnly. And his eyes moved from the stack of rocks on the table towards the desk, where the journal from the night before sat. "The mine," he whispered, the color draining from his face. "It's…it's cursed. We were warned…"

The declaration hung in the air, heavier than the disappointment that enveloped them. Silence followed for a few moments as the men took in Jacob's words. But Mitch wouldn't have it. Suddenly, he leaned in, his face just inches from Jacob's. Then he yelled in rage. "Cursed!? You're actually buying into those damn old wives' tales? You rube!" he roared, spit flying from his mouth as he berated Jacob, who could only sit there in shock. "We're from the city, Jacob, not superstitious fools from the hinterlands!"

Jacob, taken aback, stammered, "But, Mitch…"

Mitch wasn't listening. The pent-up frustration erupted; he stood up straight, backed away from Jacob a step or two, and then swung a fist, catching Jacob square on the jaw. Jacob's head flew to one side, and he slunk to the side of his chair, holding his face in his hands. Jack jumped up from his chair and quickly stood between the two men.

"What is wrong with you?!" Jack bellowed, his eyes blazing as he stared down Mitch. Jacob stood, holding his jaw in one hand, eyes now blazing with anger. He was ready to fight. Jack, who was larger in frame than either of the men, formed a barrier between them. "This ain't the time for violence!" He yelled at the two, "Our bodies have had enough for the day!"

Jacob nodded in agreement, stepping back hesitantly. But Jack's attempt to defuse the tension did little to thin the palpable unease enveloping the room. In a surge of frustration, Mitch seemed to channel his anger towards the very source of their despair. "Damn you, Yik-Yak Mine!" he cried out, arms outstretched, voice bouncing off the walls and filling the haunting void.

From the abyss of the encompassing forest outside came a response. An unsettling, uncanny laughter pierced the night, trailed by a croak. "Yiikk Yaaakkkk!" The tone, otherworldly and reminiscent of a deep-throated frog, froze them in their tracks. All three stood stock-still, a mix of terror and disbelief widening their eyes.

Taking a deep breath to steady himself, Jack finally broke the silence. "I've had enough," he declared with grim determination. "Our only option now is to leave." His words, though meant for all, were directed more at Jacob, who seemed the most grounded amidst the chaos.

"At night?" Jacob queried; his voice laced with exhaustion.

"In the morning," Jack declared with gravity. As his words settled, there was an unspoken accord between him and Jacob. They subtly withdrew from the sitting area, their movements reflecting a mutual desire to distance themselves from the day's inexplicable events and to seek the refuge of sleep.

The terrifying cry from the forest still played on Jacob's nerves as he ventured outside, clutching two large buckets. Moonlight washed over the porch, illuminating the nearby pump in a ghostly light. Water would be essential for the chores at hand, so he ventured forth. Each of his steps felt fraught with tension, the weight of every footfall heavy with silent bravery.

Inside, the soft gurgle of whiskey being poured filled the room. The golden liquid shimmered under the lantern's light as Jack treated himself to a hearty drink, seeking a momentary escape from the day's horrifying events.

Mitch, overcome by grief, slumped into the comforting folds of the couch. His slouched form was the picture of exhaustion and turmoil, his face obscured by his hands as he grappled with the incomprehensible.

Their shattered dreams painted the cabin walls with gloom that night. Each man was lost in his own thoughts, their silent despair punctuated by occasional grunts of disbelief. The whiskey, which they'd thought would be their celebration, was now a bitter balm to their crushed hopes.

Mitch was uncharacteristically silent, brooding by the fire. His eyes, reflecting the dancing flames, bore a vacant look, as if he was questioning the very foundations of his beliefs.

Every once in a while, he would pick up one of the chunks of rocks and examine it one more time, only to be disappointed once again.

Jack, having calmed himself with both whiskey and some food, ventured back to the desk in the corner. He reached into the drawer, pulling out the journal he had read from the night before. The time-worn book felt heavy in his hands. He dreaded looking at it again, but after the events of today, he knew he had to take one more look. Jacob watched with eager anticipation as Jack opened it. Unable to read himself, he depended on the elder man's ability. Jacob drew near to listen to the words Jack now read aloud. Jack began.

"'We can't believe our luck! What an unexpected treat to have a fully equipped cabin to rest in after such a long journey. We will sleep tonight and get to work in the morning.'"

Jack paused for a moment, and said, "the next entry." "'We were about to settle in for the night when we heard the most terrifying noise. I know it sounds crazy, but all of us heard it. It was laughter, coming from the forest outside. Thank God for this cabin. We are all too terrified to go back out there, even for some extra water.'"

Then another pause before Jack read the next entry. "'Today we hit the mother lode. I can't believe it! Gold, everywhere! I am the first to return to the cabin after an incredible day. We were down there for probably 10 hours, chipping away at the veins. It was incredible. Gold seemed to run through the entire wall in front of us. Unfortunately, Larry struck me with his pickaxe. The weirdest thing. I swear he did it on purpose, so I had to return to bandage myself. I will go back and help them carry the load we gathered but am taking a moment to recuperate.'"

Then, after another pause, turning the page. "'Nothing makes sense. The rocks we excavated are all just rocks; no gold to be found. Larry is going nuts, and the others had to hold him back from attacking me. We will return in the morning.'"

Then Jack hesitated to read aloud, taking a moment to scan the page ahead before reading it aloud. Jacob looked on in anticipation.

"What happens next?" Jacob asked inquisitively.

"Nothing," Jack said in despair. "There is a new entry from a new group."

"Read that one," Jacob said, his voice shaky with fear and anticipation.

Jack cleared his throat and began reading the next entry. "'We arrived at the cabin today with a mix of anticipation and exhaustion. Our journey was long, and we are tired, but inexplicable whispers and peculiar bangs keep occurring in every corner of this place. Sam, with his usual bravado, is telling us to dismiss them as the wind playing tricks. But Father O'Malley, a former member of clergy, looks deeply troubled. He is currently holding a crucifix tight in his hand and praying quietly to himself. I do hope we get some needed rest tonight.'"

Jack turned the page and then began the second entry. "'This morning we headed out for our first excavation, but just a few steps into the shaft, we unearthed the grisly remains of former miners — a rusted helmet, a worn-out shoe, and most shockingly, skeletal remains that disturbingly still have rotting flesh in them. A heavy weight of responsibility and reverence came upon us. Father O'Malley was adamant that before we lay claim to any gold, we must first lay these souls to rest. The others agreed so, setting aside our avarice, we spent today gathering the scattered remains and giving them a dignified burial, with Father O'Malley performing a somber last rite. We were going to go back into the mine to attempt a shortened excavation, but Peter began behaving oddly, his voice suddenly filled with unfamiliar tones, and his movements becoming erratic. We have returned to the cabin, in hopes that we can shake him from this strange illness. But I am afraid this place may not be the best location to ease a troubled mind. The walls around us continue with their strange whispers, and those odd knocks on the windows and floorboards have not ceased.'"

Both Jacob and Mitch were listening intently. Though Mitch remained on the couch, he could not help but turn his head and drop his jaw a little as Jack continued to read the entries aloud.

"'The walls of this old cabin are my only protection now. That thing in Peter - it's taken him over! This morning, we ventured into the mine, and indeed we rejoiced when we saw veins of gold, like nothing I could have ever dreamed of. Huge shining veins fill the walls of that mine! We had only just begun to chip into the rock when suddenly Peter attacked us. It was a horrifying sight, watching as Peter brutally struck down Father O'Malley and then turned his frenzied attack on Sam. I tried my best to stop him; I even stuck him with my own axe, but he was like a demon. His strength was beyond human. I fled…I feel like a coward. I left Sam to die. But I managed to escape. I ran back to the cabin, the chilling sounds of Peter's twisted laughter chasing me as I went. Now, he's out there, waiting, occasionally thudding against the cabin's walls. The shadows play tricks. Sometimes, I swear I can see Father O'Malley's spirit, hand raised in a final blessing — or perhaps a warning. Oh God, he's opening the window! I must go now…'" And that was where Jack ended his reading, looking up from the page with terror in his eyes.

145

"That's the end?!" Jacob gasped.

Jack nodded solemnly. He flipped through the pages, scanning them vigorously. "It's all the same. Every entry goes like this. They start hopeful, but once any group enters the mine, they tell of horrible events. Violence, ghostly apparitions…murder!" Jack whispered the last words.

Laying the journal down, Jack stood, the room falling into silence as his two companions only stared back in horror. His face was pale under the lantern light, eyes reflecting a dread that was mirrored in the other men.

"Boys," he began, his voice wavering slightly, "we need to leave. We need to leave as soon as dawn breaks."

The words hung in the room like a tangible thing. Mitch finally looked away from the fire, his gaze hard, while Jacob shifted uncomfortably, his unease apparent.

"That mine…" Jack continued, holding up the journal. "It's haunted. There's a cursed spirit in there, something…something beyond any ghost. And it's got a hold of us. This," he said, tapping the journal, "is the account of the miners before us. The same gold turning to rock, the same laughter…and then, murders, many of them."

Mitch shook his head violently, as if cleansing himself from the fear that had formerly gripped him. His eyes opened wide, and he grinned as if the most fantastic realization had just crossed his mind.; "Boys! This curse, or whatever it is… It doesn't want us to take the gold! That's what it is! The illusion is not that there is gold, the illusion is that there is not gold!" he said, suddenly ecstatic with joy. "These rocks, they are full of gold. We just can't see it!" Mitch's eyes gleamed with a crazed glare. He lifted a chunk of rock from the table again, gazing at it with that mad look in his eyes.

But Jack continued, ignoring Mitch's insane suggestion. "Don't speak the name of the mine again. It seems to be a trigger. A call to whatever resides in there. Remember when we spoke the name of it, in front of the mine's entrance? We all heard that awful laugh." Jack was adamant, he looked to each of the men with a staunch expression of authority, demanding agreement.

Jacob shuddered, wrapping his arms around himself as if trying to ward off a chill. "A demon?" he whispered; his voice barely audible.

Jack nodded gravely. "Yes, Jacob, a demon. We've trespassed, and now we will pay the price if we stay any longer. We must leave before it's too late."

Just as Jack's words faded into the charged air, a sudden gust of wind surged against the cabin with a force so violent that it shook the very foundations. The windows rattled in their frames, and the whole structure creaked ominously, as if straining under some colossal burden.

Jacob, gripped by fear, sprinted towards his bunk, curling up in an attempt to find some semblance of safety. Jack stood still, his body as rigid as a steel beam, eyes wide and filled with terror.

Mitch, however, only grinned - an eerie, malicious grin that did not fit the situation. His eyes twinkled with a gleam of madness, and he threw his head back and laughed, a sound that chilled the blood in the other men's veins. And then, he uttered the name that Jack had just warned them never to speak again.

"Yik-Yak!!" Mitch screeched in a horrifying tone.

The words echoed in the cabin, and the other two men screamed. Jack, in a fit of anger and fear, stormed towards Mitch. "You damned fool!" he roared, grabbing Mitch's collar and shaking him violently. But Mitch was unaffected. He only stared back at Jack with a strange, almost unhinged, gleam in his eyes, as if he was a puppet possessed by a malignant spirit.

Enraged and horrified, Jack trudged off to his own bunk, snapping at the others over his shoulder. "When the sun's up, I'm out of here!" he declared with finality. Jacob, his head already buried under the covers in a feeble attempt to ward off the horror, grunted his agreement.

Helped by the numbing effects of the whiskey, Jack eventually succumbed to a restless sleep. Jacob shook in his bunk for a long time, unable to calm himself. He tried not to open his eyes, but whenever he did, he peered over to the couch, where Mitch remained, still fawning over the chunks of rock that lay on the little table. Eventually, late in the night, he succumbed to sleep as well.

***

The first light of dawn roused Jacob from his uneasy slumber. Despite the lingering taste of cheap whiskey in his mouth and a mild headache, his youthful resilience helped him spring out of bed with relative ease. His eyes fell on the other bunks, and he noticed with a pang of worry that Mitch's was empty. A quick scan of the cabin revealed that his boots and jacket were gone too.

Reluctantly, Jacob ventured outside, his heart pounding in his chest. His gut knew where Mitch had ventured to, remembering his crazed ideas that the gold was in fact real. There was no doubt in his mind that Mitch had returned to that accursed place. A chill ran down his spine at the thought of entering the shaft again, but his concern for his friend overpowered his fear.

Fueled by a sense of duty and concern, he picked up his lantern and steeled himself for the journey ahead. Plunging into the abyss of the Yik-Yak Mine, he ventured forth, the echoes of Mitch's pickaxe hitting rock serving as his grim guide. As he ventured deeper, the chilling sound of laughter mixed in with the sound of metal striking rock. Jacob's stomach churned with unease; the reality of Mitch's manic obsession was sinking in. He called out to his friend, his voice trembling, "Mitch? It's me, Jacob!"

There was no answer. Only the constant rhythm of the pickaxe hitting the rock. With a mix of concern and apprehension, he continued his journey deeper into the mine, the light from his lantern casting long, monstrous shadows on the tunnel walls.

Finally, Jacob reached the end of the tunnel. The sight that greeted him stopped him in his tracks. Working away at a manic pace, drenched in sweat, Mitch was relentlessly chipping at the rock face. Mitch's lantern sat on a pile of new mounds of what looked like...gold.

"Stop it, Mitch! We need to get out of here!" Jacob called out in panic as the sight unfolded before him. But his plea fell on deaf ears.

As Jacob watched the unfolding of his friend's sanity, his eyes couldn't help but return to those piles of gold that were accumulating around Mitch. As he came close, Jacob kneeled down to examine the chunks of golden-veined stone. The glimmering yellow metal twinkled in the lantern light; its allure impossible to resist. The dreams he had tasted just the day before returned to his mind. He picked up a piece, its weight solid and real in his hand. His mind teetered on the edge of disbelief and wild anticipation. "Is this real?" he murmured, entranced by the glittering specimen.

Suddenly, the striking of the pickaxe ceased. Jacob looked up to see Mitch turning towards him. With a wild, frenzied gleam in his eyes, Mitch responded in a voice barely above a whisper, "It is!"

But then, a wave of clarity swept over Jacob, his sense of reality pushing back against the intoxicating allure of the illusionary gold. He dropped the deceptive stone. The clinking sound of it hitting the others as it fell to the ground rang through the tunnel. He straightened up, looking at his friend with a resolute gaze. "No, it isn't," he stated firmly. "And we need to leave. Now!" His voice echoed off the rocky walls, the gravitas of his statement hanging heavily in the dim, confined space.

Mitch looked at Jacob, his eyes glowing with a dangerous intensity. "You're wrong," he spat out, each word infused with venomous defiance.

Jacob didn't waver. He stood his ground, his conviction stronger than the illusion the haunted mine presented. "Once we take this out of the mine, it will revert back to stone," he argued, the fervor in his voice failing to mask the worry etched on his face. "Because that's what it is, Mitch. It's just stone."

And with those last words coming from Jacob's mouth, Mitch drove his pickaxe into the top of poor Jacob's head. The young man, mouth still agape, breathed out the last letters of his final statement. His face staring blankly back at Mitch, his body crumpled to the ground, the long metal spike making a squishing sound as it was released from the young man's skull.

**

The sound of delirious celebration reverberated through the morning air, rousing Jack from his intoxicated slumber. Mitch's ecstatic cries were tinged with an edge of insanity that sent a cold ripple of apprehension down Jack's spine. "I've cracked it!" Mitch was shrieking, his voice echoing through the woods around the cabin. "The secret...it's mine now!"

Jack, his head throbbing and stomach churning from the remnants of the whiskey in his guts, staggered to his feet, his pulse quickening as he began to comprehend Mitch's words that rang out through the windows around him. Could Mitch have truly found a way to circumvent the mine's bewitching curse? Could the gold exist outside the shaft?

The notion seemed fantastical, but the echo of Mitch's laughter fueled a tiny spark of hope in Jack's chest. He was fully aware of and remembered the horrific journal entries he had read the night before, yet he couldn't help but be intrigued by the prospect of the gold being real. As he stumbled out of his bunk, he steadied himself against the wall, shivering with anticipation, and the chill of the early morning air.

In the soft glow of dawn, Mitch stood tall, his mining gear slick with sweat, beside a mining cart filled with an ominous bounty. Jack's heart fluttered in horror as he stepped forward, his gaze locked on the overflowing cart. As he approached, the glimmer he had hoped to see within the cart was absent. Instead, a gruesome sight met his eyes. The cart was filled with rocks, plain gray rocks, rocks that did not shimmer with the glint of gold, but he did see a tinge of moisture on them. And there were oddly shaped pieces of things amongst those rocks, mingling with the cargo.

The sight of it froze Jack in his tracks, his blood turning to ice in his veins. He squinted, his eyes adjusting to the morning sunlight, his breath hitching as the grim reality of what he was observing began to take shape…

His heart pounded in his chest like a drum, each beat echoed with his growing horror. As he leaned in for a closer look, his worst fears were confirmed. It wasn't gold glistening within the cart, nor was it moisture from the dripping ceiling of the cave. It was blood, still fresh and wet, mingling with those mundane rocks in a grotesque spectacle. The sickening metallic scent wafted into Jack's nostrils, making his stomach lurch violently. And the strangely shaped pieces scattered amongst those rocks were dismembered hands, feet, and what he thought might be Jacob's face, peeking out from beneath the piles of stone.

A stone-cold shiver ran down Jack's spine as his gaze slowly rose up to meet Mitch's. The man's eyes, which were once filled with a bright sparkling determination, now glowed with an eerie, unhinged madness that chilled Jack to the bone. Mitch's lips pulled into a grotesque grin as he raised his bloodied pickaxe, gesturing with his head towards the horrific contents of the cart.

"I found the secret, Jack," he hissed through gritted teeth, his voice echoing ominously in the still mountain air. "A blood sacrifice, that's what it needs. That's what this cursed mine wanted all along!"

The words hit Jack like a punch to the gut, leaving him breathless with shock. His gaze involuntarily flitted back to the cart. It was the head of poor Jacob, face half buried in the bloody rocks, but he could see it now, the face of the innocent young man who had been so unlucky as to be conned into this ridiculous journey.

His breath came out in a choked gasp. "Jacob..." He stumbled backwards, the horrifying truth hitting him like a freight train. Mitch, in his crazed pursuit of wealth, had committed the unthinkable. The joyous cheers from earlier wrung out in Jack's ears like a nightmarish chorus, the chilling reality of Mitch's victory sinking deep into his bones.

With every fiber of his being screaming at him to flee, Jack whirled around and made a desperate dash down the worn pathway they had journeyed on just days before. His middle-aged body protested against the sudden exertion, the aftermath of the whiskey's grip making his vision blur and his head pound mercilessly.

His heavy boots stumbled over the uneven terrain, loose rocks skidding beneath his desperate strides. He could barely hear his own labored breaths, the wind whistling past his ears and the pounding of his heart echoing in his skull were the only sensory intake his body would allow during his desperate flight.

Over this symphony of fear, one other vibration passed through his ears. The chilling sound of the determined footfalls that followed him. Then Mitch's voice cut through the thin mountain air like a knife, a threat veiled as a playful taunt, "Oh, no, you don't!"

Jack's breath hitched in his throat as terror sliced through his mind. Mitch's footfalls grew steadily closer, the younger man's athletic build giving him a terrible advantage in this deadly chase. Despair mingled with Jack's terror, the seemingly inevitable outcome looming over him like the shadow of the haunted mountain. He tried his best to flee, but a misstep sent him tumbling to the ground. Lifting his gaze, he saw Mitch looming above him, pickaxe held high above his head…

***

As the day meandered towards its end, a final burst of sunlight gilded the facade of the town bank. Inside, the bank manager methodically packed up his paperwork, the humdrum rhythm of his routine providing a comforting end to another day.

This quiet comfort was violently shattered when the bank doors were thrust open with a sudden bang. A chilling breeze trailed in, carrying with it the tang of iron and something else that made the banker's stomach churn. His eyes snapped up to the door, and all color drained from his face.

He recognized the man, that stubborn leader of the nearly penniless group of miners who had been here a few days ago. An unhinged grin splitting the man's face as he pushed a minecart through the door. Its contents were a gruesome sight: blood-soaked gray stones along with horrifying chunks of what must have been human remains. Each time he trundled the old cart forward, the thump of something disturbingly soft and wet banged against the cart's metal. The sound sent waves of nausea through the banker's body.

"I did it!" Mitch's voice, unusually jovial, was laced with a manic edge. His bloodshot eyes gleamed with madness. "I won, and I'm here to make a deposit!"

The declaration echoed ominously through the bank. The manager could do nothing but stare in abject horror at the macabre spectacle. It was indeed his own fault; he had damned these poor men to a horrible fate. As Mitch's laughter rang out, unhinged and jarring, the setting sun gleamed a golden hue over the stones, and for just a moment, the banker swore he saw a cartload full of gold.

JULIANA'S CHILD

Arlo walked out of the general store at a hurried pace, pulling his young son along by his hand. There was an angry look on the man's face, and he scowled at the boy once they were outside.

"But Dad, that lady had blue skin!" the portly boy of about ten years cried out in a whining tone.

The man did not speak. He lifted the heavy lad up, jumped aboard his carriage, and then set the horse off to a good pace. Once they had pulled away from the store and were on the road home, he finally turned to the boy.

"You should never point at people. It's rude," Arlo chided his son. The boy looked down at his feet, confused. "I know. She had blue skin. It startled you," the father said, easing up his harsh tone a bit. "But that is a very dangerous woman, and I want you to promise me to keep away from her, is that understood?" Arlo said sternly.

"I will," the boy said in that same irritating whine. "But why?" he asked curiously.

"I guess you are old enough now, and you are going to learn about it soon enough from the other kids at school," Arlo conceded. "Let me tell you the story of where she comes from. It's a story every parent in Finchester tells their child when they are around your age. We have to make sure our children realize the importance of never going near that lady," Arlo said. And as they rode further, Arlo recited this tale to his boy:

***

Once, not long ago, there was a woman named Juliana. Juliana Windword, the epitome of beauty and grace, faced a harrowing tragedy that forever altered the course of her life. In the town of Finchester, a darkness unfurled that changed her very being, from a once wonderful, kind, caring mother, into an insane and evil menace.

In the heart of her home, Juliana's kitchen stood as a testament to her passion. Here, surrounded by the familiar tools of her culinary craft, she had often lost herself in the joy of cooking, each dish a masterpiece of flavor and presentation. Yet, all that changed on one

ill-fated day. A momentary lapse, a slip of her usually steady hand, caused a tray collecting dripping fat to tumble. Flames, ravenous and untamed, surged forth, ensnaring Juliana in their destructive and malevolent embrace.

Her anguished cries pierced the tranquil evening, resounding through the streets of Finchester. In a frenzied panic, she stumbled forward, a human torch in the clutches of despair. The once enchanting features that had captivated the hearts of many men were changed forever, disfigured, twisted into a fearsome and grotesque form.

Arnold Trussel, who owned a barber shop across the street, was cleaning up his establishment when Juliana's burning body came running from the front door. Spotting her from the store's front window, he immediately sprang forth like a guardian angel, armed with nothing more than a barber's cape. With swift determination, he smothered the flames that threatened to claim Juliana's life. Though her life was spared, her scarred flesh bore witness to the infernal ordeal she had endured.

Though the flames had been snuffed out and her life had been saved, the physical pain of healing from such a horrible injury was more than the human spirit could endure. The flames had seared not only her body but also her fragile psyche. Seeking refuge from the prying eyes of a judgmental world, she retreated to the solitude of the attic, a place that would become both her sanctuary and prison.

In the dimly lit expanse of the attic, Juliana fashioned a strange, forlorn space for herself. A worn mattress lay on the cold floor, a pitiful respite for her weary body. Nearby, a bathing tub, unadorned and barren, became the theater for her daily ritual of agony. There, she would sit, hunched and trembling, meticulously cleansing and redressing her wounds, each touch a torment that sent shards of pain coursing through her veins.

At first, Juliana yearned for her husband's comfort, his touch to soothe the relentless agony that plagued her existence. But as time passed, the pain was too unbearable, his tender words and encouragement only sending her into fits of rage. The physical and emotional chasm between them grew wider with each passing day.

Her husband Ralph, once her source of solace, became a mere vessel for practical duties. Ralph would ascend to the attic, his footsteps heavy with reluctance, to bring her fresh bandages, gather her bed sheets, fill and drain the water in the tub. He would bring her meals that she rarely ate. His presence to her now was a cruel reminder of the life she had lost.

Juliana's physical transformation after her accident was a grotesque testament to the horrors she had endured. Her once radiant skin, now marred by the relentless flames, resembled the scales of a reptilian creature. The scars etched upon her face, once a canvas of striking beauty, now created an otherworldly visage that repulsed and scared those who beheld it.

Ralph, who had once been captivated by her charm and grace, now could hardly look upon her. This, paired with her a new short-tempered and cruel personality, made his love wither like a fragile blossom touched by frost. The accident had shattered his perception of the woman he once adored, replacing it with a deep-seated revulsion that gnawed at his morality.

Their young, innocent children, still untouched by the cruelties of the world, recoiled in fear at the sight of their mother's transformation. Her new appearance, like something from a nightmarish tale, terrified them. Yet their young minds still sought understanding and comfort from the woman they had once known as their mother.

But Juliana, consumed by her own pain and inner demons, could no longer offer comfort to her children. Instead, she became aloof and distant, her words to them laced with bitterness and cruelty. The tender bonds that once connected her to her offspring began to fray, replaced by a growing chasm of fear and mistrust.

Juliana's sanity appeared to be fraying as well. Whether this deterioration was her mind's way of grappling with the excruciating pain she experienced, or if it was influenced by a darker, more malevolent force, only Juliana could truly reveal. However, her husband Ralph, reflecting on those haunting days following her accident, firmly believed that more than mere psychological strain was at play.

During Ralph's brief visits to her attic refuge, she would recount peculiar tales. Initially, her words seemed mere ramblings, but Ralph soon discerned a recurring motif of the supernatural and the macabre within them. She often spoke of a green mist emanating from the floorboards, seemingly attempting to infiltrate her through her breath. Although she claimed to have resisted its advances so far, she confided in her waning determination to do so. She warned him that she would inevitably give in to it and was unsure of the consequences. Disturbingly, she also professed to be able to read Ralph's thoughts, accusing him of harboring dark sentiments towards her, and attributing to him the most vile and disturbing intentions. She even extended these unsettling assertions towards her own children.

On another day not long after her troubling confessions about the green mist, during a routine visit to bring her new bandages, Ralph noticed another change in Juliana. The perpetual anguish that previously clouded her eyes seemed to have lightened slightly, replaced by an unsettling, manic smile. Hesitantly he ventured: "Juliana, there's something different about you today. It's been so long since I've seen you smile, and while it's a welcome relief... it seems somewhat disturbed." His voice trailed off, tentative, wary of her now frequent and unpredictable outbursts.

Juliana, much to his surprise, responded without any hint of anger. With an almost exuberant tone, she shared, "Oh, Ralph, you wouldn't believe what happened last night! I let the green mist in. I stopped evading it and instead I took a breath, and something changed in me. Though the pain persists, and every nerve ending in my damaged skin still screams at the slightest touch, it's as if clarity has returned to me. I've grasped how to navigate this torment."

Attempting to match her newfound enthusiasm, Ralph responded, "That sounds wonderful, Juliana." Yet, he couldn't shake off a sense of foreboding. Her smile, far from being reassuring, seemed to be teetering on the edge of madness. With a mixture of hope and trepidation, he asked, "Does this mean you'll be rejoining us outside the attic soon?"

Her countenance shifted abruptly as she responded curtly, "No. But I now see a path forward, a future for me." The manic brightness in her eyes faded, replaced by an emotionless void. She gazed at Ralph intently, then whispered, "Something greater than this pitiful existence with you is on the horizon."

Ralph, momentarily taken aback, considered pressing her for details. However, he thought better of it, fearing another barrage of delirium or worse a furious argument. He also took note of the distinct phrasing she had used. Specifically, she had stated, "I now see a path forward, a future for me' — not 'for us.'" With a heavy heart, he withdrew from the room, the weight of despair pressing on him. He was left with the chilling realization that the Juliana he once knew was irretrievably lost to him.

Ralph, burdened by the weight of his shattered dreams and the venom that now so commonly dripped from Juliana's lips, grew to despise the woman he had married. He believed the accident had not only disfigured her physically but had also destroyed the kind and gentle soul he had once cherished. The once-vibrant woman had become a hollow shell, haunted by her own pain and something incomprehensibly sinister seemed to lurk within her soul.

As the days turned into weeks and the weeks into months, Ralph's resentment festered like an open wound. The once-happy household had become a battleground, with love replaced by bitter resentment and accusations. Almost continual arguments and spitefully cruel words deepened the chasm between husband and wife, pushing them further into the realm of their own private hells.

One evening, as darkness cloaked the town of Finchester, Ralph Windword was roused from a fitful slumber by a haunting melody weaving through the night air.

He rose from bed in hopes to locate its source. As he reached the window, a glimmer of hope sparked within him as the music still danced in his ears like a spectral symphony. But, to his dismay, as his eyes scanned the moonlit streets, the melody abruptly ceased, leaving only a silence that hung heavy in the night air.

Ralph peered into the shadows, straining to catch a glimpse of the unseen musician who had enraptured him. But the darkened alleyway remained empty, devoid of any presence that might explain the enchanting melody that had stirred his soul.

On subsequent nights, Ralph found himself haunted by the same mysterious music, which was soon accompanied by a series of other puzzling disturbances. Over the course of a few weeks, while the children were nestled deep in dreams, Ralph would lie in restless anticipation, straining his ears for the uncanny melodies that seemed to waft from the outdoors, followed by unsettling noises emanating from the attic. These sounds suggested a clandestine gathering; faint footsteps, barely discernible rustlings, and the hushed exchange of words he couldn't quite decipher.

More than once, he'd rush up the stairs, driven by a mix of curiosity and concern, to confront Juliana. But she always kept the door securely bolted, leaving him no choice but to inquire through the timber barrier. Her responses were predictably terse, often tinged with annoyance, as she insisted she'd merely been pacing in the night and talking to herself.

On subsequent nights, he tiptoed up the stairs, hoping for a glimpse of shadows under the door or to hear the mysterious intruder's voice. But, as if alerted to his approach, the subtle disturbances from the attic would cease the moment he drew near. Though his inspections were constantly evaded, and eventually the strange occurrences ended, deep down a part of him knew, with an unsettling certainty, that something ominous had occurred on those nights.

***

Over time, still confined to the attic, Juliana's behavior grew increasingly peculiar as she spoke more and more about the new life she needed to pursue. Abruptly one day, after never having ventured outside the attic, she walked down the stairwell dressed in formal attire. She entered the foyer where Ralph happened to be mending a broken chair.

He stood, startled, and asked her, "Where are you going?"

Juliana replied, "To the bank. I am going to look into purchasing my own home."
Upon further inquiry, she told Ralph she was going to find out if there were any nearby estates for sale with the intent of purchasing one for herself. She had resolved to relocate away from town. Ralph, taken aback, felt an unexpected wave of relief rather than sorrow at her intention to depart. With eyes wide in bewilderment, he stepped aside. As confident as if nothing strange had occurred, she exited the home and made her way towards the bank.

When she returned later that day, she announced that she had indeed purchased a small homestead in the heart of the wooded countryside, a ways outside of town.

She claims to have used a small sum of money from a savings account left to her by her father. This was peculiar, as Ralph had never heard of such an account. She even showed Ralph the deed she carried in her hand, and indeed it held her name as its owner.

Within only a few days, Juliana moved out. Ralph took her to the home himself. Loading a cargo of clothes and household items into his wagon, he helped her on her exit from their once jovial abode. The ride out to the estate was long, over three hours, the road growing increasingly bumpy as they went. Finally, upon arrival at a little side road, Juliana's new home came into view.

The house, cloaked in shadows, stood as a haunting presence. It seemed to swallow the feeble rays of sunlight that dared to pierce its decaying facade. It stood an impressive three stories tall, with a square turret at the front that rose to a fourth-story tower window. The exterior walls, once sturdy and proud, now sagged under the weight of neglect. A heavy scent of must from inside the home wafted outside, a testament to its years of abandonment. The wooden siding was rotten, and pieces had fallen away, the stairs leading up to the entrance looked like they might collapse, and most of the windowpanes were missing. Ralph was horrified at the sight, but to Juliana, it might as well have been a palace; it was the first genuine smile he had seen on her face since the accident. She asked for only her things to be brought into the foyer, insisting she would handle the rest herself.

Juliana had the key. She approached first, ascending the creaky stairs, and opened the front door to allow Ralph's entry with her belongings.

Ralph followed behind with his arms full of luggage. He walked carefully on the steps, the weight of the bags causing the planks to bend beneath him, but, to his relief, they did not break.

When he set the bags down on the floor inside the foyer, a chill went down his spine. The interior was just as foreboding as the exterior. Its decaying timbers and cobweb-laden corners bore the weight of years gone by, a testament to forgotten dreams and desolate solitude. A grand foyer opened up to a large stairwell and three arched doorways leading to darkened rooms beyond. The floorboards creaked with each tentative step, their once-lustrous surface now worn and faded. However, as Ralph tried to look further into the house, Juliana stopped him in his tracks.

"Thank you, Ralph, I appreciate your help. But that is all I need; please leave now. I have too much to do before evening," Juliana said firmly. The look in her eyes told Ralph not to press her any further. So, he exited the place, glancing back a few times, only to see Juliana already at work moving the luggage further into the dark interior of the home.

Ralph took one long look around the property before ascending back up to his wagon. Surrounding the home, the forest loomed, its ancient trees reaching upward, blocking out the sun and casting a perpetual twilight upon the land. It was a foreboding place. The Juliana he had married would have been frightened to set foot in these lands even for a moment, let alone to stay here on her own for the night. Within the dense undergrowth, dangers lurked, unseen and unnamed. Beasts with feral eyes prowled in the shadows, while the whispers of unseen entities carried on the breeze.

Despite Ralph's fearful observations, the house was transformed in Juliana's eyes. They were illuminated by a flickering flame of madness or perhaps a deluded enchantment. To her distorted perception, the decaying walls became a canvas for her twisted imagination, the cobwebs like delicate threads of ethereal beauty. The desolation and decay that repulsed others held a mysterious allure for her, an invitation into a world that defied conventional understanding.

As Juliana bid her final farewell waving at Ralph from the doorway, a haunting smile tugged at her lips, revealing a happiness that had long been absent from her countenance. The weight of her past life fell away, replaced by the anticipation of solitude and a newfound kinship with the unseen forces that whispered through her mind.

And so, in a bittersweet moment, Ralph waved back with a faint smile of his own before heading home. He turned to look back a few more times, hoping she might come running out of the doorway, but deep down he knew that was only his final hope for her returned sanity. Instead, she closed the door and disappeared into the house, into the embrace of her newfound sanctuary. It was a departure marked by both sorrow and a sense of liberation. Ralph knew deep down that their paths had diverged irrevocably, each destined to follow separate roads into the unknown.

***

As Juliana settled into her reclusive lifestyle, new interests and studies filled her days. A mind once distracted by domestic duties and menial tasks bloomed like the twisted flowers of a forgotten garden, expanding into more worldly and academic matters. She was entranced by sciences and histories from distant corners of the globe. An increasingly peculiar flow of deliveries was brought to her desolate abode, as she filled the empty rooms with macabre antiques and foreign furnishings. Books, brimming with ancient knowledge and esoteric secrets, arrived in a ceaseless stream, feeding her insatiable thirst.

Ralph, burdened by concern and a lingering sense of responsibility for his estranged wife, found himself drawn back to the house time and again to check on her well-being. With each visit, he hoped to glean some semblance of understanding, to grasp the nature of Juliana's new personality. But his efforts only deepened his despair and discomfort as she evaded his attempts to unravel the enigma she had become. Her only responses were filled with cruelty and aloofness. Even mentioning her children seemed to have no effect on her.

On one such visit, Ralph arrived at the home to find a stack of books on Juliana's doorstep. He couldn't resist perusing the strange and morbid titles, such as "Demonology of the Caucasus," "Rites of the Mongolian Death Worm," "Occultic Taxidermy," and other dreadful topics. He carefully picked up the leatherbound volumes and cradled them in his arms before knocking. After three tries to which there was no reply, he decided to try the door and found it unlocked. Calling out her name, Ralph crossed the threshold into the foyer. His eyes surveyed the ever-transforming interior. A gallery of curiosities met his eyes, and startlingly, standing in the dim entrance to the parlor was Juliana's face, shrouded in shadows, a mask of secrets and distant contemplation. She stared back at him, acknowledging his presence with only a slight smirk.

Unable to contain his curiosity any longer, Ralph mustered the courage to confront her. His voice, tinged with a mix of concern and trepidation, probed the depths of her enigmatic world for answers. "Juliana," he began, his tone cautious yet determined, "I cannot fathom the nature of these books you surround yourself with. The knowledge they contain...it feels malevolent, dark. What draws you to such sinister topics of research?"

A flicker of fury ignited in Juliana's eyes, transforming her distant smirk into a blaze of intensity. The air grew heavy with tension, as if a storm were brewing within the walls of the house itself. Her voice, now carrying an otherworldly timbre, cut through the silence with the precision of a spectral dagger.

"Answering such an inquiry would be a waste of my time," she hissed through clenched teeth, her words dripping with venomous spite. "Poor Ralph, your pretty little maid is gone... Life must be so treacherous without someone to take care of you!" She whined with mocking concern. "Maybe you could get one of the town whores to come clean your mess. I deal with more important things these days." She spoke in such a hateful tone that Ralph shuddered.

Angered by her words, he retorted, "Should the town whores also raise your children?" allowing his own venom to show through.

"If they're such a burden, just drown them in the tub on their next washing day," she replied, amusedly. Her indifference was so pronounced that she almost sounded horrifically hopeful. "Surely you are strong enough to hold them under the water for a few minutes?" she continued. The fact that she could linger on such a description made Ralph's stomach drop. He stared back at her with utter disgust.

"I don't know who is in control of this body I speak with, but it is not Juliana," Ralph replied, attempting to reflect her callous tone, but his voice wavered just slightly.

They locked eyes there for a moment, in that eerie, dimly lit foyer. Ralph found himself inexplicably entranced by the transformation she had undergone. Summoning his courage, he asked, "What dark forces have you welcomed into your life, Juliana? If our marriage vows hold any authority, I command you! What name do you invoke in your pursuit of this dark knowledge?"

A haunting silence filled the air as Juliana's lips curled into a wicked smile. With a voice that seemed to resonate from deep within the bowels of the earth, she uttered an alien name, laden with ancient power and dread.

"Throg Tuk," she whispered, her lips quivering reluctantly as if uttering the words caused her physical pain.

In that moment, a flicker of green light ignited within Juliana's eyes, an eerie luminescence that shimmered with an alien glow. Her irises, once a mirror of her pain, now seemed to reflect something far more sinister, a malevolent presence, like some sort of parasite had taken root within her soul, and in that moment, it had shown itself to him.

Ralph's breath caught in his throat, and a chill raced down his spine. He felt an inexplicable connection to that name, a name that resonated with ancient terrors and cosmic forces beyond mortal comprehension. His mind recoiled, struggling to process the implications of Juliana's invocation.

A primal intuition was warning him of the horrors tied to that name and to this damned house. That eerie green flare in Juliana's eyes would be seared into his memory forever, as was the whisper of that accursed name, "Throg Tuk." He instinctively understood the gravity of uttering it aloud or sharing its significance with others. It was more than just a symbol of Juliana's madness—it was a manifestation of a genuine supernatural force, one that had taken his wife forever. This realization would plague Ralph, shadowing him with guilt and filling his nightmares. Had he done something that had allowed this? Could he have prevented it? A braver soul would have acted, ending her suffering right then and there. God knows, it would have been for the better, not just for her, but also the inevitable victims such an evil would ensnare.

Consumed by terror and a deep-rooted instinct for survival, Ralph felt an irresistible pull to escape. As he turned to flee the foyer, sinister laughter resonated through the house, its haunting timbre interwoven with the dark echo of the ancient god's name that had so corrupted Juliana's soul. In his haste, Ralph tripped descending the porch stairs, and as he scrambled to rise, he felt the eerie touch of diminutive hands clutching at his neck. Shaking off the chilling sensation, he made a frantic dash to his wagon, spurring his horse towards Finchester with desperate urgency.

***

Juliana, with her unsettling behavior, had already alienated herself from the few remaining friends and family she had. Leaving her with all but one peer, Egbert Throngbolt, the peculiar owner of Finchester's bookstore. From here on, it is mainly through this peculiar man's recountings, and a few other delivery drivers, that we gain most of the information of what happened next. What was most strange was that Ralph had never known of Egbert before this time. To Ralph's knowledge the two had never been friends prior to her move to that remote house, but perhaps her numerous purchases from his establishment had created some form of bond between the two.

As for Ralph, he found it too repellent to continue with his own visits to Juliana's cursed property. Following that last harrowing experience, he relinquished his role as her caretaker. He withdrew, ceasing to be her bridge to the outside world. In his absence, only Egbert and the few delivery men, who frequented her residence with unyielding consistency, became the chroniclers of her life within those dense woods. Their tales of eerie encounters found eager audiences at local taverns, and soon, whispered accounts permeated every corner of the town.

The reports from these men painted a disturbing picture. Juliana's purchases had grown increasingly bizarre, extending far beyond books and odd antiques. Whole loads of raw building materials were being brought to her home in those desolate woods, as if she had planned to embark upon a grand renovation project of some sort. The costs escalated far beyond what Ralph's meager allowance was offering, and Ralph grew anxious, his concern mounting with each passing day. And then: the unimaginable, something far worse. Reports came in that Juliana's belly was swelling, that she was pregnant.

Aside from her death, this news was likely the only thing that would have brought Ralph back to that house. But unlike the report of her death, which would have come with a sigh of relief, a report that she may be bringing new life to this world filled Ralph with such anxiety and dread that it made his head spin. Unable to resist the gnawing curiosity that plagued him, Ralph resolved to make one final visit to the house. He knew he had to confront Juliana, to see if this most horrendous rumor was true.

***

Upon his return to the house, a sense of foreboding weighed heavily upon him. The once-dilapidated structure now stood as a bizarre amalgamation of old and new. An architectural chaos in the midst of construction that defied reason stood before him. He wondered if it was Juliana herself assembling these structural components, perhaps using her new cursed abilities to fuel such an endeavor. The air hummed with an otherworldly energy, a potent mixture of fascination and unease filled Ralph as he approached.

When he arrived, the door was open, as if awaiting him. He knocked lightly on a porch beam and called Juilana's name, but there was no reply. Somewhat reluctantly, Ralph entered through the open door. There, standing in the dimly lit foyer, was Juliana. Ralph's gaze fell upon her, her once beautiful countenance now twisted by the scars of her accident. The shadows in the room only illuminated them, making her appear even more grotesque. But it was her swollen belly that caught his attention. Her hands lay rested upon that enormous bulge, and she gleamed at him with a wicked, prideful grin. A wave of repulsion washed over him as he realized the impossibility of being the father of this child. It had been nearly half a year since she had moved out to those woods, and their last intimate encounter had occurred long before her accident, many months prior to that.

The revelation struck him like a hammer's blow, shattering any remnants of his former affections. Juliana's repulsive appearance and her impending motherhood marked the final blow to any remnant of attachment he had left for her. Disgust mingled with a deep-seated sorrow as Juliana delivered one last nail of insult into the coffin that was their marriage.

He said nothing to her, nor did she speak to him. Silently, Ralph turned away, his footsteps heavy with resignation and a sense of bitter finality. The truth had been laid bare before him, a truth that spoke of a connection severed and a bond forever broken. He left the desolate house behind, carrying with him the weight of the past and the lingering echoes of a life that had crumbled into ashes. As he walked back to his wagon, he heard soft laughter, cruel mocking snickers that sounded like they came from a crowd of onlookers, though there were no other people there. He took one last look towards the open door before he left. There he saw the small frame of Juliana standing, and he called out to her. "Juliana, I hope that whatever became of you, you are at peace. I know this is not you I have visited today." And with that, he urged his horse to quickly depart.

As Ralph journeyed through the dense woods en route to Finchester, he found himself deep in thought over the unfolding situation. To the residents of the town, the enigma surrounding Juliana's pregnancy, steeped in secrecy and scandal, would undoubtedly become fodder for eager tongues and wagging whispers. The realization that many might revel in the cruel jest of his adulterous wife stung, but only just. Dominating his psyche were feelings of profound concern—for the yet-to-be-born child and for the very fate of the citizens of Finchester.

***

Egbert Throngbolt, the enigmatic owner of Finchester's bookstore, stood tall and lean, with a notably effeminate demeanor that often became the subject of town gossip. His unwed status and distinctive quirks marked him as an outsider. Yet, with Juliana, he had forged an unexpected alliance. Their relationship might have been cemented by Juliana's frequent and valuable purchases, many of which were rare and obscure books. However, others believed it was Egbert's own captivation with her and her peculiar interests that drew them together. Regardless of the reasons, Egbert made it a point to personally deliver her orders, further strengthening their unique bond.

Reports from Egbert claimed that Juliana was embracing her newfound solitude with vigor. She had become a renaissance woman of sorts. Self-taught, she had taken on the role of contractor for a seemingly ridiculous renovation. The desolate house was undergoing a startling metamorphosis, from dilapidated farmhouse to some kind of Oriental mansion, alien in form. She employed a number of immigrant workers, whom oddly enough all came from the far east. Peculiar indeed since there were very few people of such heritage in the surrounding area. No one knew where she had found such laborers. They must have resided on the property itself, for no one ever saw them in town.

Even more fascinating was the news that came about Juliana's child. Rumors spread like wildfire. Apparently, Juliana had given birth within the walls of that remote mansion. It was of course Egbert who had brought back the tale. With a tremor in his voice, he recounted the day he had met the child for the first time. He said he was delivering a particularly rare and delicate manuscript that had been shipped all the way from India. He was greeted by one of the laborers, a large dark-skinned man who did not speak English but knew Egbert from previous visits. When he saw the manuscript, his eyes brightened with eager attention, and he led Egbert to the study, where Juliana often resided in the day.

Upon entering the study, he was shocked at what lay before him. In the corner of the room, lying in an ornately decorated wooden crib, was a baby. And around this baby stood a number of Juliana's workforce. Two even bowed down as if in reverence, and a third was reading passages softly to it in a foreign tongue. But what was the most amazing part of the spectacle was the child itself. The baby boy sat up in an unconventionally mature position. It stared at Egbert in a surprisingly alert manner, and its skin gleamed a surreal shade of royal blue.

As Egbert gaped at the boy, eyes wide in astonishment, Juliana neither mentioned nor referred to the child. Instead, she concentrated on the document Egbert held. With great anticipation, she snatched it from his hands, having her hired hand lead him back outside immediately.

The news spread like whispers on a lonely wind, stoking the fires of speculation and fear. The townsfolk, already unsettled by Juliana's transformation and the swirling rumors about her, now found themselves facing an enigma that surpassed their darkest imaginings.

The surreal shade of blue that colored the child's skin became a symbol of the unnatural forces at play, further fueling stories of demonic origins and otherworldly influences. Fear gripped the hearts of those who dared to contemplate the fate of Juliana's offspring, their minds filled with visions of foreign gods and supernatural beings.

Amidst the growing unease, the grand and unusual mansion was erected and stood as a haunting reminder of Juliana's descent into madness. Its peculiar Asian architecture and mysterious allure became a fearful landmark in the countryside, casting a forbidding presence that sent waves of strange and malevolent energy toward anyone who dared to travel past.

***

The child was named Nolan, as Egbert learned in future visits, Juliana would speak of her new infant with utmost pride. However, she never uttered any references to her former children. Amid rumors of her alleged adultery, Ralph obtained a legal divorce and severed all financial ties with Juliana and her remote abode. Nevertheless, deliveries to the mansion continued unabated, and the frequency and magnitude of the deliveries steadily increased. No one knew how she had obtained the funds.

No expense was spared in the pursuit of knowledge and enrichment for young Nolan. An unending array of luxuries poured into the mansion, fueling his insatiable thirst for exotic decadences. A barn was built to house horses, cows, and all sorts of other animals from lands far and wide. Even further renovations were undertaken to create a magnificent library, a sprawling sanctuary of knowledge within the twisted walls of the mansion.

Animals of all kinds and species were delivered over the years, filling the once desolate grounds with the sounds of strange, exotic creatures. Their purpose remained shrouded in mystery, their existence adding to the enigmatic aura that surrounded the estate.

As the mansion expanded its opulence, so too did the eclectic retinue of servants from far-off shores. Each steeped in their own enigmatic origins and idiosyncrasies, they were, to the best of the town's knowledge, bereft of English. Yet, Egbert attested that Nolan was versed in various Eastern tongues and would converse with them in their indigenous languages. These foreign denizens added an exotic aura to the estate, their cultures and dialects unfamiliar and arcane to the simple folk of Finchester. Within the imposing and eerie walls of the mansion, they dwelt, their dealings with the outer world minimal and cryptic, enveloped in an air of silent intent.

Rumors of these exotic servants, distinguished by their foreign features and the peculiar circumstance of their cohabiting on Juliana's estate alongside her child, spread like wildfire, fueling the most intense speculations Finchester had ever witnessed. The town, already simmering with suspicion and unease, regarded the mansion's residents with a mix of fascination, mistrust, and subdued fear. Wild speculations emerged about the mansion's undertakings: some believed Juliana was leading an Eastern cult, while others conjectured that the illustrious abode had evolved into a sanctuary for pilgrims of a distant religion. While a multitude of these surmises stemmed from unfounded, xenophobic apprehensions, a consensus emerged that there existed, at the very least, a disconcerting anomaly within the mansion's confines.

Egbert and the delivery men, serving as the main conduits of information, whispered tales that seemed to grow more and more absurd. Some swore to have seen rituals being performed on the property, and still others claimed to have heard horrible, agonizing cries from within the ever-growing number of storage sheds and barns that were being built there. These rumors continued to sow the seeds of intrigue and speculation. As Nolan matured into a young man, the stories painted a portrait of someone even more peculiar than his mother. He was of a diminutive stature, standing only just above five feet in height. But Nolan possessed a surprising handsomeness that mirrored the once-beautiful features of his mother's face.

It was Egbert who had the most direct contact with the bizarre little man. The strange blue hue that colored his skin, coupled with his short stature, were only the beginning of what set him apart from the ordinary. His personality was even more strange. It was as if he was not of this world. He spoke with a strange accent, possibly from having been raised by so many foreign servants. He was stoic to a level that was malevolent, always glaring with eyes that seemed to bore into one's soul. In spite of his small stature, his body was incredibly robust and perfectly healthy, his limbs strong and capable. He moved with an agility that defied his height. Egbert had witnessed the man engaging in numerous sports, archery, hunting, and various athletic pursuits across the expansive lands surrounding the mansion.

There was no doubt that the young man had an incredible thirst for knowledge, with a heavy focus on the sciences. As Nolan matured, he demanded more and more from his mother. His needs seemed to have no bounds, and somehow Juliana always found the funds to appease him. She acquired the neighboring properties, mostly empty parcels of forest and some hills. She would offer absurd amounts to the more stubborn landowners in order to expand her holdings.

Over time, Egbert himself became more distant, recounting less to those he still spoke with. Some said the contact with Juliana and her boy might have plagued him with whatever madness was occurring out there. His eyes grew hollow, and he became a frail shell of himself. No doubt, he was earning a small fortune playing the middleman for all the items he delivered. But the increased wealth only seemed to plague him with demons. Perhaps he knew more about what was going out there than he admitted.

The last few reports that came from Egbert were troubling. He said that Nolan was becoming more and more prone to mad fits of rage, where he would not only yell but physically assault the people around him. Most of the time the abuse was aimed at the servants who constantly surrounded him. According to Egbert, horrible acts of violence were commonly committed to these poor foreign men and women, but increasingly they were directed at his own mother. In spite of this, the residents of Juliana's mansion never swayed in their reverence for him. Even Juliana herself seemed to kowtow in fear and subservience to the little blue man.

On top of this, the deliveries began to take on a more mechanical and practical nature. Books now only made up a fraction of the deliveries. The bulk of the purchases were more like what one might find in hospitals or sanitariums—skeletal models of anatomy, surgical equipment, dental equipment, an assortment of chemicals, alongside other unidentifiable instruments.

It was around this time that Egbert disappeared. He had been growing increasingly distant. And one day, seemingly out of the blue, he sold his establishment and his house and left town. What was even more disturbing was that more than one account claimed that after cashing in on his estate, Egbert was seen taking his carriage towards Juliana's estate. He was never seen again.

***

From this point forward, firsthand accounts regarding the activities on Juliana's property dwindled to a mere trickle. The most reliable source of such tales was one Emily Junker, a close confidante of Nayomi, one of Juliana's tragically abandoned children. As the relentless sands of time passed, nearly two somber decades elapsed since Juliana's devastating accident. During this span, the children Juliana had borne to Ralph grew into their own, without the maternal presence they were born to. A nascent curiosity, however, took root in their hearts. This was especially pronounced in Nayomi, the youngest and most sensitive of the Windword brood. Merely an infant when the catastrophic incident occurred, her perception of her mother was not drawn from memories but rather from terrifying tales. These stories painted a figure so intimidating, Nayomi grappled with recognizing Juliana as her mother. Her father, Ralph, maintained a stony silence on the topic, offering only a stern warning to his children: they were never to seek her out.

But blood runs thick and is sometimes unavoidably linked. As reported by Emily, her dear friend grew increasingly melancholic, curious about her long-estranged mother. Now mature enough to venture out on her own, it was noon on a crisp autumn day when Nayomi asked her dear friend Emily if she would accompany her to the hinterlands of Finchester, to Juliana's infamous property, to finally quench her fascination. A good and loyal friend, Emily agreed, only because she had witnessed the yearning of her dear friend firsthand and the pain it seemed to be causing her. Emily had hoped this visit might put that to rest. Bravely, the two headed through the forested hills towards the legendary estate.

As the pair stepped onto the property later that day, their eyes widened in awe and confusion. The sight that unfolded before them was a spectacle of mechanical contraptions, cranes, and heavy building machines. A barn housing horses, and other creatures stood nearby, while warehouses loomed in the distance, their contents shrouded in mystery. But it was the house itself that was most astonishing. Of course, they had both heard the tales of it, but they never could have pictured the odd form of that structure without seeing it for themselves. It stood four stories in height, though it could even have been five. It was hard to tell. The floors themselves didn't appear uniformly level.

Tentatively, they approached the door, stepping onto the wide wooden porch, the beams and railings in a style unlike anything they had ever seen. Everything about the place seemed alien in nature. It was Nayomi who dared knock three times on the door. There was silence for a moment. The two stood in anxious anticipation. Finally, the door opened, and to both of their astonishment, standing before them was the incredible figure of Nolan.

He smiled at the two of them politely, looking almost abashed as he averted his eyes downwards to the floor. In spite of this, Emily described the man's stature as strangely prodigious. It was as though the man, who must have stood at most five feet two, loomed above both of them. His skin was a surreal royal blue, just as the stories had said it would be. He wore no shirt, only a tanned leather vest with red and black bead patterns and linen pants cut above the ankle. He was muscular and oddly handsome. Though sheepish, his authority was unquestionable.

They heard a call from one of the adjoining rooms, the voice of a woman, somewhat hollow and gravelly. "Nolan, please have our guests see me in the parlor."

Emily took Nayomi's hand in hers. She could sense her friend's anxiety was even greater than her own. Nolan stepped away, leaving them to enter the parlor on their own. Once inside the lavishly decorated room, Emily witnessed the peculiar reunion between mother and daughter. Juliana's appearance was horrific, but the scars on her body were only a portion of what made her so terrifying. It was her demeanor that was more disturbing. She seemed almost predatory; her eyes, like an animal's, watched her daughter with a strange hunger. Emily recounted that very little attention was paid to her, from either Nolan or Juliana. It was understandable, she thought, since Nayomi was their relation. But there was something very disturbing about it. It did not seem the right kind of attention to be given to one's daughter, or half-sister. It was like they wanted to devour her. Juliana did not hug her daughter, only smiled broadly and gestured for the two of them to sit across from her at a little table.

The sitting room blazed with heat. It was not a particularly cold day, but a huge fire was burning. Servants brought tea made from herbs that Emily had never smelled before. They sipped it tentatively, seated in uncomfortable chairs with elaborate carvings. The room was decorated with oriental furnishings, every detail of foreign design. None of the items in the room could have come from the shops in Finchester.

"Thank you for seeing us," Nayomi said nervously, filling the silence. Neither Nolan nor Juliana seemed to be good at socializing. "My brothers send their hellos," she continued, struggling to find the right words. It was terrifying the way her mother stared back at her, and Emily was tempted to grab Nayomi's hand at that moment and run. Yet there was not even a single acknowledgment of her words. A few awkward moments later, as Nayomi was about to speak again, Juliana put a finger to her lips in a universal gesture for silence. Nayomi obliged.

Finally, Juliana spoke. She asked no questions, made no comments about her daughter. Instead, she began to tell them the story of the accident, delving into the tale without introduction, as if it was precisely what they had come to hear.

***

"I was a very good cook," was how she began. "And that day was like any other. I was busying myself with my household duties. What an exemplary wife I was," she sneered with disdain. "But everything changed that day. I spilled the dripping tray all over my apron, and somehow it lit on fire. Probably when I leaned over the stove to grab the cloth I used for cleaning. I lit up like a Christmas candle!" She cackled at her own horror story, a horrible guttural laugh that Emily swore sounded like two or even three voices laughing at once.

"The pain was excruciating. Like nothing I had ever felt before. Every nerve ending fired at full blast. And only more so after the flames were extinguished. Ralph, he was useless, and I was equally as useless at helping myself. There was no solution. His attempts at tender touches and kind words just made me fill up with rage, and I despised him. He tried his best to help, I guess, but his repulsion was as clear as day to me, I don't blame him really. There was no one and nothing to ease my suffering. I locked myself in the attic as a means to find solace, but there was no escape from that pain. If anyone ever tells you that you get used to pain, they are lying. No, it goes on, and on, and on. Your nerve endings will keep firing relentlessly forever as long as they are damaged. It's enough to drive one mad. I probably would have jumped out of that attic window had it not been for the blue minstrels.

"I would sit at the attic window and stare down, urging myself to jump. But come nightfall, after the entire household was enshrouded in the veil of sleep, they would emerge. At first, I thought I must have been dreaming or was in some kind of pain-induced delusion. Down the desolate alleyway behind our home, a troupe of minstrels would emerge, their presence both enchanting and unnerving. They were not like ordinary minstrels but rather otherworldly beings, blue-skinned, short in stature but broad in body, dressed in clothes from the far east, like warriors from the Mongol hordes arriving from the great steps, now here in my alleyway. Their attire swirled with vibrant colors that contrasted against the shadows of the night.

"The musicians wielded their instruments with skill, weaving a tapestry of haunting melodies that carried on the breeze, enchanting me and soothing me. Their music was like a siren's call. It beckoned me from the depths of my anguish, offering me the respite I had yearned for. I knew right away what they wanted. They wanted me to let them in. And how could I resist? They alone could proffer me the sanctuary of hope and peace that I so desperately sought.

"Among the trio of minstrels, there was one who stood out, the smallest of them all. His piercing gaze, framed by pure black eyes, held an otherworldly allure that both frightened and fascinated me. It was as if his gaze possessed an ancient knowledge, a secret language that spoke directly to my tormented soul.

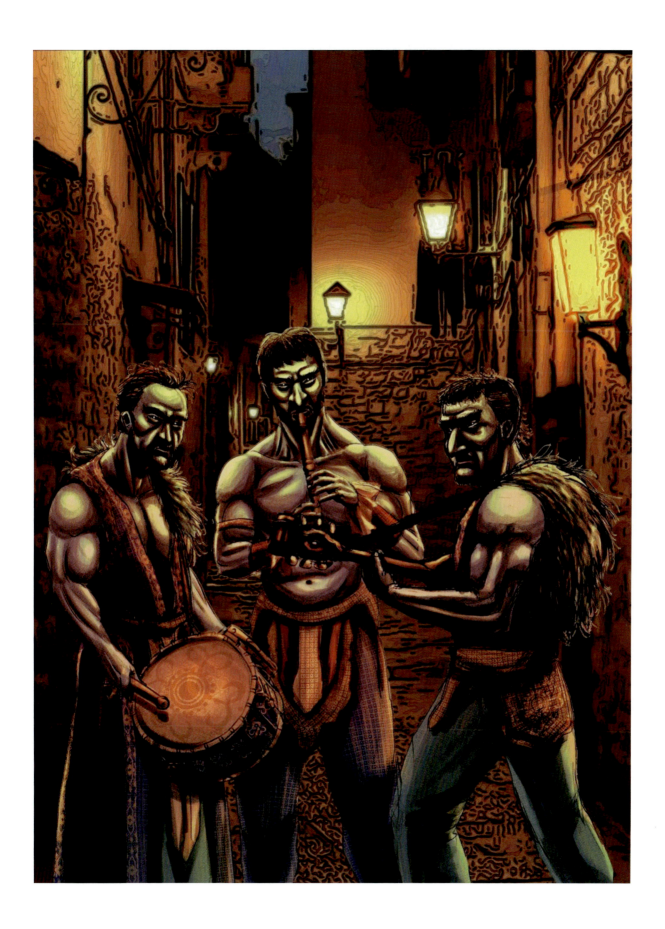

"In a surge of reckless abandon, I extended my hand from the open window, beckoning the blue-skinned figure into my sanctuary. The ensemble of musicians halted their tunes. With an elegance tinged with mischief, the men stacked upon one another like seasoned acrobats, hands gripping legs, forming a human ladder until the tiniest among them stood precariously on the second man's shoulders. He reached for my outstretched hands, I hoisted him up, and he crept inside, bridging the gap between the surreal and my all-too-real realm of pain and suffering. As he stepped over the threshold, his gaze locked onto mine, and a strange understanding passed between us.

"From the moment that we embraced, the pain that had plagued me for so long not only dissipated but was replaced by a sense of joy and pleasure that I had never experienced. It was a rare and intoxicating moment of quenched desires, as though the boundaries of reality had blurred, and a world beyond the mundane had intertwined with my own that offered more than relief; it offered ecstasy.

"It was the first night in so long that I had actually slept. That alone was a priceless reward. But when I awoke the next morning, beside the bed, there was an enormous bag filled with gold coins. And this happened again and again for the next week. Each night, another bag of coins was left. After that week, they never returned again, and I realized why afterward. I had been ovulating. That was what the blue men had wanted; they wanted to impregnate me…"

And that was all she said to them. Juliana stood and left the room, leaving the two girls sitting there, dumbfounded. It was the most unusual conclusion to such an anticipated event. Relieved that the meeting was over, Emily stood to leave. But Nayomi sat there, not ready to go yet, as if in some sort of trance. Emily said she had to physically pull her out of her seat. As she finally managed to get the girl moving towards the door, Nolan reappeared, blocking their path.

He said only one sentence: "I hope you visit again, Nayomi." And then he moved from the doorway, allowing Emily, who was about ready to scream in terror, to pull her friend with her out the door and down the steps back to their wagon, where they quickly headed away from the dreadful estate. Emily recalled her friend's strange silence on that long journey home, but had chalked it up to the intensity of the visit.

***

After Nayomi returned from her first visit to her mother's home, she was never again the same. She appeared distant and detached from her brothers, creating an invisible barrier that left them saddened and worried for their normally warm-hearted sister. They eagerly confronted her, hoping to hear the tale that Nayomi had brought back from their long-disavowed mother, but she told them nothing.

From that day forward, Nayomi made clandestine visits to the mansion, often occurring under the cover of darkness. She ventured to that cursed realm time and time again, her actions cloaked in secrecy and mystery. The truth of what transpired within those hallowed halls remains unknown. She refused to yield to the curious gazes and probing questions from her brothers, who had discovered her missing in the night.

Whispers of Nayomi's nocturnal journeys traveled through the town, igniting curiosity and speculation. Some wondered if she had succumbed to the same peculiar illness that had claimed her mother's sanity, while others contemplated the possibility of a darker influence drawing her back to that grand and sinister mansion. The truth remained hidden, buried within the depths of Nayomi's soul, as the mansion stood as a silent sentinel, its dark presence casting a long and haunting shadow over the lives of those entangled in its mysterious embrace.

After enduring a heated interrogation by her father, Nayomi made a life-altering decision. Without any words of explanation or argument, only a silent resolve, she packed a single bag and left that night to the mansion, and she never returned. Whispers, laden with vile insinuations, spread through the town, igniting rumors of an incestuous relationship between Nayomi and her half-brother, sending a chill of repulsion down the spine of anyone who dared to entertain such thoughts.

Rumors of incest in relation to that cursed property came as little surprise to the townsfolk. Over the years, so many tales had been told of what went on there that no one knew what was true. No real evidence of anything sinister had come forth as yet. It was all whispers with no substance. But it was the tales of this relationship that became the final straw, breaking the back of the town's tolerance. The whispers grew louder, an anger was growing that would soon need some kind of resolution.

The townsfolk, torn between their morbid curiosity and their innate repulsion, grappled with conflicting emotions. Many had known and loved Nayomi, as well as her father and brothers. They watched from a distance, their gazes filled with a mixture of judgment, fear, and concern. An inability to fully comprehend why such a kind girl as Nayomi would abandon her family for her insane mother and bastard blue-skinned brother cemented the belief that evil forces were at work in that sinister abode.

***

In the end, it was not the relationship between Nayomi and Nolan that caused an investigation of the property, but something even more horrible. One fateful sweltering summer evening, a grotesque event occurred. The door of the local pub swung open with a jolt, and a foreign man entered. His face was grotesquely contorted by what looked like numerous skin grafts and rudimentary operations of a horrendous nature. As he limped feebly forwards into the establishment, the patrons looked on in horror. Dripping blood as he went, at first it appeared the man was dressed in some kind of cow hide, but as the visage clarified itself, it became evident the man was naked. What looked to be hides were actually patches of bovine skin entwined with the poor man's own flesh. Onlookers gasped and screamed as he approached.

Unable to speak English, the poor soul garbled in a foreign tongue. Blood streamed from his eyes, staining his face with crimson trails, while half-performed surgeries adorned his body, a grotesque mosaic of stitches crisscrossed his skin. His ears seemed to be those of a pig's. The patches of undulate skin were somehow integrated into his own. Seemingly, he had been in this condition for some time. But perhaps the most chilling sight of all was his left arm, which had a hoof attached to its end. A shudder of revulsion passed through the crowd as they witnessed the unnatural fusion of flesh and animal appendage. To their disbelief, the arm exhibited faint signs of life, a twisted semblance of movement that defied reason.

The man, unable to communicate, babbled incomprehensibly, his desperate gaze always returning to the forest he had fled from, as though terrified of what might have followed him. It was a chilling revelation, a most bizarre and repulsive piece of evidence to the horrors that awaited within the depths of those woods. The townsfolk, their fears now validated, knew all too well the significance of the man's panicked gestures.

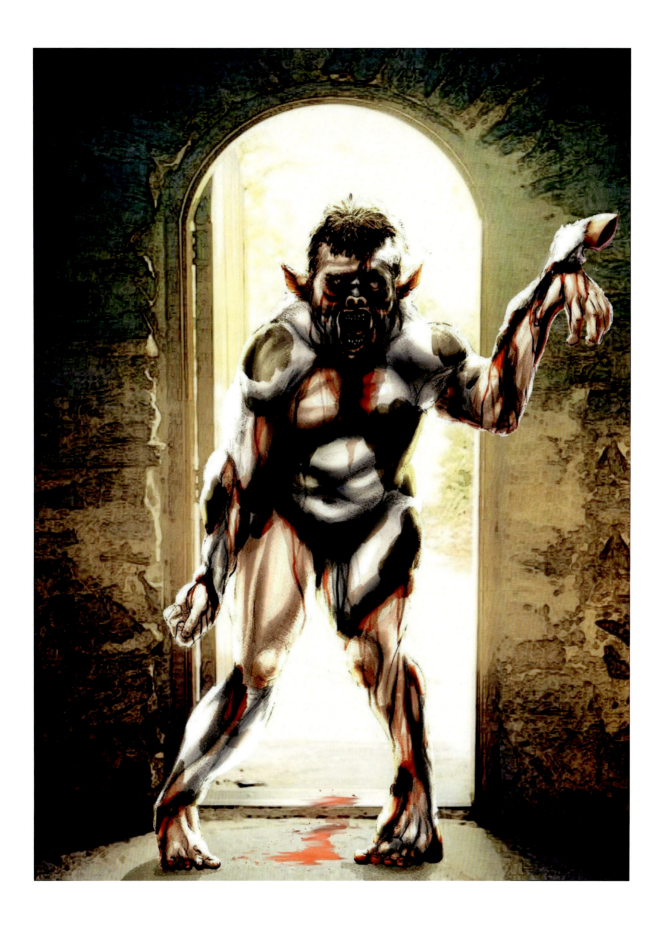

The patrons of the pub, in a desperate flurry of activity, did their best to aid the poor soul who was clearly in agony. Yet, despite their most valiant efforts, by the time they managed to rush him to the hospital, life had left him. The attending physicians were met with a sight so confounding; it left them utterly horrified. The man's condition stood in stark defiance to all established medical knowledge. Several among the shaken staff couldn't help but whisper among themselves, suggesting that the man's state bordered on the unnatural, perhaps even entering the realm of the paranormal.

The tragic demise of the servant sent shockwaves through the town, igniting a sense of urgency within the authorities. A swift investigation was launched into Juliana's estate. A team of officers and inspectors with legal consent were sent to the house, armed and ready if any violence broke out.

Upon the authorities' arrival and thorough examination of the mansion, they discovered no solid proof to back the townspeople's horrendous allegations. Juliana, despite her evident madness, demonstrated an uncanny cleverness that evaded their scrutiny. She and her son, Nolan, portrayed the perfect picture of cooperation, permitting the investigators unobstructed access throughout the property. Much to the investigators' frustration, they uncovered no signs of violence or any form of malevolence. The mansion remained a steadfast bastion of mystery, fiercely shielding its sinister secrets.

Lacking concrete evidence, and with the sole witness now silenced forever, the authorities found themselves at an impasse. Frustration simmered within the hearts of the townsfolk, their fear and outrage mounting with each passing day. It seemed that the darkness that had enshrouded the mansion was immune to the reach of justice, a malevolent force that taunted them from behind a veil of obscurity.

Desperation settled upon the town as they grappled with the realization that their efforts to expose Juliana and Nolan's atrocities had been thwarted. The authorities, bound by the constraints of the law, could do little to appease the collective desire for justice. The nightmare continued to unfold, unabated and unchallenged, as the fearsome duo remained untouched by the consequences of their heinous actions.

***

Things might have fallen back into their original pattern of whispers and gossip with no action, if it was not for Ralph Windword. Juliana's former husband was resolute in finding justice. Not only had he lost a wife, but now also a daughter, to this demonic presence. And when news came that Nayomi was pregnant, his focus became singular. There would be a resolution found, be it legal or illegal.

The news of Nayomi's pregnancy sent one more round of shockwaves through the already weary town of Finchester. The once-unthinkable notion of an incestuous relationship between siblings now appeared to be an undeniable reality.

Ralph, consumed by a mix of anger, sorrow, and desperation, refused to accept the abomination that was unfolding before him. He raged against the dark forces that had taken hold of his family. Demanding that action be taken, he did his best to round up a group of vigilantes to bring an end to the depravity that had infested their lives.

United by their shared horror and a collective desire for justice, quite a large number of the townsfolk rallied behind Ralph's impassioned plea. With Ralph at the head, the group demanded the authorities take a more aggressive action against Juliana and her son, arguing that following regular protocol and legal procedures should be overturned in this obviously abnormal situation. They demanded the presiding officers to cast aside their hesitations and confront the diabolical presence that had plagued the area for far too long.

Ralph's pleas echoed through the corridors of power, reaching the ears of the authorities who, chastened by their previous failures, felt the weight of the town's mounting unrest and recognized the urgency of the situation. They assembled a task force, determined to investigate the obscure manor once again, to uncover the truth and put an end to the fear it brought upon the region.

The fate of Nayomi's unborn child hung in the balance; a symbol of innocence tainted by the darkness that surrounded its conception. The townsfolk felt that a moral obligation supported their infraction of the legal system. Their hearts were filled with a mix of hope and trepidation, as they organized a final confrontation. Their collective breath held in anticipation, they yearned for an end to the nightmare that had haunted their once-peaceful town.

The sheriff accompanied the mob of angry townsfolk, but only as a face of legitimacy. The true leader of the group was Ralph, but urged to keep their identities hidden, the men wore sacks over their faces. It was an ominous sight, and a symbol of the true intent of the crowd. It seemed inevitable that violence was going to break out. Under the cover of night, the mob traveled the road to the mansion.

This time their arrival seemed to be truly unexpected. As the wagons filled with men trundled up the pathway to the home, shadowed figures could be seen emerging from the entrance. Both male and female servants were running to the numerous sheds and warehouses on the estate. The road to the entrance of the house was long, and there was ample time for these men and women to get to those sheds. The wagons increased their speed, sensing the urgency to stop whatever was transpiring.

By the time the mob arrived at the porch, most of the men and women had already returned from the storage barns and sheds, retrieving what looked to be other figures, being carried from those storage sheds back to the house. Only two stragglers were left. A man and a woman were running to the door of the house when a group of men from the mob jumped from the wagon to intercept them. They screamed in terror as they were dragged to the wagon. The man managed to escape for a moment and immediately pulled a knife from his belt and slit his own throat. The woman, in a similar frenzy, managed to throw herself onto a machete being held by a mob member, ending her own life. Her lifeless body dragged her and the man wielding the massive knife to the ground.

Other members of the mob made a run for the door, but by the time they got to it, it was locked. It was clear that time was of the essence, the residents were clearly conspiring to conceal whatever horrendous activities they had been engaged in. Ralph, witnessing the hysterical acts of suicide, feared for the life of his daughter. He yelled out to the crowd to break down the door.

After a few futile attempts at ramming the door with their bodies, the mob organized a battering ram made from a quickly felled tree. The combined force of the crew soon crashed through the threshold. Men flooded into the foyer of the mansion. But to their astonishment, as the mob raged through the rooms of the house, they found that all of the rooms lay empty. The echoes of their footsteps reverberated through the abandoned halls, accompanied only by their own yells to one another and the faint whispers of the wind. The furniture, artwork, and countless treasures of the mansion stood as silent witnesses to whatever had unfolded within these walls.

Other members of the group decided to check the many warehouses and sheds dispersed around the estate, where the servants had hurriedly collected people from. The sight that greeted them fulfilled their hopes to find evidence of malice, but what it revealed would forever scar the minds of those who took witness. It was a scene of unspeakable horror, a grotesque tableau of blood-stained instruments, discarded medical equipment, and the remains of animals, as well as humans, sacrificed to dark experimentation. Like the poor soul who had stumbled his way to town, the victims had an assortment of different animal appendages and skins attached to them.

The investigators recoiled in revulsion, their eyes widening in disbelief at the evidence of twisted surgeries and macabre practices that had unfolded within those structures. The weight of the atrocities became almost unbearable. Some turned away, unable to face the full extent of the horrors that had been concealed for so long.

After witnessing such atrocities, the realization that the perpetrators had managed to escape fueled a renewed sense of urgency and desperation. Ralph and the crew reasoned that there had to be a secret passage somewhere. The mob began tearing the house to shreds looking for any sign of a hidden door or cellar entrance.

Then, a cry came from one of the men in the study. There, behind the desk, a lever was discovered. And once pulled, a hidden doorway opened up to a stairwell that went beneath the house. A narrow hallway, who's width would not allow for more than one man at a time to go forward, lay before them, making whoever went first susceptible to attack. It was Ralph who suggested that he lead the way. It was his daughter they were there to retrieve, and thus, it should be his chance to take.

With a knife drawn in front of him, Ralph descended the stairs with a long line of men behind him. He called out for his daughter, but the only response was silence. The spiral stairwell opened up to an enormous chamber that lay beneath the house. The sight that Ralph beheld was worse than anything he could have imagined. There, beneath this ominous mansion, was a kind of demonic chapel. Rows of seats were lined in front of a grand altar, on which were carved strange occult symbols. In the seats, a scatter of servants sat, all of whom had had their throats slit. Blood covered the floor.

On top of the altar lay the deceased bodies of both Nayomi and Juliana. Sprawled out like some form of grotesque offerings, their hearts had been removed and lay on the floor in front of the altar. Taking in the gruesome visage, Ralph began to wail in despair, and the men who had followed him took in the sight themselves as they entered behind him. It was so revolting that some of the men had to turn and leave, back up the stairwell. But those with stronger stomachs came forward to investigate the macabre scene. Nolan was nowhere to be found.

Then the sound of a baby's cry came from beneath the altar. One of the men closest to it peered beneath that blood-soaked table, where he found a newly born child. Within a little wicker basket, wrapped in a blanket, was a blue-skinned baby girl. He cautiously lifted her and showed her to the others.

"We have to kill it!" one of the men cried.

"It's the spawn of the devil!" another yelled out in fear.

But Ralph, still freshly stricken by the grief of his daughter, saw only the last vestiges of his beloved child in that blue face and immediately grabbed the basket away from the men. He refused to do such a horrible thing and declared the child innocent. The sheriff, who had only just arrived at the scene, caught wind of what was occurring and quickly came to the aid of Ralph. He told the men to get hold of their senses and that any man who lay a hand on the child would be severely punished by the law.

Ralph, basket in hand, quickly exited the disgusting chamber and took his grandchild to safety. As he glanced down at the newborn, he was astounded by its resemblance to both his daughter and his former wife. He prayed to the heavens that she was not shrouded by whatever cursed activities had occurred only moments before.

***

Nolan's body was never found. And the mob of crazed men slowly gave up in their search for him. While the victims' bodies would provide the physical evidence needed to validate this unlawful raid, the discovery only slightly relieved their lingering fears. Unanswered questions gnawed at their minds, leaving a haunting sense that the true depth of what had happened out there would never be revealed.

When the news of what the mob had found arrived back in Finchester, the townsfolk recoiled in horror, their reactions an array of emotions, from anger to pity and revulsion. The child's physical appearance, with its surreal blue skin and obvious family resemblance to its incestuous parents, served as chilling proof of their suspicions. Whispers of anger and vengeance filled the air, some demanding the child be extinguished to eradicate the taint of evil. But the compassionate sheriff, touched by the innocent vulnerability of the baby, stood resolute in his legal defense.

Amid the lingering discontent and murmurs of dissent, a lawful decision was reached by the courts to establish a trust for the infant, who was clearly the only living heir to the estate. The funds were secured by the hefty sums of money found inside the mansion, ensuring her well-being and protection. An experienced nurse was appointed to help Ralph care for the child, providing her with a nurturing and loving environment to bring an end to the evil of her family's legacy.

Though met with discontent from some corners of the town, the laws that safeguarded the rights of the innocent prevailed. The child, named Cassandra Windword by Ralph, was the sole heir remaining and would be granted ownership of the estate on her eighteenth birthday. The decision, while not without controversy, served as a testament to the importance of justice, even in the face of darkness.

Ralph did his best to help raise Cassandra, but he was never quite the same after the event. His health diminished in the following years. The appointed nurse attended Cassandra's upbringing. Shielded from the public due to her strange appearance and the horrible stories surrounding her past, she was a solitary girl. When she reached her eighteenth birthday, she returned to that house. It was not without much grumbling from the residents of Finchester, but there was nothing they could do to stop it. And there she lives, to this day.

***

"And that, my boy, is the story of the blue woman you saw in town today, Cassandra Windword," Arlo said, patting his boy's head. The boy was now lying nuzzled in his bed, the long journey home well since over. The man had carried on with the story all the way home from town and then all the way up to the boy's bedroom. He had continued it as he had tucked the boy into bed.

The boy looked terrified and appalled at the dazzling tale he had just been told. His innocent brain had never envisioned such horrors, but that indeed was the point. Arlo smiled and rustled the boy's hair.

"So," Arlo asked his young son, "are you ever going to approach the blue woman again?"

The boy looked like he was about to be sick and shook his head vigorously.

"Good boy," Arlo said and left the room, leaving his poor boy to be terrified all night. And, indeed, that was the point, for the citizens of Finchester never, ever wanted those horrors to happen again.

© 2023 Grant Crowther. All rights reserved.